LAST ORDERS AT MULBERRY LANE

ROSIE CLARKE

First published in Great Britain in 2024 by Boldwood Books Ltd.

Copyright © Rosie Clarke, 2024

Cover Design by Colin Thomas

Cover Photography: Colin Thomas

The moral right of Rosie Clarke to be identified as the author of this work has been asserted in accordance with the Copyright, Designs and Patents Act 1988.

All rights reserved. No part of this book may be reproduced in any form or by any electronic or mechanical means, including information storage and retrieval systems, without written permission from the author, except for the use of brief quotations in a book review.

This book is a work of fiction and, except in the case of historical fact, any resemblance to actual persons, living or dead, is purely coincidental.

Every effort has been made to obtain the necessary permissions with reference to copyright material, both illustrative and quoted. We apologise for any omissions in this respect and will be pleased to make the appropriate acknowledgements in any future edition.

A CIP catalogue record for this book is available from the British Library.

Paperback ISBN 978-1-78513-111-0

Large Print ISBN 978-1-78513-107-3

Hardback ISBN 978-1-78513-106-6

Ebook ISBN 978-1-78513-104-2

Kindle ISBN 978-1-78513-105-9

Audio CD ISBN 978-1-78513-112-7

MP3 CD ISBN 978-1-78513-109-7

Digital audio download ISBN 978-1-78513-103-5

Boldwood Books Ltd
23 Bowerdean Street
London SW6 3TN
www.boldwoodbooks.com

AUTHOR'S REMINDER

This is book number ten in the *Mulberry* series so we thought it might help to have a little recap for readers. Some of you won't need it, others might find it helpful.

Main Characters

Peggy's family:

Peggy and Able Ronoscki and their twins, Freddie and Fay. Peggy's eldest daughter, Janet, and her brother, Pip, by her first husband, Laurie.

Peggy is now in her sixties, Able is a couple of years younger. The twins are now 19. Janet is 39 and Pip is 37; they both have children.

Maggie is Janet's daughter by her first husband and Peggy's first grandchild and is now 21. Janet and Ryan, her second husband, have a son, Jon.

Pip is married to Sheila, they have two children, Chris and Sarah. Pip works as an aeronautical designer.

Peggy has always run the Pig & Whistle pub in Mulberry Lane in the East End of London, apart from a period when she went away to the seaside and Sheila ran the pub. However, in 1958, Maggie and Fay started to take over. Peggy also has a boarding house, which is managed by Pearl. Pearl's mother, Mrs Maggs, helps at the Pig & Whistle washing up. Able has a partnership with Tom Barton in the building trade.

* * *

Maureen's family:

Maureen is in her late forties and Gordon is slightly older. Gordon's daughter, Shirley, is in her late twenties now and Maureen and Gordon's son, Gordy, is a teenager. Maureen also had a son, Robin (not Gordon's), but he died of a childhood illness.

Gordon is suffering from a weakness of a heart muscle but is better than he was in the last book. He still manages the grocery shop that came to them through Maureen's family, but it is much bigger now, though he only goes in for an hour or two and has a youthful manager. Maureen still helps out in the pub and the restaurant kitchen sometimes. Shirley is a doctor and married to Ray.

* * *

The Barton family:

Tom and Rose Barton have two children, Molly and Jackie or these days, Jack. Tom and Able are now partners in a building business and doing well. Rose sometimes helps out in the pub kitchens. She and Maureen are Peggy's best friends and they've always done things together. They are several years younger than Peggy and Maureen and in their thirties.

All the characters are well and continuing to thrive now that life is so much better after the long years of war. This is a time when things aren't too bad for folk in Mulberry Lane, but, of course, life always has surprises round the corner...

1

Maureen Hart glanced at her husband Gordon as he sat in his favourite shabby, but comfortable, chair by the fire. He looked pale and tired and it wasn't just the chilly February air that made him shiver. His cold had kept him at home for a couple of days and she'd felt concerned as she saw him cough, his whole body racked with the fever that had made him feel so ill these past few days. Was it just a bad cold or something more? She was always anxious when Gordon was unwell, because of the underlying heart problems with a weakened valve, he'd had a year or two back. A doctor had warned her at that time that he might not have many years to live. But then after Shirley's husband Ray, a renowned heart surgeon, had performed a small operation, he'd seemed better. However, Maureen still worried that the condition might worsen and that she could lose her beloved husband.

'Would you like a cup of tea, love?' she asked, hovering solicitously. 'Or some nice hot soup?'

'I'd like you to sit down and talk to me,' Gordon replied and something in his voice made her do so at once. 'I need to discuss the future, Maureen. This cold has really pulled me down, love. It has made me think about things...'

Maureen's heart did a little skip of fear. It wasn't like Gordon to speak so seriously. She sat down in the chair at the other side of the black range, which she polished every few days; it shone with her efforts and was the source of both heat for their water and her main cooking area. Gran's old house didn't have many modern conveniences; the kitchen was old-fashioned but cosy, and only the bathroom had been renewed, though they'd kept the outside painted and she'd decorated the sitting room just before Christmas. It was home all the same and she'd been happy here all these years with Gordon. Maureen couldn't imagine it without him – or her life.

'What do you want to talk about? Shirley and the baby – or the shop?'

Shirley was Gordon's grown-up daughter by his first marriage, but Maureen loved her as if she were her own, and was thrilled with the prospect of becoming a grandmother later that year.

'I want to talk about you.' Gordon looked at her lovingly. 'I've always considered myself lucky because you married me, Maureen. I was eight years older than you and I'd been married before.'

'Best day's work I ever did,' Maureen replied with a smile. 'Best part of twenty years – and a war raging. Now we're in 1962 and I'm still thanking God we met.'

'I was the lucky one. You're a lovely wife and you've been a wonderful mother to Shirley and our Gordy, and Matty too – though we never see him since he won that scholarship to boarding school.' Matty was an intelligent boy and, at the age of twelve, had won a place at the King's School in Ely. His teachers had recommended that he be allowed to take the place, because it was felt he would benefit from a more relaxed atmosphere in a small cathedral city and the education there was suited to his needs.

'He comes home for the holidays.'

Gordon shook his head. 'If he isn't off with his schoolfriends somewhere. I know he loves us, but I sometimes wish he hadn't won that damned thing; I'd rather he'd been with us.'

'I know what you mean, love, but it is better for him. His teachers told us he needed the kind of education he would get there; he is in the cathedral choir, very wrapped up in his music studies, and he's happy, and surely that is all that matters?' Maureen looked at him anxiously. He didn't often complain and she thought it was the long winter blues catching up with him.

'Yes,' he acknowledged with a sigh. 'I miss him, that's all.'

Maureen nodded. She missed her son, too, but knew he needed a different life. 'Gordy is still here and I think you'll find he won't stray too far. He's a real homebird; Matty is clever, but Gordy is sports-mad.'

'He's a good lad, hardly seems possible he is ready to leave school,' her husband agreed. 'I love all the kids, but the house seems empty without Matty. Gordy is always out with his friends or upstairs working in his bedroom.'

'Yes, that's true and I miss him, too, but we *do* still have Shirley and Gordy. I love them all equally,' she told him with a smile. 'I loved Robin, too, but we lost him too soon.' Her son, whom she'd conceived from a brief affair with a man who had deceived her and broken her heart, had died of a childhood illness when still very young. 'I always hoped we'd have more, but after that last miscarriage, I knew we wouldn't.' A little sigh escaped her.

Gordon's eyes conveyed sympathy as he nodded. 'Robin was a little darling and we all miss him,' he said. 'I watched you struggle with your grief, love, and I was proud of you...' He paused, then, 'You were brave when you lost Robin and I want you to be just as brave when I go—' Now he'd said what was on his mind and her throat caught with emotion. This illness had really pulled him down.

'Don't!' she cried, her heart catching. 'Please, Gordon. I don't want you to think that way, love. You mean too much to us all.'

'We have to face up to the possibility that I don't have long,' he said gravely. 'I'll fight to the end, don't worry – but I'm not throwing this cold off as I would once, and it has made me think.' He drifted off into thought for a moment or two and then looked at her. 'Will you want to keep the business on if I am not around, Maureen? Or would you rather we sold it now?'

She was taken by surprise and just stared at him for a moment. 'I hadn't thought about it. If it is too much for you, just leave it to Ginger, he seems to be able to manage well enough.' Ginger Thomas was their assistant at the corner grocery shop that had once belonged to Maureen's father. It had been just a small shop then, but under Gordon's management it had grown and prospered into a thriving business. 'We could take on another assistant and let Ginger be in charge. That would just suit him.'

'Yes, it would,' Gordon agreed and smiled. 'I just wondered if you would like to make a change – go somewhere else to live. Perhaps by the sea?'

Maureen hesitated and then shook her head. 'I like a nice holiday by the sea and I wouldn't mind going for longer in the summer if you felt like it, Gordon, but my friends are here in the lanes.'

Gordon nodded. 'I thought that might be your answer. You and Peggy Ronoscki are joined at the hip, but supposing Mulberry Lane wasn't there any longer? What would you feel then?'

'Mulberry Lane not there?' Maureen was puzzled, a queer little shiver down her spine. 'I don't understand?'

'I heard there is a possibility that they might designate all these lanes as a clearance area. They are saying in the council meetings that all these old back-to-back terraces should make way for new homes and shopping centres. High-rise flats were suggested for Mulberry Lane.'

'No! Surely not?' Maureen was shocked. 'That would mean the Pig & Whistle would go...' The thought of all Peggy's and her granddaughter Maggie's hard work in building up the new restaurant being swept away by a bulldozer was so devastating that she couldn't think straight for a moment. It was outrageous! 'Can they do that?' she asked her husband. 'Can they simply take away everything Peggy and Maggie and Able have built up? All we have? Able spent a lot of money buying that property and renovating it, and so did we on the shops over the years. Doesn't that count for anything?' It was so overwhelming, too much to think about.

'Several people in Mulberry Lane have bought their houses in recent years,' Gordon replied. 'Tom Barton owns three as well as his building yard. Owners will be compensated for the value of the property, but perhaps not what they're worth in terms of community and comfort. I suppose the council will offer new homes to those who can't afford to buy elsewhere or those in rented accommodation, which most are, of course.'

'Many of the houses won't fetch a lot,' Maureen objected. 'The rents are cheap though and some could do with repair...' A sudden thought struck her. 'Will our home be included in the clearance?' She saw the answer in his eyes and horror filled her. 'So they will take away our homes and our businesses just like that to build their monstrosities? That's what I call those dreadful flats they are building all over!' Her breast heaved with indignation as anger spurted. 'How can they just sweep in and take it all away? Surely it isn't legal?'

'I am afraid it is, if the council consider it in the best interests of the general public.' Gordon sighed heavily. 'I agree with you and I think they will realise one day that it was a mistake, to sweep away all these communities, but they say it is progress – and some of the houses are in terrible repair. I suppose they do need knocking down rather than patching up.'

'Surely they could build new houses, bit by bit?' Maureen questioned. 'I think it's a rotten shame. Isn't there anything we can do to stop it?'

'It hasn't been passed yet,' Gordon told her gently. 'It was only suggested at the last meeting and may go no further, though I think there have been meetings and rumours about it for a while now – but when I was told that it is now being seriously considered, it made me think about what you would do, love. If I shouldn't be here and you had to leave everything you know and care for, it would be difficult for you – so I wondered if you would rather sell now and move away. Matty is settled at his school for at least three years; Gordy has only this year at school and then he'll go into training as an apprentice. Plumbing is a good trade and he can work anywhere.'

'All his friends are here...'

'As are yours,' her husband agreed. 'But what if they had to move, too? I cannot imagine Peggy living in a high-rise and I think she and Able might go to the sea. It might be better for you to do the same.'

Maureen sat in silence for a moment or two, her head buzzing with objections. There was merit in what he said, but to just uproot like that... it was a huge step. 'We need to think about it, Gordon. There is Shirley, too, remember. I promised I would be around to babysit and help out when the little one arrives.'

'Yes, I have thought of that – so perhaps you'd like a little house nearer her and Ray and the baby but stay here in London?'

'The honest answer is – I don't know,' Maureen told him and sighed. 'Why can't these interfering councils leave well alone? There are a lot worse areas than Mulberry Lane.' Most of the houses were very old, and some had been damaged in the war, but many had been repaired now and, to her eyes, the area was familiar and safe, despite some peeling paint and a cracked window here and there.

'Have you really looked recently?' Gordon asked her. 'Much of the area is a bit dilapidated, love. Yes, the Pig & Whistle looks smart and we've looked after the shop and this place, but some of the other houses are not fit to live in.'

'Well, I did notice that Alice's old house had the windows boarded up. No one has lived there for a while now and some kids broke the glass.' Alice had been an old Londoner, cheerful and outspoken; her jokes had often kept them going during the war and everyone in the lanes had turned out for her funeral. Maureen still missed her. She sighed. 'It used to have sparkling white net curtains at the window, but Tom Barton was saying he might buy it and renovate it.'

'I've had a word with Tom,' Gordon said. 'He popped round to see how I was the other morning when you were shopping. I doubt he will buy it now. He'll wait and see if the proposal goes any further. After all, as you say, there are other areas they might choose to rebuild first.'

'So it might not happen?' Maureen looked at him hopefully.

'It might be delayed for a few years,' Gordon admitted. 'If that were to happen, things could get much worse as folk move away. Seeing the area go into decline would be the worst of all cases. If you are going to make the change, it is better sooner rather than later. You are still young, Maureen, plenty of time to make new friends and a new life.'

Maureen looked at him hard. 'You've asked me what I want to do – what do *you* want, Gordon? Would you like to move away somewhere?'

'Not particularly,' he replied. 'I think we should have longer holidays in the summer and perhaps a weekend away now and then when the weather is decent, but I like living amongst friends – but we do need to consider how we would feel if the clearance goes ahead.'

'Yes, I suppose you are right,' Maureen agreed. 'I wonder what Peggy thinks about it all…'

'Why don't you make us that cup of tea you suggested and then go round and see her later?' Gordon suggested. 'It might help you to settle your thoughts.'

'Yes, I will,' she said. 'Would you like a sandwich, too?'

'I'd like a piece of that almond Madeira cake you made earlier,' Gordon said and smiled. 'I think my chest feels a little easier now. I've been worried about how I was going to tell you the news.'

* * *

Peggy looked up as Maureen walked into the big warm kitchen at the Pig & Whistle, where she was preparing the cottage pies that were on that night's menu. 'I know what you're going to say,' she blurted out as she saw Maureen's look. 'Tom told me. It is outrageous! I couldn't believe it, but Able has checked and it is true – they are seriously considering a clearance of the area so they can build those horrid flats everywhere. I know it has been mooted a few times, but I thought it was just talk. Now it seems as if it's serious.'

'I couldn't believe it either when Gordon told me,' Maureen said. 'We've built the shop my grandmother left me after Dad died into a good business. It isn't fair they can just decide to take it away – and look what you spent only last year on the Pig & Whistle. What will Maggie do if they knock it down?' Maggie was Peggy's eldest granddaughter and did most of the cooking these days at the restaurant; she lived with Peggy and was engaged to Greg Hayes, who had been a famous racing driver until the accident that had left him with facial scars, but was now a consultant designer of Formula One cars and quite wealthy.

'I expect she and Greg will open a restaurant elsewhere once they are married,' Peggy said. 'She was disappointed at the news, because she enjoys working with me and says it won't be the same if I'm not around – but what can we do?'

'Fight?' Maureen suggested. 'We could petition the council, get lots of signatures to say that we like our community the way it is.'

'Would that work?' Peggy considered. 'I suppose it might delay things a bit, but could we get enough signatures? I was talking to Mrs Brown the other day and she says there are cockroaches coming out of her kitchen walls. She complained to her landlord, but he refused to do any repairs. I asked Tom Barton if he could do anything and he says the walls need to be stripped and disinfected and then replastered. I offered to pay and he says he'll do it at cost price... but I doubt if she would say no if she was offered a nice new flat.' Tom Barton had been brought up in the lanes and was now Able's partner in a building firm. He was a good businessman, but still did little jobs for neighbours and friends for next to nothing.

'Nor would I if I had cockroaches,' Maureen said with a shiver of disgust. 'I didn't realise some of the houses here were that bad, did you?'

'I sort of knew because people moan about it in the pub,' Peggy told her. 'Able reckons Tom has his eye on a larger yard elsewhere and is thinking he'll get it just in case. They can do with the extra space anyway. Tom says the business can carry on, because it isn't limited to one area and he's expanding all the time.' She laughed. 'I can remember when he was a lad and just starting to do odd jobs...' She shook her head. 'It makes me feel old sometimes. When I think about the war... so many years.'

'You're not old, only sixty-ish,' Maureen said and stared at her. 'So what will you and Able do? Move into the suburbs or to the sea?'

'We've talked but haven't decided yet,' Peggy said. 'Able thinks he will get decent compensation for the pub, so we could take over another one somewhere – or just retire. Tom doesn't need Able to be here. He has always been a sleeping partner in the building side of things – they talk a lot, but Able isn't involved on a day-to-day basis. Able does most of the paperwork, getting the building permissions and keeping the books.'

'Yes, Tom is good at what he does but can't be bothered with all that stuff – that's why they make a good team.'

Peggy nodded her assent. 'What will you and Gordon do if it happens? It isn't certain yet, only at the proposal stage. I expect it will take two or three years to buy all the property once they pass the planning anyway.'

'Yes, that is true,' Maureen said, feeling slightly better. 'We haven't made up our minds yet. Neither of us really wants to move, but if we have no choice… perhaps we'll go right away, try something different. Gordon thinks once they start to compulsory purchase properties, the area will go downhill fast.'

'Yes, I suppose so.' Peggy looked concerned. 'I thought you would opt for London, just another area?'

'I might because of Shirley and the baby – but it wouldn't be the same if you and the others weren't around. You and Rose have been my closest friends for a long time now. What does Rose say?' Rose was Tom Barton's wife and helped out in the bar sometimes.

'She is happy to do whatever Tom wants,' Peggy replied. 'They will stay in London. He is a young man and he'll be a rich one, in time. Able says he has a good head for business. They will stay, just move to another area.'

'I'm not sure what I want,' Maureen sighed. 'I'd rather it all remained just the way it is.'

'Oh, don't let's think about it,' Peggy said and made a wry face. 'How is Shirley?' Her pregnancy was approaching the uncomfortable stage and Shirley was used to being a busy doctor and running around after everyone. The last time Peggy had seen her, she'd been feeling down in the dumps and complaining of backache.

'She is getting tired now and has decided to stop work this week,' Maureen told her. 'Shirley says she just can't stand for long enough in theatre to be any use and she's too big. She'll just take it easy for the next few months.'

'It will be a spring baby; due sometime in April, isn't it?' Peggy nodded her approval as Maureen agreed. 'Lovely. I think Maggie is planning a summer wedding. They had thought this spring, but both of them are so busy. They see each other briefly and then Greg is off somewhere and Maggie is always busy with the restaurant, though we have more cooks these days.' They had two trained chefs as well as part-time helpers.

'How are you doing with Fay's catering business?' Maureen asked. 'You said it had started to pick up before Christmas.' Fay and Freddie were twins, born to Peggy when Able was still missing during the war.

'Yes, but it went dead in January. Hardly anything has come in this past month,' Peggy told her with a wry look. 'Fay would be annoyed if she were here. Thankfully, judging by her last letter, she is sunning herself in Hollywood and having a wonderful time catering for pool parties. It sounds like something out of a movie...' Peggy laughed. 'She has actually met Elizabeth Taylor and Johnny Weissmuller, amongst others. You know, he was in all those *Tarzan* films we used to love.'

'He was so handsome!' Maureen said and laughed. 'It all sounds very posh. Just think of your little Fay all that way off, Peggy. Has she said anything about whether they will come back in the summer?' Fay, Peggy's youngest daughter had married a famous rock star the previous year and gone off to America to live with him, leaving Peggy to manage her catering business here.

'She says Jace has a European tour in the summer,' Peggy supplied the information with a laugh. 'He has been approached to do a big feature film but isn't sure about it yet. Apparently, the studio knows what they want to do, but they have to get the money men interested. That isn't likely to happen until much later in the year, so if Fay comes with him on his tour, we may see her in the summer.' She finished cutting her pastry and wiped her hands absentmindedly on a tea towel.

She observed her friend curiously. 'What are you thinking, Peggy? I know something is going on in your head.'

'Able is talking about another holiday in America...'

'After what happened to you the last time?' Maureen frowned, because Peggy had been involved in an unpleasant incident that had resulted in a stay in hospital and given her amnesia for a time; bits of her memory still hadn't returned, though most had now.

'Well, that was awful,' Peggy said, 'but I understand we enjoyed ourselves until the accident, though that has never come back to me. Able thinks I would like it where Fay is – and she says if I ever want to help out, she could do with my touch… whatever that means.'

'I should say she is missing her mum,' Maureen said with a smile. She caught her breath on a sudden thought. 'If Fay decided to live there for good – would you consider emigrating too?'

'I don't know,' Peggy admitted. 'I would have said definitely no – but if they pull down Mulberry Lane… why not? After all, Able is an American. Janet seems to be enjoying renovating properties and Pip is settled. Freddie is at college and will probably go out there for a holiday when he finishes his course. I might go for an extended visit anyway.'

Maureen nodded. How things had changed over the years. Who would ever have thought so much could happen to two ordinary young women when they were helping each other survive in the worst of times? Peggy's children had spread their wings. Her eldest, Janet, had at last found a job she enjoyed renovating houses; Pip, Peggy's second born, was highly paid and working as a designer for an aerospace project, whatever that meant, Maureen had no idea. The twins, Freddie and Fay, were both busy and seemed to have ideas for their futures that would send her head spinning. How time had flown.

Peggy smiled as Maggie came bustling into the restaurant kitchen, her arms filled with parcels of fresh food for that evening's service. 'We don't know what the future will bring, so why worry about it?'

Maureen nodded, but, after a few minutes spent chatting to her friends, she was still thoughtful as she walked home. Perhaps there was no sense in worrying about the future. The idea that Mulberry Lane and the surrounding district might disappear had shocked and distressed her, but beyond complaining and upsetting herself, there was little she could do. Yet it was ironic that an energetic council could do what all the bombs in the Blitz hadn't manged and destroy their homes and their lives as they knew them.

2

Janet Hendricks stood back to look at her handiwork. She'd been renovating this small flat for the past three months and it was finally finished. Now she had to decide whether she wanted to move in or sell and continue to live with her mother at the Pig & Whistle. She thought there was a reasonable chance of making a profit if she sold and her step-father, Able, agreed. He'd recently suggested to her that if she wanted to join the building firm he and Tom owned, as a planner and advisor, he would welcome her. Janet had told him she would think about it; for the moment, she rather enjoyed working as an independent. She enjoyed doing a lot of the renovating work herself, but had employed skilled workmen to do the electricity and plumbing, which had needed expert attention. However, a lot of it had been just planning, taking out the old kitchen and decorating, and she'd made the curtains to give it a finishing touch. As she let her gaze travel round the rooms, she was pleased with how it looked.

Hearing a ring at her newly installed doorbell, Janet frowned. She wasn't expecting anyone. Unless Able had decided to take another look, though he'd visited yesterday and there wasn't much more to see. She'd only had a bit of painting and cleaning to do this morning. Answering the summons, Janet looked blankly at the man who stood there. He was a stranger to her, possibly late thirties, good-looking with dark blond hair that brushed his shirt collar and blue eyes and he was a bit on the tall and lanky side.

'You are Mrs Hendricks, yes?' His accent told her he wasn't English and she guessed he might be Swedish or perhaps from another Nordic country.

'Yes, I am,' she agreed. 'And you are?'

'I am Lars Stevenson, from the apartment below you,' he replied with a smile that made Janet catch her breath. His smile reminded her of Mike, her first husband, who had died of his war wounds. 'I learn that you may sell this apartment and I want to ask if I can see it, please?'

'I haven't made up my mind yet,' Janet admitted. She hesitated, because he was a stranger. She hadn't seen him about and thought perhaps he'd been at work while she was renovating the place, because she'd had no complaints about the noise. 'But you can come in and see what I've done, if you'd like to?'

She stood back, allowing him to enter. He didn't look dangerous and Janet felt quite safe, despite all the stuff in the papers these past weeks about the A6 murders and the trial of James Hanratty. Her mother would tell her she was a fool to invite a stranger into her flat, yet Janet knew that Peggy was often impulsive herself.

Lars walked through the empty rooms, which still smelled strongly of paint, ahead of her, almost as though she wasn't there, and Janet smiled inwardly. He was only interested in the flat.

Watching him open dresser drawers and inspect the new bathroom, she waited patiently for his verdict. The question was on her lips as he finally turned to look at her. 'What do you think then?'

'It is good what you do here. Much nicer than the flat I rent below – how much is it?'

'I haven't decided to sell yet.'

'I give you £6,500, yes?'

Janet caught her breath. She'd bought it for £3,000 because of the work that needed to be done and that had cost her just over another£1,000 – not counting her own time and effort – so she would make a decent profit. 'I suppose I might sell for that,' she agreed. 'But don't you need your wife to see it first?'

He laughed, a nice open sound. 'No wife. I'm too busy to have time for courting ladies... You will sell to me, please?'

'Well, yes, I will,' Janet said, feeling relieved to have made up her mind. She knew her mother would be content to have her stay on at the pub for a while longer and her son Jon was happy there. 'I'll give you the name of my solicitor. What is the number of your flat so that he can contact you?'

'Number five, Rembrandt Court – but, of course you know the address.' He smiled at her again and this time it was even more warm and friendly. 'You come down and have some coffee before you leave, yes? We talk a little?'

'Yes, why not?' Janet smiled at him. He was nice and there was no harm in being friendly. Her husband, Ryan, had moved to Wales the previous year, something he'd known neither she nor Jon were happy about, but he'd done it all the same, which was why they were separated for the time being. Janet missed him, more than she'd thought she might when they had quarrelled. 'We can exchange details in comfort. There is nowhere to sit here yet...'

* * *

Walking home an hour or so later, Janet thought how swiftly the time had gone. Lars was an interesting man. Settled in London now, he travelled a lot and was an engineer. It meant that he spent a lot of time in other countries, working on projects, often the kind that brought water to parched areas like Africa. Because of his work, he'd chosen to rent his flat at first, but now he'd decided he would buy.

'I have seen you leaving at night,' Lars had told her, 'but I was always too late to catch you. It is good that I have now – yes?'

Janet had nodded.

He was a very attractive man – but much younger than her.

Janet caught herself up with a little laugh. Whoa! What was she thinking? Yes, he was outrageously good-looking and she would be lying if she pretended that she didn't fancy him.

Sighing, Janet put the thought out of her head. She still loved Ryan, if only she could understand why he'd suddenly gone off on his own to Wales, after previously agreeing they would live in London. Several times she'd been tempted to just drive there and have it out with him, but she hadn't.

Anyway, it didn't matter. Lars was just someone she was selling a property to and once that was settled, she would never see him again. As far as Ryan was concerned... well, maybe she would try telephoning again, though he never answered these days. Janet sighed. She'd been busy with the flat, but she really should go to Wales and discover if there was anything left of her marriage to save.

Catching sight of a newspaper stand, she saw the headline and went into the shop to buy a copy of the *Evening Standard*. She frowned as she read the headlines. The smallpox outbreak in Cardiff was spreading, and some people had died in South Wales. Janet shook her head. She hadn't been vaccinated so perhaps she would leave visiting for a while, just phone Ryan and tell him she would come later in the year.

* * *

Able nodded as, later that day, Janet told him that she'd accepted Lars Stevenson's offer for the flat. 'That is a very good price, Janet,' he told her. 'I'm glad you sold the flat. I didn't think it was suitable for you and Jon to live in. You need a proper house and garden – something more like you had before you moved to Scotland, but here in London – perhaps Islington? Or somewhere in the suburbs?'

'She doesn't need a house at all yet,' Peggy said, putting a cup of steaming-hot tea in front of her daughter. 'You have time to decide what you want to do, Janet. Have you decided for definite that you won't go to live with Ryan, love?'

'Jon hates the idea,' Janet said, uncertainly. 'I prefer living in London; Ryan knew that when he went ahead and bought that small-holding, Mum. He knew that Jon wanted to live near you. He is happiest when he is with you – look how much he has improved, both mentally and physically, these past months.' In his mid-teens now, Jon had been involved in a road accident that had left him with a weak leg as well as a balance problem, which had seemed gradually to improve now that he was settled and happier living with his grandmother and mother.

Peggy nodded her agreement. 'Well, you are both welcome to stay with us wherever we live.'

Janet looked at her anxiously. 'Do you believe the slum clearance will go ahead? What do you think, Able?'

'It will happen,' he said decisively. 'The only question is when – this round or the next? There is more than one area under consideration and I doubt they have the money to do them all. If they go ahead now, I suppose we may have three or four years here if we hang on to the last, which I wouldn't, because it will only become a desolate area as the houses are closed up one by one.'

'Poor Maggie,' Janet said. 'She so wanted to make this place successful.'

'She has done and that will reflect in the price we get for it,' Able said. 'I think at the moment Maggie's mind is focused on getting enough time free to marry Greg. After that, I dare say they will move down Devon and Cornwall way before long. He has a family home there and I think a restaurant in one of those areas will do well, so it should be just a change of venue for her.'

'What about you and Mum?' Janet asked, frowning. 'You've put so much work into this pub over the years – and you spent a lot of money getting it extended for Maggie.'

'That should also be reflected in the price we get for it,' Able said. 'I would say there is a case for leaving the Pig & Whistle as it is and building round it – after all, folk will still need a pub to drink in, even if they live in a high-rise flat.'

'It wouldn't be the same,' Peggy cut in instantly. 'All the friends we've known for years will be scattered. I'd rather make a new start elsewhere.'

Able looked at her for a moment in silence and then nodded. 'Yes, I agree, but I would have fought for it to stay if you wanted.'

'It's people I care about, not places,' Peggy told him with a loving look. 'Even if my family is scattered, we will always keep in touch. Freddie is in Cambridge on that teaching course, but he telephones often, and if he doesn't, Greta does. They come home whenever they can – and wherever we are will be home to him.' Greta was Freddie's girlfriend, though as yet they were not engaged.

'She followed him down to Cambridge,' Janet said, a wry twist to her mouth. 'I thought Greta was supposed to be a timid little thing, afraid of her own shadow, but she seems determined enough when she wants something.'

Peggy laughed at her eldest daughter's censure of the young girl Freddie had brought home to them the previous year. She'd been running from her aunt's scolding tongue then, but it seemed Freddie was her world and he didn't appear to mind that she stared at him with adoring eyes. 'Don't be jealous, Janet. Greta is young and in love and I think Freddie feels the same, though I'm not sure he is in a hurry to marry. Greta says she doesn't mind waiting.'

'Well, I still think he is too young to marry her for years yet.'

'You married before you were twenty,' Peggy reminded her. 'Freddie is twenty this year – not that I think he will marry just yet. He is sensible enough to know he needs a good job first and he says they will travel a bit when his teaching training is finished, and that's not for a while yet. He has to do a year at college, so that will be done this summer, and a practical year as a pupil-teacher before he can get a proper job on full salary.'

'Do you think they sleep together?' Janet asked and her mother frowned.

'I sincerely hope not! Greta is a decent girl. Freddie should put a ring on her finger first. I may be old-fashioned, but I'd be disappointed in him if he didn't.'

'He will,' Able said unruffled. 'He is in no hurry for marriage and all the ties and responsibilities that brings, but he won't hurt her. I think he loves her – but Freddie is one to take his time and Greta will have to be patient.'

'Yes, I agree,' Peggy said and then looked at Janet. 'What are you smiling about? Do you think otherwise?'

'Oh no. I wasn't thinking about Freddie at all,' Janet disclaimed. She'd drifted into a dream, thinking about a man's smile. Mike, her beloved first husband, as he'd been when they were young and so much in love. Just for a little while she'd seen that same smile on another man's face and, for a moment, she'd felt youthful and carefree, but, of course, she wasn't. She was in her forties and it looked as if her second marriage was over. 'It's nothing, Mum. I'm just pleased I've sold the flat, that's all.'

Peggy nodded. 'You will tell me in your own good time,' she said. 'We'd best go upstairs. Maggie wants to start preparing for the evening service and I need to change into my working things.' The busy restaurant was booked out again that evening and Peggy would help with the preparations and some of the cooking.

'Where is Jon?' Janet belatedly realised that she hadn't seen her son since she got home that afternoon. 'Surely he should be back from school?'

'He has gone to a football match with Gordy. Gordy is the captain of the school team and he has arranged for Jon to be one of the helpers, collecting kit and practice balls. Your son loves being around Gordy and his friends, even though he can't play football himself.' She shook her head. 'He is lucky to be walking.'

Janet nodded. 'Yes, he is. After that accident, we're lucky he is alive.'

'Yes, that is true,' Peggy replied, looking at her troubled expression. 'You don't still blame Ryan for that, do you?'

'It happened because he was too hard on Jon. Instead of talking to him to try and understand why he'd taken things that didn't belong to him, he punished him,' she said and her mouth set in a firm line. 'I did try to forgive and forget, Mum, really, I did. And what happened? Ryan just went off to Wales, regardless of our feelings.' Janet sighed. 'I didn't want to go to live in Scotland with Ryan, but I went to save our marriage. I've done everything I could to make it work – but I married him on the rebound after Mike died, and I think now it was a mistake. I've never stopped loving Mike in my heart and Ryan knows it. It has been there between us like a shadow the whole time...' She shook her head, the tears close. 'It's probably my fault he doesn't want me near him – but I can't believe he just deserted his own son the way he has. He never answers his phone and I'm sure he's there sometimes. It's as if he's just cut us out...'

Peggy looked at her and Janet saw the sadness in her mother's eyes. 'If that is truly the case and you're happier without him, then perhaps it is best you've separated. Will you divorce in time?'

'I'm not sure,' Janet replied. 'That is such an ugly thing, Mum. Unless Ryan wants to marry again, I probably won't. I'm nearly forty-two and I have a grown-up daughter who is soon to marry the man she loves and a young son. I am not likely to find love again at my age.'

'I don't know,' Peggy glanced at her husband fondly. 'I was only a few years younger than you are when I met Able.'

Able nodded in agreement and then looked at Janet. 'You'll find love if you want to,' he said. 'You just have to open your heart – but, next time, don't carry the regret of losing Mike with you.'

Janet stared at him, and then inclined her head. 'You are right, Able. It wasn't fair to Ryan. He wanted me and set out to get me but he didn't get what he'd hoped for, because, although I did love him, I could never forget Mike. I don't suppose I ever shall...'

* * *

Janet left her son watching the new craze on TV – the noise of a car chase following her as she went into the hall. *Z-Cars* had taken the viewing audience by storm and Jon had begged to be allowed to sit up and watch it. She'd given in, because it was hard to say no, even though she knew he'd be difficult to get out of bed in the morning.

Picking up the receiver, she dialled the telephone number Ryan had given her. It rang several times, but there was no answer. Janet replaced it, feeling peeved. That was the third time she'd tried to contact him this past week and he hadn't answered it once. Surely he couldn't be out day and night? She was sure he knew it was her and just wouldn't answer.

She returned to the sitting room. Able and Jon were watching the

TV, clearly enthralled by the exciting action. Janet wasn't in the mood. She left them to it and went to her room, intending to read a book. Hearing the phone ring, she went back out into the hall and answered it, half expecting it to be Ryan calling her back, but the voice that answered wasn't his.

'Janet... Mrs Hendricks,' the deep tones she vaguely recognised sent a little tingle down her spine. She'd given him the pub number but hadn't expected him to ring. 'It is Lars – I wondered if we could meet for a drink?'

'When?' Janet asked, hoping he hadn't changed his mind about the flat. 'Have you had second thoughts about buying the property?'

'No. I just wanted to see you,' he said. 'This evening – or lunchtime tomorrow?'

'I'd prefer lunchtime tomorrow,' Janet said, wondering why he'd asked her out. Yet a part of her knew. The attraction had been mutual. 'I have a son to get to bed after he's seen *Z-Cars*...'

Lars laughed and she enjoyed the sound of it.

'This I do not understand, but the English like these things. I prefer to listen to music or enjoy the company of a beautiful woman.'

'Are you flirting with me?' Janet asked, not quite certain how to take this direct speech.

'Yes, just a little – do you mind?'

'I don't know you...' she said hesitantly and heard him laugh again, but it was such a pleasant sound that she was not disturbed by his teasing.

'You will know me one day,' he told her. 'I should not perhaps have been so direct – forgive me?'

'I will have a drink with you,' Janet said. 'You can come here to my mother's pub at lunchtime and we'll talk – if you'd like to?'

'I shall be there,' he promised. 'Do not be afraid of me, Janet. I do not bite... well, only sometimes...'

'I'm not afraid,' she told him and she wasn't. 'As I said, I don't know you – yet.'

She heard his throaty laughter at the other end and smiled.

'Do you know where to come? I did tell you I lived at the Pig & Whistle in Mulberry Lane, didn't I?'

'Yes, you did,' he agreed. 'I will be there at twelve-thirty tomorrow.'

As the phone went dead, Janet smiled. It was nice to feel attractive and desired and she'd known as they had talked in Lars' flat that he'd found her so.

Frowning, because the brief moment of pleasure was followed by guilt, she picked up the telephone receiver once more and dialled Ryan's number. This time, it was answered and she said, 'Ryan, it's Janet. I rang earlier but you didn't answer.'

'Janet...' Ryan sounded far away, weary. 'I was asleep when the phone rang; it woke me. I thought it might be you. How are you – is Jon all right?'

'Fine. He is watching that new police series on TV,' Janet told him. 'How are you, Ryan?'

There was a brief silence, then, 'All right. Fine. Is there anything you need, Janet?'

'I just thought we could talk—'

'What about?' he interrupted brusquely. 'I don't think there's much left to talk about, do you? I don't think there is any point in prolonging —' Suddenly, the phone went dead. Janet stared at it for a moment. He'd put the phone down on her. Why? She hadn't deserved this, surely?

She replaced the receiver, picked it straight up and dialled again. It rang for several minutes but he didn't answer, so she replaced it and went back to her bedroom, feeling angry now. He was still there; he just refused to talk to her. What was wrong with him? It was as if he'd blocked her out of his life. Once she'd told him Jon was all right, he didn't want to talk to her. It was useless to even try.

3

Freddie looked around the tiny room Greta had rented when she'd followed him down to Cambridge. It was clean and adequate, with a bed, wardrobe, chair and a small fold-up table on which stood her typewriter and some exercise books with a pot of pencils and various bits.

'It isn't much of a home for you,' he said, frowning. 'Are you sure you wouldn't rather be back with Mum and Dad? You were settling in well there last year.'

'You know why I came,' she replied. 'It wasn't the same after you left and Fay went off to America. Your parents are lovely and so is Maggie – but I missed you. I had no friends in London and I was lonely.'

'We don't see that much of each other now,' Freddie pointed out. 'I study and I train with the rowing club – and you have to work, too.'

Greta had found employment as a waitress in a small café in the centre of the city. It was busy and she was on her feet several hours at a stretch, but the owners were pleasant people. They paid her well and she had plenty of time to work on her stories. Greta couldn't help the stories tumbling into her mind; they came along like steam trains, but she'd never thought of trying to sell them until she met Freddie. She'd been working in a small boarding house for her aunt when Freddie came to do a seasonal job helping to keep the beaches safe. She'd hated how she was living then and Freddie had made her believe she could actually have a different life.

'We see each other every weekend and on Wednesday evenings if you don't have a training session. If I went back to London, I'd only see you at the end of term. You don't have time to travel home every weekend. Besides, I like Cambridge. I like the older parts of town, the punts on the river and the colleges. It is so pretty along the Backs. I like seeing the market stalls when I go to work and shopping in the Petty Cury. I like the antique shops and – oh, just the feel of it...'

'As long as you're not miserable on your own here?' Freddie studied her face, his concern for her in his eyes.

'I don't even notice,' Greta assured him. 'When I write, I get lost in my stories. I'm going to start a proper book soon.'

'Really?' Freddie looked at her with interest. 'What will you write about?'

'I'm not sure yet.' Greta wrinkled her forehead. 'I think it might be a historical romance.'

'I like a good mystery where I can't guess the ending,' Freddie remarked. 'I thought you were concentrating on your local articles for a while?'

'I sold one,' Greta told him with a sigh. 'They returned the others and said they couldn't use them.'

'Oh, I see.' Freddie nodded in sympathy. 'Well, maybe you'll have better luck with those stories you sent to a women's magazine.' Greta shook her head. 'Did they come back too?'

'All but one – and that is a longer story, so I doubt they will want it. I've got some more to send out this week...' Greta sighed, because sometimes it seemed impossible to get anything published, and she always had a sinking feeling when the large brown envelopes came back.

'Cheer up,' Freddie said. 'In time, they will get accepted. I am sure of it.' He hesitated, wanting to please her. 'I know, let's go to the pub by the river. Some of my friends are meeting there this afternoon. We could do with a bit of fun and they're planning a quiz, all of us in by the fire in the snug.' It was nearly the end of March now and still chilly.

'Yes, all right,' she agreed and raised her head defiantly. 'Don't feel sorry for me, Freddie. I'm disappointed when I get rejections, but it won't stop me writing. I write because I enjoy it, and perhaps one day, I'll be good enough to be published regularly.'

'I think your stories are good,' he told her loyally. 'Perhaps a little bit too serious for those women's magazines you've been sending them to. Why don't you write a mystery story and see what happens? I think that might sell better.'

'I'm not sure I could.' Greta looked at him doubtfully. 'All my stories are about love and being happy...' She was thoughtful for a moment. 'I suppose I could write about a love affair that went wrong and ended in murder...'

Freddie saw the sudden gleam in her eyes. 'As long as you don't want to practise the dastardly deeds on me,' he teased. 'No, I think it is a good idea. Now put your coat on, wrap up well, because it is still cold out, and let's have some fun. Tomorrow it will be back to the grindstone for me. I have some mid-term exams coming up and I have to swot if I want to pass them.'

* * *

Freddie worked long into the night to catch up on his studies. He'd spent the afternoon and most of the evening with Greta before taking her back to her little room. Leaving her there was hard, because he loved her and wanted her to be warm and comfortable in a home she could call hers. When he'd taken her to his parents' home, he'd thought she would live there for the next year or two. It had surprised him that she'd had the courage to follow him to Cambridge and live by herself in that boarding house. She'd chosen well, because it wasn't too far from the college and her landlady was pleasant and friendly. Unlike many landladies, she trusted them enough to allow them a little time alone in Greta's room. Had he wanted to stay the night, she might have had something to say, but she allowed him to come and go at weekends and he didn't abuse the privilege, despite being tempted more than once.

Sighing, he finally lay down his pen at four in the morning and tumbled into his single bed. His own room wasn't much better than

Greta's, except it was slightly larger and looked out over college greens towards gardens rather than a drab street. He was studying English literature, Medieval history, maths and sport. His main purpose was to become a sports master, but the other subjects would qualify him to teach them if need be. Freddie understood that many schools would need their teachers to have more than one specialist subject.

It wasn't long before Freddie was sleeping. His alarm set for seven, he had football training at half-past and would grab a couple of biscuits or a sandwich to eat on the way. Life at college was fast-paced and exciting for a young man who loved to throw himself into everything, and Freddie was enjoying the debating sessions, as well as the rowing and other physical activities. He rushed from one lecture to the next, his long, striped scarf wound round his neck, hair slightly too long, blowing in the wind, eating on the go as he snatched a snack whenever he had a chance. Normally, he ate in the college dining room at night but bought food for himself the rest of the time. He missed his mother's home cooking and was looking forward to spending a part of his long summer holidays with his family, but he wouldn't have changed his life if he could. College was a great experience and he was loving every minute, his only real worry was that Greta might be unhappy spending too much time alone in her room.

He woke when his alarm rang, groggy at first, but, after splashing his face with cold water in the bathroom, he was wide awake and ready for the sport he loved. Freddie was a keen footballer and the team trained regularly all year long. That and the rowing, which he did five mornings a week and some evenings, kept him fit and lean despite his constant snacking on starchy foods. Bacon rolls bought from a café nearby were his favourite, but he probably ate more cakes and biscuits than he should. It was a habit he'd got into because all his female family seemed to cook delicious sweet things.

A lot of the students spent their evenings in the pubs. Freddie went once a week and usually took Greta with him. He saw no point in getting drunk every night like some of the other young men. The evenings he didn't see Greta, he spent either studying or at the debating club. Freddie had joined because he was pestered into it by one of the masters, but he'd discovered that he enjoyed it. Sometimes it became very political and biased, but one evening, he'd taken the opposite view to one of the most prolific speakers and argued his case when the older student was castigating the government over being too slow to clear the slums. His argument was that it wasn't just a matter of pulling down old buildings or even of the cost in monetary terms – but the disruption to people's lives. The suggestion that poor housing could still be valued because of the community spirit was met with raised eyebrows. He got only a smattering of applause when he took his seat, but the master who oversaw the proceedings spoke to him later.

'That was an interesting proposition of yours, Ronoscki. People often don't see beyond the obvious – new, clean and warm homes are needed, but what happens to the old sense of community when the slums go?'

'As I said in the debate, sir, I think we are solving one problem only to replace it with another. During the war, people in the London backstreets and terraces supported each other and everyone knew everyone else. Once that goes, it leaves a vacuum. Loneliness is a soul-destroying thing.'

'Have you experienced it yourself?'

'No, sir – but I know people who have.'

The master had looked at him for a moment and then nodded. 'You're a deep thinker, Ronoscki. You plan to teach, I believe?'

'Yes, sir.'

'Good. I think you'll do well...' He had turned to walk away and then halted, 'Ronoscki – just a word of warning. You opposed Crawford this evening. He didn't like it much because some of your arguments made his look shallow. Don't do it too often.'

Freddie had caught the veiled warning. Crawford was one of the senior students, taking a three-year course, and most of the others hung on his every word. He had a lot of first-termers running errands for him in the hope of a kind word, but he was vain and pompous in Freddie's opinion. Was he also dangerous? The master, who was Freddie's history teacher and known as Old Fart behind his back but called Mr Henry, had seemed to be warning Freddie. As he was taller, broader, and fitter than Crawford, who was thin and pale and never exercised, Freddie felt able to cope with him so he dismissed the warning. What possible harm could Crawford do him? Freddie could knock him down with one punch if he chose but he wasn't the aggressive kind and would only use his strength if it he had no choice...

4

Maggie looked at Greg, her fine brows raised. He'd arrived early that morning with a large bunch of red roses and a bottle of Chanel perfume, telling her that he would be based in London for the next month and then he might have to go abroad again for a few weeks. As a test driver and consultant for racing cars, he was often asked to test-drive new models, and worked on a freelance basis, for various teams, attending several of the races held overseas, as well as working in the factory. Maggie teased him about his glamorous lifestyle, gadding off to all these exotic countries, like Italy, France and Spain, but she knew that most of his time was spent inside working on the cars, or testing for performance on various tracks.

'It is impossible to plan our wedding, isn't it?' she said with a wry laugh. 'You're never in the same place long enough.'

'I know it has been difficult,' Greg apologised. 'We do have the next few weeks, Maggie darling. Could we just jump in with both feet and do it... say, *in* two weeks?'

'Two weeks?' she almost squeaked. 'I don't have a dress or anything—'

'Three?' The look in his eyes made Maggie's heart catch. 'Otherwise, it may just drag on into the autumn...'

Smothering a sigh, because she'd hoped to plan a fancy wedding with all the trimmings, Maggie smiled. 'I might just manage to do it in three weeks,' she said. 'Yes, why not?' She laughed, catching the excitement in him, her love for him coming to the fore as she agreed. 'Oh, Greg, I do love you.'

'Not as much as I love you,' he teased.

'I love you more...'

'I love you more and more.'

'Soppy,' she said, amused by the game he played whenever he rang her from his travels.

'If we're married you can come with me on my next trip. Ferrari are having some problems with their latest car, and Enzo asked if I would do some test driving for them,' Greg said, reaching out to kiss her again. 'I thought we could make it an extended honeymoon. I'll be working some of the time, but there are a lot of wonderful things to see in Italy and we'll have plenty of time to explore together. Think of all the sleepy villages, the scenery, and the wonderful old buildings, the art – and the clothes in Milan.'

'Italy? All that wonderful food to try!' Maggie saw the laughter in his eyes. 'Oh, I'd love to come and I shall. Granny Peggy will make sure everything is all right at the restaurant and she has plenty of helpers now.'

'Are you still as busy?' Greg asked, looking lovingly into her eyes.

'Yes, we are, which makes it even sadder that we may lose it...'

'Have you heard anything more about the clearance?' Greg raised an eyebrow. He'd been upset for her when she'd spoken to him of it during one of their long phone calls. Maggie thought he must spend a fortune on them, but she loved it that he wanted to talk to her whenever he could. 'I know a good lawyer who will get you the best compensation – and he won't charge you a penny, because he is a cousin and if he did, I'd kill him.'

Maggie laughed as was intended. 'Give his name to Able. He says he isn't going to let them have the Pig & Whistle for nothing. He sold his other property in Mulberry Lane years ago, but he spent a lot of money on restructuring the Pig & Whistle. I think Tom Barton owns some houses as well as his yard.'

'The council will try to get them all as cheaply as they can, but Able has a good case. The Pig & Whistle isn't a slum building, so if they want to knock it down, they have to pay the market price. There is also the matter of your business; they should pay some compensation for that, but it doesn't always amount to much. Their standpoint is that you can go and do it elsewhere.'

'And I can if I have to,' Maggie said. 'It doesn't seem fair that we have to just uproot, though in my own case it doesn't matter so much – but Maureen's shop is profitable too and she doesn't know what she wants to do if they clear all the lanes and she loses her home.'

'I dare say a lot of the residents feel the same,' Greg nodded his agreement. 'I know slum clearance sounds like a good idea, and Mulberry Lane is a bit run-down, but it isn't a slum when you compare it to other areas in London, so, perhaps, we're all worrying for nothing.'

'Able doesn't think so,' Maggie said. 'He knows some of the men on the council and they've told him privately that they believe the lanes are due to be restructured, whatever that means.'

'It could mean they intend to leave some properties in situ.' Greg looked thoughtful. 'I know complete clearance hasn't always worked in the past, so they might plan round buildings they consider of interest.'

'You mean like the Pig & Whistle?' Maggie considered the idea. 'I'm not sure it would be good for business if they did. There will be disruption and mess for months on end and all the regulars will have been driven away. We might become a fashionable oddity.'

Greg burst into laughter at that. 'So what are you going to do if they do pull it all down?'

'Who knows?' Maggie said with an eloquent little shrug. 'Become a full-time wife and mother?'

'I'd enjoy that, my beautiful Maggie, but would you?'

Maggie shook her head. 'Not completely. I still want to cook and run my own restaurant. I would employ others, of course, so I didn't work every day, but it's something I love to do.' Maggie was never happier than when she was creating a special dish or discovering a new taste.

'Well, we can find somewhere else for you to do that,' Greg told her and she nodded.

'I know. I'm not going to worry about it. I have a wedding to plan to the man I love, in a hurry – and, besides, Granny Peggy told me not to let the problem of whether we'll have to move upset me. She says things have a habit of working themselves out. She will be far more concerned about whether we can book the church in time.' Maggie gave a little gurgle of excitement. 'Oh, Greg, it's wonderful. We'll be married at last.'

'Not before time,' Greg murmured as he drew her into his arms and kissed her softly. He stroked her cheek with one finger as he released her. 'What will Peggy say when you tell her the wedding is in three weeks?'

'She won't mind. Granny Peggy just wants us all to be happy – but...' A naughty twinkle lit up Maggie's eyes. 'Everyone else round here will count the months to the birth of our first child...'

Greg's shout of laughter set her off and they were laughing together when Peggy walked into the kitchen.

'I thought I heard your voice, Greg. So what is causing such gales of laughter?' She looked from one to the other.

'We're getting married in three weeks,' Maggie told her. She smiled as Peggy arched an eyebrow. 'No, I am not pregnant – but it is what everyone will believe.'

Peggy chuckled. 'Yes, a few will undoubtedly, but they won't say so in my hearing or they will get a flea in their ear.' She looked from one to the other. 'Why the rush?'

'Because Greg has been asked to test-drive for Ferrari – and we have a few weeks before he has to leave, so—'

'You are going to use it to get married. Good idea.' She smiled at Greg. 'I thought you worked for Lotus – the British team?'

'I work for whichever team needs my expertise,' Greg explained. 'I have a talent for setting up cars to get the best performance on a certain track – that is why we test-drive. Not all racing drivers can do that, so the teams employ freelance drivers like me to test their car and sort out any little problems.'

'Ah, you're one of the clever ones,' Peggy nodded as if she understood. 'I'd expect that, because you had the sense to choose my Maggie. Well, what are we going to do about this wedding? I hope we can get the church at such short notice...'

'Oh, Granny Peggy, I do love you,' Maggie said. 'I told Greg you would say that. You don't mind, do you?'

'I am looking forward to it. It's what we could all do with just now, something to be excited for,' she assured them. 'Three weeks will just give us enough time to buy a wedding dress for you and a new hat for me. I've got loads of outfits I bought for our holiday and never wore. I've put on some weight since I got home, so they should fit me again now.' A look of satisfaction entered her eyes. 'You will be a beautiful bride, Maggie love – but you always look beautiful, doesn't she, Greg?'

'Always,' he agreed promptly. 'I was just telling Maggie I know a good lawyer who will fight for your interests if the council try to get your property for nothing.'

'Do you think he would do a group claim for us and friends who own houses and shops in the area?' Peggy asked. 'I wouldn't bother to fight against the clearance. I think Hitler's bombs did quite a job of clearing some of the slums – but at a terrible cost in terms of people's lost lives. At least this time it is just a case of relocating.'

Greg looked at her with interest. 'I thought you would be more upset than that, Peggy?'

'I would have been once upon a time,' she agreed. 'Now, I understand that people you care about are all that matters. I know some of my friends will be really upset if it goes ahead. They will lose not only their homes but the community we've known all our lives – and during the war we all supported each other; it got us through. Things have been gradually changing over the years and I think this drive for modern homes is both good and bad. We do need them but the right kind. I believe all these flats are a mistake.'

'I think you might be right. If the old London disappears completely, things will be different. I doubt they will have that same sense of camaraderie in the suburbs.'

'No. It isn't the same.' Peggy frowned. 'I had some friends that it happened to a few years back. Mary wanted to stay in London when her area was redeveloped, so she moved into one of those tower blocks, but when I met her once in Oxford Street, she said she'd hardly spoken to her neighbours for weeks. Everyone was at work all day and they kept pretty much to themselves at weekends. Mary said she thought she would rather live in the country, where there might be a better community. She and her husband were looking for a nice village to move to. Mary had been a Londoner all her life but she couldn't settle after they forced her to leave her home. I often wonder if she is happier in the country.'

'Not everyone can just up sticks and go,' Greg observed. 'I agree with you, though, Peggy. For me it's the people, not the place.'

'We moved around quite a bit when I was young,' Maggie said. 'Mum and Ryan seemed happier in Scotland but...' She shook her head, feeling sad. 'I don't know why Ryan had to go off to Wales when he knew Mum wanted to be in London...'

'Don't place all the blame on Ryan,' Peggy told her. 'Your mother admits she is just as much at fault for their troubles.'

Maggie nodded. 'Where is Jon – did you take him to school again, Granny Peggy?'

'Yes. Janet had to see her solicitor about that flat she is selling,' Peggy said. 'She said once the sale has finalised, she wants to buy another one and renovate it. She had got her eye on a house in the lane, but now she needs to look elsewhere and there is another flat in the same block, so she might get that if hers is sold.'

'Tell her to be careful,' Greg advised. 'She puts a lot of work into her renovations and if the area is run-down, she might lose out.'

'Yes, she knows that,' Peggy said. 'Able had a long talk with her last evening. He and Tom have decided to stick to new build for a while in areas that have already been either cleared or rebuilt. Some of the old property appears cheap, but not if it gets a compulsory order on it.' She gave a little shake of her head. 'Let's forget about it now. We've got a wedding to plan – and a lot of cooking to do. We'll have the reception here, of course. Oh, it is so exciting!' Peggy's face lit up. 'Just wait until I tell Maureen. She was wondering when the wedding would be...'

5

'That is wonderful, Peggy,' Maureen exclaimed when her friend told her the news about Maggie's wedding. She'd popped round specially and they sat down for a cuppa and cake. 'I am so pleased. I've been feeling a bit mixed up since we heard they might knock everything down. This will help to take my mind off things...'

'You have Shirley's baby to look forward to,' Peggy reminded her. 'You were so thrilled about becoming a granny.'

'I still am,' Maureen told her, eyes lighting up. 'I've knitted loads of things already – but I promised Shirley I'd be here for her and I don't want to let her down, Peggy. She needs me to be close enough that she can leave the baby with me when she's ready to return to work.'

'I know Shirley trained hard and she takes her work as a doctor very seriously,' Peggy agreed, 'but surely she will want some time off to be a mother?'

'Yes, a year or so,' Maureen concurred. 'She wants a family, Peggy, but doesn't see why she should give up the job she loves. Ray agrees with her. He says they can pay a nanny and she can do less hours than before – but Shirley would rather I was around to look after her child, at least some of the time.'

'Yes, of course she would.' Peggy sighed. 'Why the council suddenly decided we're due for clearance, I don't know... Although the lanes do look a bit run-down when you really look. Tom and Able had plans to renovate them bit by bit, but now they've put those plans on hold until we know for certain.'

'Gordon says we can buy a house in the suburbs,' Maureen remarked. 'He says Shirley can pop back and forth in her car now she has learned to drive – but I don't think that will work. It was just a short drive for me, but it will take a lot longer if we go out further.'

'What is the alternative?' Peggy asked. 'You couldn't move closer to Shirley – in an apartment perhaps?'

'There are some not too far away and that would be better, but I wanted a garden for the pram, and for us, too,' Maureen said. 'We've looked at houses in her area, but they are too expensive.'

'Will they stay in their apartment now?' Peggy enquired. 'Wouldn't it be better if they bought a house somewhere out of the city centre? You could probably get something close to them and Shirley and Ray could do the travelling back and forth, leaving baby with you.'

'That is what Gordon thinks,' Maureen said. 'He believes Shirley should just stay home for a few years anyway. She says that if she did that she might have to retrain, because medicine is changing all the time, getting better, but she needs to keep up with it.'

'I see her point – and I kept working when I had children, but things were different then. There was always someone to keep an eye on them in an emergency.'

'That's it exactly. We all knew each other,' Maureen reminisced. 'Alice would look after Robin if I asked her and so would Mrs Tandy. Poor lady; she was so good to me.' She sighed for lost friends, both dead now. 'I miss them, Peggy – and I shall miss you if we are forced to move on.'

'Wherever we go, you'll be welcome to visit,' Peggy told her. 'You know that, Maureen. We don't know what we want either. Able needs to continue his part in the business with Tom, but he says he can travel in by train if necessary. One minute I think we'll stay in London, the next I decide we're off to the country, then I ask Able what he wants and neither of us truly know. I'm waiting to see what Maggie and Janet do before I decide.'

'What do *you* want to do?' Maureen asked her.

'It depends what happens,' Peggy replied thoughtfully. 'I don't have to live in my children's pockets, but I want a nice home for them to come to on holidays. Pip is considering another offer to live and work in America. I think he might go this time as his contract here is almost completed. Able says we can visit him, go on a ship next time, perhaps spend some time travelling there – and if Maggie settles in the country, we can visit her. I'm not sure what Janet will do...'

Maureen shivered suddenly. 'I hate seeing families break apart, even though they grow up and move on. It always used to be that you lived close to your parents and could help them as they got older – unless you were a man and serving in the forces, of course – but even then, you came home.'

'I think it is the way things are moving,' Peggy said. 'I'm not sure I like it either – but I've got used to the idea. Janet went off to Scotland with Ryan for years and we didn't see much of them. Pip and Sheila are near his work – and now Fay is in America, and of course Freddie is at college in Cambridge.'

'I can never quite believe that,' Maureen murmured with a shake of her head. 'It only seems like yesterday that I helped to deliver the twins.'

'And where would I have been without you through all that time?' Peggy asked. 'I do agree with you, Maureen love, and I hope it doesn't happen – but I'm not sure my family will stay in London even if they change their minds about the clearance. Freddie thinks he wants to travel when he finishes college and then do his teacher training – take a few months off before he starts a permanent job. That is several months down the line, of course – but there is no telling if he will take a position in London. He might go anywhere once he is qualified.'

'I thought that was his plan, to come home eventually?' Maureen was surprised.

'Yes, it was – but I don't think Greta likes London much,' Peggy explained. 'She is happier there in Cambridge, or so he thinks, and he might look for work in a smaller town or city.'

'Why does everything have to change?' Maureen said crossly. She saw Peggy looking at her and gave a rueful laugh. 'I am sorry. I am just out of sorts. I know things do change and young people like adventures. I went off to be a nurse during the war without the blink of an eye – well, almost. Gordon says it will be all right. I think he would quite fancy village life. He says we could have a shop or something there...'

'Why not a boarding house?' Peggy suggested. 'I wouldn't mind taking one on again. Oh, I know I let Pearl have the lease on the one I had, but there was the restaurant and Fay's business... But, as I said, I'll have to see what happens. We might be worrying for nothing.'

'Able doesn't think so and nor does Gordon.' Maureen sighed. 'Oh, well, I shan't change things by moaning, shall I?'

'It never helped during the war and we had a lot more to complain about then,' Peggy said.

'They were good times, though,' Maureen argued. 'I sometimes wonder how we got through the way we did – but I put it down to good friends.'

'Yes – and sheer stubbornness.' Peggy nodded. 'We were determined not to be beaten and so we weren't – but it was a close-run thing at times...'

* * *

Maureen sat staring out of the kitchen window after Peggy had gone. Her friend had cheered her up, but that was what she would miss most: the little chats over a pot of tea; the cooking sessions and the evenings spent in the Pig & Whistle, talking to friends. There was no sense in dwelling on it she decided and got up to start preparing their evening meal. Gordon had gone into the shop as he was feeling better but would be home any time now and she hadn't done a thing.

She turned on the wireless and heard a voice announcing that the A6 murderer, James Hanratty, had been hung. It sent a little chill down her spine and she shook herself as she turned off the radio just as the same voice was saying the new Panda crossings were causing confusion.

Fancy, going from a hanging to something like that! Maureen tutted to herself; she'd best get busy.

Just as she'd started to peel the potatoes, the telephone rang. Maureen went to answer it. 'Hello, Maureen Hart speaking—'

'Mum, it's Ray,' her daughter's husband sounded strange. 'I don't want to alarm you, but Shirley is in hospital. She fainted at work this morning and I booked her into a private clinic immediately. As far as we know, there is nothing much wrong, just that she has probably been overdoing it.'

'Oh, Ray. Why was she at work? She told me she was going to stop until after the birth?'

'She was – *is*,' he said. 'I asked her if she felt up to helping me with a delicate procedure and she said yes, of course she did – and she never made a murmur until we were done and then she suddenly fainted in my office. I'm the one to blame—'

'Don't go down that road,' Maureen countered. 'Shirley should have said no if she wasn't feeling well.'

'She particularly wanted to see the operation done as it was on a heart valve. We're working towards the time when we may be able to do a bypass, Maureen – and that could save a lot of lives, prolong them at least.'

'You are thinking it might work for Gordon?' Maureen's heart thumped.

'Yes; in time I think we'll be able to do it – and that is why Shirley wanted to see this procedure. It wasn't a bypass, but we're getting close to it. So, naturally, she thinks of her father and you.'

'Yes, that would be such a relief,' Maureen said breathlessly. 'I understand now. Shirley would want to see anything that might help her father. I'm not quite sure what you mean by a bypass, but you can explain another day. Just tell me – is Shirley going to be all right? And the baby?'

'As yet, they haven't done any tests. They are just letting her rest. I pray she is, Maureen. She is strong and healthy, and I can't see any reason why she shouldn't be – but I am anxious and I felt I should tell you.'

'Of course you should,' Maureen said. 'I've got a pen here. Give me the details of her hospital and I shall visit her tomorrow.'

'Yes, of course. They've told me I can visit for a few minutes this evening, but they want to keep her quiet, so it will only be a short visit.' He repeated the address for her and she wrote it down.

'You will let us know if there is any more news?'

'As soon as I can,' he promised. 'I told you, I can't think it is anything but tiredness – but I wanted to be sure.'

Maureen thanked him and he rang off. She felt her eyes prick with tears as she replaced the receiver. All day she'd been fretting over the future if they had to leave the lanes – and now her darling daughter was in hospital. If anything happened to Shirley or the baby... But no, she wouldn't let herself think that way. Maureen had to be careful. She mustn't let Gordon get upset, as he would do if he thought his daughter or grandchild was in danger.

She went to the kitchen sink and splashed water on her face, just managing to dry it before she heard Gordon's key in the lock.

* * *

'What else did Ray tell you?' Gordon asked, looking at her anxiously after she gently told him the news. 'Is she going to be all right?'

'He doesn't know much yet... He thinks so.'

'Thinks so? Thinks so!' Gordon exploded. 'He's her husband. He should damned well know. He should never have let her help him in theatre at her stage...'

'Shirley was interested in what they were doing,' Maureen said without enlightening him as to what it entailed. 'You know how stubborn she is, Gordon – a bit like her father. You keep working when there is really no need...'

For a moment, his eyes glittered with temper, but then he sighed and nodded his head. 'I know what she is – but she is my little girl, Maureen. She always will be.'

'Of course she is, love. Ray told me not to worry. He thinks Shirley is just tired. You know she still does that clinic as well as her theatre work. It is time she gave that up in my opinion.'

Gordon sat down heavily in his chair. He looked tired and drained. 'I know you're right. I'm just as bad. I should leave the shop to Ginger. He is a good lad and he told me to go home an hour ago, but I didn't. I wanted to finish stock-taking. It is the only way to know where we stand. I'm thinking of the future – but my little girl is more important right now. When can we see her?'

'In the morning,' Maureen replied. 'Ray is going to pop in this evening – but I remember now that Peggy's daughter-in-law, Sheila, was rushed off to hospital when she was having her second child, and she was fine and the baby healthy.'

Gordon closed his eyes for a moment. 'I am sure it happens, love – but it is different when it is your own.' He looked round the kitchen. 'Where is Gordy? Why isn't he home?'

'He was going to stay late at school for sports practice,' Maureen reminded. 'He said he might be in the cricket team this summer.'

'Football in the winter, cricket in the summer, that boy is sports-mad,' her husband said. 'I'll ring Ray later this evening. See if there is any more news.'

'Yes, you do that,' Maureen agreed, understanding how worried he was. She was anxious, too, but believed that Ray would let them know if anything more serious was happening.

* * *

When Gordon rang him later that evening, Ray sounded weary. 'I haven't been told anything more,' he assured Shirley's father. 'She was resting and they'd given her something to settle her, but her tests aren't complete yet, so we shan't know what is wrong until they've finished them. I'm hoping it is just exhaustion.'

'She should have stopped work before this,' Gordon replied, a slight censure in his tone.

'I agree,' Ray said easily. 'She hasn't been doing theatre work for the past few weeks but still goes to that clinic. I've tried to stop her, but she is passionate about her work there, as you know. I let her help with the procedure today, but, truthfully, she was only observing most of the time.'

'She will have to stop working at the clinic now,' Gordon said. 'I've tried to tell her myself, but you need to put your foot down, Ray, and make her rest more.'

'I'll do my best,' Ray replied ruefully, 'but you know Shirley. The more I tell her she shouldn't do something, the more stubborn she is...'

Gordon sighed and agreed. 'I know. I also know it isn't your fault she collapsed, Ray, but I couldn't bear any harm to come to her or the baby.'

'I believe both Shirley and the baby will be fine; it was just a precaution,' Ray said. 'I think she will be more sensible after this, Gordon. If she thinks she could lose the baby, she will be less inclined to take risks.'

'I hope so. Well, you sound tired, so you'd best get some rest.'

The two men said goodnight.

Gordon looked to Maureen as he replaced the receiver. 'I know he is right. She was always a stubborn little thing...'

'Try not to worry too much,' Maureen sympathised. 'Shirley is strong and that's why I believe she will be fine.'

6

'You should buy a second-hand cycle,' Greta said when she and Freddie were sitting by the River Cam in the spring sunshine one Saturday afternoon. Around them was the noise and chatter of students, and on the water, laughter as a punt got stuck midway between the banks and the young man poling seemed to have lost control, causing it to go round in circles rather than straight ahead. 'There's a small shop just off the market place in the Petty Cury. He does them up so they are in good condition.' Greta had discovered it when she was shopping in Woolworths and went around the corner to look in the windows of Roses, the big fashion shop there.

'I'm not sure I really need one,' Freddie replied, turning his face up to the sunshine to enjoy the rare warmth; the weather was still changeable, but that day was perfect. 'I suppose it would be useful, though. I could get to yours that bit quicker than walking.'

'It would make it easier for you to get about and you can put your books in the basket when you get them from the library,' she said. 'The man in the shop says you can sell it back to him when you no longer need it. I thought I might borrow one for a couple of bob – he does that too. We could go for rides out into the countryside on a Sunday afternoon in the summer...'

'That's a good idea,' Freddie agreed. Most of the students cycled madly round town, to and fro lodgings and the pubs they frequented, and, if they didn't own one, some of them weren't above borrowing any bike they happened to spot. 'Make sure you get a chain and padlock, Greta. If you leave it outside a shop, you might find it was unofficially borrowed by the time you came out again.'

Greta laughed. 'The man in the repair shop told me that, too. He says he often gets one of his bikes brought in by a student looking to sell it. If he knows who the owner is, he only offers them a couple of bob. When they take his offer, he knows they pinched it, but at least he can return it to the owner who is happy to pay the two shillings.'

'It isn't right, though,' Freddie said. 'I know the sort that do it. They actually have plenty of money and one of them has a sports car, but he still borrows other students' bikes if he gets the chance.'

'He doesn't sound very nice?'

'No, he isn't,' Freddie agreed. 'I clashed with him in the debating club and he and his friends make a point of sneering every time we pass each other in the quadrangle. They say things they think will upset me just loud enough for me to be aware and then get this superior look on their faces if I turn round and look.'

'You should be careful of them,' Greta warned, looking anxious.

'I just wish he'd try something,' Freddie said and grinned. 'I'm bigger and fitter than he is, so there's no chance he'd risk it. No, if he does anything it will be underhand.'

'That makes him more dangerous, not less,' Greta pointed out. 'Promise me you won't deliberately provoke him, Freddie.'

'I try to avoid him as much as I can,' he assured her. 'Don't worry. I don't believe he would risk getting expelled. His father is in politics and is expecting him to go into law and then perhaps a diplomatic career. He can't afford to be thrown out of Cambridge.'

Out on the river, one of the girls had taken over the punt and was now showing the hapless young man how it should be done.

Greta nodded. 'Shall I see you tomorrow?' she asked as a clock chimed four somewhere and she knew they had to make a move.

Freddie had keep-fit training to go to later that evening for the rowing team.

'Well, we have a couple of hours' training on the river in the morning and I need to do some work on my project for my English exam – but I should be able to get away by three. We can spend the evening together if you've nothing else you want to do?'

'I'll finish a story this evening and send it off,' Greta said. 'I did sell another one of my articles, after all, Freddie. The cheque came today for four guineas.'

'That is brilliant,' he said. 'Did they ask for more?'

'Yes. It was about the colleges and student life. I used little things you've told me and described some of the Backs... remember we walked that way together?' Her cheeks were pink. 'They've asked me to write about the rowing and the punts on the river... but I'm not sure I know enough.'

'We will talk about it tomorrow and I'll help you,' Freddie said. He pulled her up from the bench they'd been sitting on. 'Shall we visit the cycle shop on the way back? If they've got any cheap enough, maybe I'll buy one.'

* * *

Freddie looked at the cycle he'd purchased with pleasure as he dismounted inside the college grounds. It wasn't new by any means, but it looked as if it might be, because it had new tyres and the paintwork had been sprayed so it was a nice dark shiny maroon and quite distinctive. He would know his bike wherever he left it. Greta had been right to suggest it. He'd got to his training ground in half the time it would take him to walk. That meant he could have a little longer with Greta when they were together. Freddie worried that she spent too much time alone. If she'd stayed in London, she would have had Maggie and his mother for company, as well as Janet and Able and all the girls that worked in the restaurant and bar.

'Oh my gawd,' a spiteful voice hissed just behind him. 'Look what the East End yokel has got now. Did it come out of the Ark, Ronoscki?'

Freddie turned and saw Crawford and his cronies watching him. They were openly sneering and deriding his cycle, hoping to provoke him into something violent.

'Ah yes,' he said calmly. 'It probably did, Crawford, but since I am the one riding it and happy do so, I can't see that it matters to you.'

'Listen to him,' Crawford drawled, his thin lips sneering. 'Anyone would think he had half a brain.' A burst of spiteful laughter greeted his words. The three other students with Crawford hung on his every word, as if he were the Messiah.

Freddie ignored the remark, though he would have liked to take the smirk from Crawford's face. He chained the wheels of his cycle so that it would be impossible to carry it away from the railings provided for their bikes, and walked off. He could hear the sniggering behind him but ignored it. If they thought rude comments about his East End background could upset him, they were wrong. Freddie was proud of being born a Londoner and it was water off a duck's back.

He suddenly felt something sting behind his ear and put up a hand, feeling a spot of blood where a stone had caught him. Turning, he looked at the group of jeering students. For a moment, his fists curled at his sides and he hesitated, tempted to go back, and give them the fright of their lives, but he held his nerve. If he did that, they had won, because if one of them got harmed in the scuffle, he would likely be sent down for the rest of the term and he couldn't afford to lose his place here.

So he just stood and looked at them and then smiled. 'Not a bad shot,' he said. 'Not quite good enough for the cricket team, Bradley, but keep trying. You might make it...'

He saw the younger of the four students colour and knew he'd guessed right. Bradley had tried for the cricket team. His bowling was good, but he'd used dirty tricks and scored the ball to make it spin faster and so the captain had turned him down.

Crawford's look of hatred shocked Freddie. Surely, he hadn't caused that simply by opposing him in the debating club? Shrugging, he walked off. They were just spiteful cowards and he had no intention of letting them get to him. Freddie's life was full and he enjoyed it; bullies like Crawford and his gang were not worth the spit.

* * *

It was very early when Freddie went out to fetch his bike the next morning; it would help him get to the boathouse quicker. However, when he bent to remove the padlock, he saw that both his tyres had been slashed.

'The bastards...' he muttered, no doubt in his mind who was responsible. It meant he would have to walk to his training – or sprint, as he'd given himself an extra few minutes in bed. He straightened up and saw that the captain of the rowing team had approached without him noticing. 'I might be a couple of minutes late...'

'Tyres been slashed?' Henry Simpson frowned. 'I'll give you a lift, Ronoscki, but report it to the students' committee. This sort of thing doesn't belong on campus.'

'Thanks. I only got it yesterday,' Freddie said and walked with him to the sports car parked just a short distance away from the college. 'Don't you worry about your car?'

'I don't have enemies,' Simpson replied with a shrug. 'You have obviously made some. Any ideas who did it?'

'Yes. I'm pretty sure I know who was responsible,' Freddie said, grimacing. 'However, I have no proof and it would be useless to make a fuss. I'll either take it back or find somewhere else to leave it.'

'That's how the bullies get away with it,' Simpson said as he started the car and drew away from the kerb. 'I've got a good idea who did it and I'll drop a few hints, but really, they need to be stopped. What kind of men will they be when they leave here? I don't fancy seeing my country governed in the future by sneaks and bullies.'

'I suspect there are always a few in and around positions of power,' Freddie answered. 'We spent several years fighting one bully, but there are others in power in other countries. Hitler wasn't the only tyrant and he won't be the last.'

'You are a deep thinker,' Simpson remarked, brows rising. 'You're not thinking of politics as a career?'

'No, it's teaching for me,' Freddie replied. 'I want to work with kids from difficult backgrounds, too, even if I do that as a volunteer in the evenings.'

'Yes, that sounds about right, but being honourable, and maybe a bit righteous, won't win you friends here, Ronoscki. Crawford and his gang are not the only privileged set who dislike being made to look like a spoiled, ignorant rabble, which is what they are, of course. You show them up for the fools they are, I fear.'

Freddie gave a shout of laughter. 'If you have opinions like that, how come you haven't made enemies?'

'Because I'm careful who I share them with,' Simpson said. 'Besides, my father knows Crawford's father and a word in his ear would soon put paid to his games. He leaves me well alone – but you are fair game to him.' He frowned as he brought his car to a smooth stop close to the river and the boathouse. 'Leave it to me. I'll let him know you're a friend of mine; that should stop him, or at least make him think a bit.'

'Thanks,' Freddie replied, surprised but pleased to have been accepted by a man he'd thought of as out of his league. Simpson was well known to be heading for a bright future, both in his chosen sport and his career in the law chambers his father owned. 'In a boxing ring, I'd show him what's what, but he'd never give me the chance.'

'No, he wouldn't,' Simpson remarked with a grin. 'Forget it now, Ronoscki. We want Cambridge to win the boat race again next year and neither of us will make the final team or even the reserves unless we put our backs into it...' Cambridge had won that year and by some five lengths, with the heaviest crew for years.

* * *

Greta was upset when Freddie told her about the slashed tyres. 'Oh, Freddie. How can they be so ignorant? What do they gain from doing such petty things?'

'They just want to get back at me for some reason. I don't know why Crawford took against me. All I did was argue the other side to his theory. I can't see why it should make him hate me. There is no point in a debating society if everyone takes the same view.'

'It probably isn't that at all,' Greta said. 'It's just who you are, Freddie. You might not realise it, but you have an air of quiet confidence and strength – it is probably just plain jealousy.'

Freddie shook his head. 'That might be the truth, but it is so foolish. I know he gets high marks in certain subjects. He's been top of the list in the maths exams twice and I was only third or fourth... and in sciences he does well. Neither of those are my specialist subjects, but I took maths as an extra and have done all right...'

'What about sports and physical training? Is Crawford any good at them?'

'Well, he doesn't do any physical exercise,' Freddie replied. 'As far as I can tell, he plays no sport whatsoever – unless he might play tennis. I think I saw a racket in his things once.'

'Then he is very likely jealous of you – you do all that well,' Greta said. 'Didn't you say one of his friends was turned down for the cricket team?'

Freddie nodded. 'Yes, I was a bit mean to him over that – but he threw a stone at me and I used words to cut him down rather than my fists.'

'Sounds to me as if that is the reason they don't like you,' Greta said anxiously. 'Be careful of them, Freddie.' A little shiver went through her. 'They are a nasty lot. I'm just glad it was your tyres they slashed rather than you...'

'Don't worry, they are just bullies and cowards; they won't try anything physical,' Freddie said. 'Let's go to the pictures this evening and forget them. I don't let Crawford and his gang worry me.'

* * *

'Well now, that didn't last long,' the man in the cycle shop said when Freddie wheeled it into the shop the following weekend. Freddie had been too busy to take it in before and he'd had to carry it over his shoulder, because it wouldn't wheel properly with slashed tyres. He shook his head as he spotted the slashes in the tyres. 'You didn't do that?'

'No. I left it chained to the railings provided and it was like this the next morning. I don't think they can be repaired and I can't afford new tyres just yet.'

'I might have some nearly new ones I can put on for you,' the man said with a frown. 'Don't worry about the money just yet. You can pay me when you're ready.'

'It's very good of you,' Freddie replied. 'I can give you a couple of bob a week until I've paid for them.' He offered his hand, feeling more was called for in the face of the shop owner's generosity. 'I'm Freddie Ronoscki. My father would send me the money if I asked, but he has already given me enough.'

'And I'm Billy Jones,' the man replied. 'I like the cut of you, Freddie. If you get any spare time, I'll give you a chance to earn a few bob, for yourself.'

'I don't get much unfortunately,' Freddie said. 'What do you need doing?'

'It's not really for me,' Billy Jones explained. 'My aunt owns the sweet shop next to the bank, just round the corner from me. She is in her seventies but still fighting fit and does most things for herself – but the bother happens when the kids crowd in on a Saturday morning. Some of them have been pinching from her. She needs someone honest to look out for her or she'll have no profits left.'

'I have rowing practice from six until eight-thirty on Saturdays,' Freddie said. 'I could be there by nine-thirty and stay until lunchtime. My girlfriend gets off work at one so we like to spend the afternoon together. Would that help your aunt?'

'Yes. It is the mornings when it happens,' Billy replied. 'I urged her to get a young assistant, but she says she couldn't afford a full-time wage, and besides, she insists she can manage for herself. But some of them cheek her and I know it upsets her.' Billy looked annoyed. 'She often gives the younger ones who look hungry a threepenny chocolate bar – but it's this gang of older boys who are causing havoc. Last week, she told them she'd send for the police and one of them threw a jar of sherbet lemons across the room and smashed it.'

'That wants stopping,' Freddie said. 'It sets a bad example to the others. If they think he can get away with it, they will try something themselves. I'll be pleased to help her sort them out, sir. I don't need any wages – just those tyres you mentioned.'

'It is a deal,' Billy said and grinned. 'I should warn you my aunt is a bit of a tartar.'

'I don't mind that,' Freddie laughed. 'I'll be happy to help.'

'You'll probably charm her,' Billy said ruefully. 'She never listens to me. Her name is Martha Jones by the way.'

'Right. You tell her I'm coming and I'll start next week,' Freddie said. 'And thank you for the chance. I'll sort those hooligans for you, Mr Jones.'

'Good lad,' Billy said. He looked at the bike. 'I'll have this ready for you by this evening...'

Freddie thanked him and walked away, feeling pleased with his bargain. He'd dealt with unruly boys before at the sports club in London, and was confident he knew how to handle them. Threats would only make them jeer and laugh, but a firm hand on the shoulder and a look would sometimes work wonders, especially when you were as large and muscular as Freddie. Usually, there was a reason behind bad behaviour and it was often sourced in the home. Dealing with unruly lads in the sweet shop would be good practice for when he started his year of being a pupil-teacher, and he would behave just as if he were about to take a class of difficult boys.

7

'I've had a letter from the council,' Able announced, walking into the kitchen that Monday morning; it was a sunny morning and Peggy had a vase of daffodils on the windowsill, which looked out into the backyard of the Pig & Whistle. 'They are having a meeting next month and I've been invited to attend. It seems the subject of the clearance is on the agenda again and some of us from the lanes have been told we have the chance to put across our point of view.'

'Good,' Peggy said and then frowned. 'Except, I am not sure it is – because that sounds as if they are serious about this restructuring. It is all very well inviting the residents and business owners to have their say, but, in the end, they will still go ahead if it's what they decide is in the public interest.'

'True,' Able agreed. 'If we all got together and protested, we might delay it, but is that fair to those that need decent homes? Mulberry Lane is much better than a lot of other lanes in the area, but some of the terraces are in wretched condition.' He looked at her anxiously. 'What do you hope for, hon?'

'If you're worrying about me, don't,' Peggy told him. 'I don't want them to destroy our community, Able, but if we have to live elsewhere, I can cope – though I feel for others; the older folk who just won't be happy in one of those high-rise flats. Yes, they will be clean and modern – but they will feel so isolated. Who do they run to when they want to borrow a cup of sugar?' She sighed. 'I know that sounds daft, but when you know everyone and then you are surrounded by strangers, how do you cope? I think some folk won't know how.'

Able nodded his agreement. 'Mind you, some of them have already accepted modern accommodation elsewhere, moved out to the suburbs. That's why a third of the houses are boarded up. I see more of it than you do. We had intended to renovate some of them, but others, well, they would be best gone...' He gave a little shrug. 'Tom says concentrate on new build, but much of that is out in the suburbs.'

'What if you get offered a contract to do some of the work when they do pull the old terraces down?'

'I expect we would accept,' Able said thoughtfully. 'No point in cutting your nose off to spite your face – but I'd still rather they didn't.'

'Oh yes, much rather they just left us alone,' Peggy agreed and sighed. 'The world never stands still, does it? Things move on whether you want them to or not.'

'Let's forget about it while we can,' Able said, and then, to change the subject, 'It is only a week now until Maggie's wedding. Have you bought a new outfit?'

'I bought a new hat,' Peggy said. 'Maggie's dress is just gorgeous. She is going to look beautiful.'

'She always does, takes after her grandmother,' Able said and reached out to pop a kiss on her cheek. 'Is everything else settled – food, church, flowers?'

'As if you need ask about the food,' Peggy teased. 'Maggie has it all planned and our cooks will prepare a banquet worthy of her. The church and flowers have been sorted by Greg.' A smile lit her eyes. 'If ever I saw a man in love, it's Greg. It just shines out of him.'

'I hope you can see my love for you shining out of me, too?' Able raised his brows.

'Yes, I can,' Peggy confirmed. 'But poor Greg looks bemused. It's as if he's hardly able to believe his luck in finding Maggie and having her love him.'

'Yes, I know. He told me he has to pinch himself to make sure he isn't dreaming. I think there might have been someone in his past that let him down, perhaps as a result of the accident that scarred him.'

'It was so touching that he had plastic surgery to make himself look more presentable for Maggie and she just didn't care about the scars. She said she fell in love with him, scars included, right from the start but wasn't sure he liked her.'

'Just as I'd expect of her,' Able said with a look of approval. 'I lost an arm in the war, but you didn't miss a beat when we met again afterwards – and Maggie is a lot like you.'

'You were still you and I was so glad we could be together again.' Peggy raised her face for the kiss she knew was coming.

'What do you want to give her as a wedding present?' Able asked.

'Maggie says they are moving into Greg's apartment for the time being,' Peggy replied. 'It is furnished, as is his home in the country. I think she might like a real pearl necklace. We can give her some money too – and, if we have to accept compensation for the Pig & Whistle, she will have her share of that when it happens.'

'Yes, I think that is perfect,' Able agreed. 'We'll give Greg something personal as well – perhaps a gold watch or a good set of cufflinks. I've noticed that he likes those.'

'I'll let you choose his gift,' Peggy said. 'We could go to the jewellers where you bought my beautiful eternity ring.'

'Yes, we will,' Able inclined his head in agreement. 'Sheila and Pip are coming to stay for the wedding so that Sarah can be a bridesmaid, aren't they?' He laughed, having spoken to their granddaughter about it on the phone and heard her excited chatter about her special dress. Maggie had asked Sheila to buy one there as there was no time to arrange for fittings in London, merely advising that it should be a pale peach in colour.

'Yes. I've booked them into the guest house, because we'll be full. Freddie and Greta will be here and I'm hoping Fay will get home for it. She said when I telephoned her that she will try to fly back but doesn't think Jace can come with her. If she manages to get here, she will want her old room.'

'I am sure she can share with Greta,' Able replied. 'She says out there they fly all the time – from one part of the country to another. So she is fine with coming alone.'

'America is a big country,' Peggy agreed. 'I've been thinking, Able. I know I said I didn't want to visit it again, but that was a reaction from what happened to me out there. I know it was my own fault for getting involved in that unpleasant business with the Freedom Riders but—'

'You wanted to help the woman those thugs had knocked to the ground,' Able said. 'That is you, Peggy. I wouldn't expect you to do anything else, though I'd stop you if I could. I was ashamed of my fellow countrymen. Next time, we'll go to places where they know how to behave, hon.'

'You said we might go over by sea and spend some time with Fay and I'd like that now and then...' Peggy looked at him wistfully. 'I miss her, Able. I know Freddie, Janet and Pip are still here – but she is my little girl.'

'Mine, too,' he said with a wide grin. 'I was hoping you might come round to the idea, hon. We'll see what Fay is planning for the future, if she manages to get home for the wedding.'

'Maggie will be disappointed if she doesn't,' Peggy sighed. 'She'd hoped they would work together for longer. I know she misses their banter – but we have to be glad that Fay is happy. I wasn't at all sure she would be. I know she was head over heels in love with Jace, but in a strange country away from her family...' She shook her head. 'I was wrong. She is having a wonderful time out there. When she isn't at a theatre or a party, she's catering for pool parties and making lots of friends. It seems to suit her.'

'If Jace gets that film contract, I imagine they will live there for the foreseeable future,' Able said. 'Not what we'd have chosen – but if Fay is happy, we can accept it for her sake, can't we?'

'Yes, of course,' Peggy agreed, but a little sigh escaped. 'Well, that's the last apple pie made. It's funny, but my old customers know the difference. If one of the others makes them, my customers look at me and shake their heads.'

'No one makes apple pie like you,' Able agreed. 'That top layer of pastry is so crisp and sweet and then the bottom layer has the tartness of the apples that have melted into it. I could eat a whole one any day!'

'You'll get fat yet,' Peggy teased, knowing he wouldn't. His lean figure never seemed to change by an inch. He was still every bit as good-looking as the first day he'd walked into the Pig & Whistle during the war. 'Well, I have finished for the day. Let's go and see if we can find some wedding gifts.'

'Good idea,' Able agreed. 'Get ready while I just pop round to Tom. We'll have lunch out somewhere too – though the best food in town is right here.'

'You can take me to the Savoy Grill,' Peggy said outrageously, a wicked twinkle in her eye. 'I've never been there for lunch, so now's the time to start...'

* * *

Peggy wrapped the gifts they'd bought with loving care, tying a wide silver ribbon around the shiny white paper with a little flourish. Maggie would enjoy the things they'd settled on for her, and Able had chosen gold cufflinks set with tiny diamonds for Greg. Peggy knew Maggie would get lots of small gifts for her home from friends and customers, but she hadn't wanted to give her something like that. There would be plenty of time once Maggie had her own home and was able to choose the style she liked.

Peggy had already bought herself a beautiful navy and white hat to go with a navy dress and jacket that she'd had new for her trip to America but never worn. Able had wanted to buy her another outfit, but she hadn't seen anything she liked as much, but she had given in and bought a pair of winkle-picker shoes in navy with a white bar across the toe. The heels were ridiculously high, but they looked elegant and Peggy would probably only wear them for the wedding.

Peggy had resisted the fashion in stiletto heels until now, but when she tried them on, she saw how good they made her legs look and so she'd let herself be persuaded into the purchase. Now she put them on and paraded across the bedroom floor, admiring their style.

'Can I come in, Granny?' Maggie spoke from outside the door and Peggy hid the parcels behind a cushion on the bed.

'Yes, of course you can, darling,' Peggy invited, smiling as her granddaughter entered. 'What do you think of these shoes? Are they too much for a woman of my age?'

'I love them,' Maggie said warmly. 'Are you going to wear them for the wedding?'

'Yes, if you approve,' Peggy replied. 'They are actually surprisingly comfortable. Able insisted I try them on, so I did and I liked them. I've got a lovely hat, too.'

Maggie exclaimed over the smart navy straw and chiffon hat. It had big white roses at the front and a swathe of white around the brim. 'It suits you, Granny. I love it and it will go so well with the navy-blue outfit you've chosen.'

Peggy nodded, but her eyes were filled with love for Maggie. 'Are you excited, darling?'

'Thrilled,' Maggie replied, her smile coming back. 'I can't wait, Granny. Greg and I have spent so little time together since we met. It will be the first time we've had more than a few days together.'

'I'm glad you are happy,' Peggy said and reached for her hand. 'I know I don't need to ask whether you're sure. You and Greg are so right for each other. Both Able and I felt it from the first.'

'Yes. I think I knew it almost as soon as we met – well, as soon as he stopped telling me off for careless driving...'

'Why, weren't you paying attention?' Peggy asked. 'Able says you're normally a good driver.'

'Oh, I had things on my mind,' Maggie said vaguely. 'Greg could smell wine in the car and thought I'd been drinking, but I hadn't; some of the wine I'd bought for the restaurant had spilled out of shattered bottles in the accident...'

'Well, it brought you two together.' Peggy nodded. 'I suppose that was about the time you heard of my accident.'

'Yes. We were all very worried,' Maggie said and moved in to hug her. 'You've always been the anchor in my world, Granny. Mum loves me and I love her, but she and Ryan – well, they had their ups and downs when I was young. My dad died and I can hardly remember it now – but you've always been there for me. I wasn't sure Ryan would be...'

'Yes, I know, but I always thought he loved both of you.' Peggy frowned. 'I can't understand why he bought that smallholding in Wales, knowing that Janet and Jon would hate it.'

'Maybe he'd just had enough,' Maggie suggested. 'They had never been truly together the way you and Able are – and after what happened with Jon, it just seemed to fall apart for them. I felt a bit guilty. If I'd been there, maybe Jon wouldn't have tried to come to London...'

'I think your brother was a mixed-up little boy,' Peggy said. 'He must have sensed that something wasn't right between his mother and father and perhaps that is why he went off the rails. He seems much happier now he's living here with us.'

'Yes, he is – though I think he misses his father. He and Ryan were closer for a while during the time Janet was in America with you.' Maggie frowned. 'That is why I don't understand what went wrong for them when you all came back. It was all so sudden.'

'Janet said he didn't give her any warning and she swears they didn't have a row. He just said he was leaving out of the blue and that was it.'

'It is a mystery,' Maggie said. 'I wrote and invited him to my wedding, said I really hoped he would come – but he hasn't replied.'

'I wrote too,' Peggy agreed. 'It is a bit strange that he hasn't replied to either of us. Ryan was very fond of you. I can't see that he wouldn't want to come to your wedding – give you away.'

Maggie looked thoughtful. 'I've wondered – but surely he would have said if he was ill?'

Peggy's gaze narrowed. 'Do you think he might be? Could that be the reason he went off so suddenly?' She shook her head. 'No, he wouldn't go to a place like that if he was ill, would he?'

'That's what I thought,' Maggie said. 'But Mum says she hasn't heard from him in months either. It was only supposed to be a trial separation... so why has Ryan cut himself off from us all?'

'I don't know, Maggie. Let's see if he turns up for the wedding. If he doesn't, I might get Able to go and see him. They get on well and if anyone can sort things, it is Able.'

Maggie agreed, looking pensive, and then her face lit up. 'Oh, I had a phone call from Jace. He said that Fay would be arriving tomorrow. She managed to get a flight at short notice; a cancelled ticket, I think, but had no time to let us know. Jace says he was supposed to have let us know sooner but has been so busy he didn't get round to it.'

'That's good,' Peggy said, feeling a thrill of pleasure that Fay would soon be with them again. 'He couldn't come with her then?'

'No, too busy, but he says he might get over in a few weeks and Fay is going to stay for a while.'

'Wonderful. I know I shouldn't, but I do miss her and I worry, too.'

'Oh, I shouldn't worry too much,' Maggie replied. 'She is having a fantastic time. Her letters are full of it.'

'Yes, I know, but I'm her mother and mothers worry,' Peggy said with a little laugh. 'I worry about all my children – except Freddie. I don't know why, but I always think he is capable of dealing with anything...'

8

Freddie saw some familiar young lads outside the sweet shop as he cycled back to college that afternoon through sleepy sunlit streets. He'd been into town to buy a gift for Maggie's wedding and was in a hurry to get back for a lecture, but immediately decided to wheel his bike towards the little shop. The lads noticed him and turned away, pushing, and jostling each other as they walked off.

Freddie smiled to himself as he went inside the shop that smelled of chocolate and boiled sweets, its glass jars filled with delicious treats arranged on shelves behind the big counter, trays of sugar mice, chewy liquorice bootlaces, and chocolate flakes in the glass counter, alongside chunky fudge, and pink coconut ice.

'Good afternoon, Miss Jones,' he said as he saw the elderly lady peering at him from behind the counter. 'Is everything all right?'

'Of course it is, why wouldn't it be?' she replied sharply, but she'd looked nervous until he spoke and he knew the unruly lads worried her.

'I just wondered if you'd had any more trouble from those lads who were here last Saturday?'

'No...' A gleam came into her pale blue eyes. 'Not after you saw them off. My grandson is an interfering nuisance, but he did me a favour sending you to me. I never saw anything that funny in my life.' A little gleam of mischief lit up her faded-blue eyes and he saw the indomitable spirit that refused to give in despite her advancing years.

'They did leave quite quickly once I went round the counter,' Freddie replied and grinned. 'I'm sorry I won't be here this weekend, but I'm going home for a family wedding. I'll come again the week after.'

'I'll be perfectly fine, young man,' she said. 'Enjoy the wedding.'

'You take care of yourself,' Freddie told her. 'Those lads are a boisterous lot, but I don't think they are malicious. If they do try to cause trouble, blow that whistle I gave you. I told them we had a police whistle and if they cause you any more trouble, they will be arrested.'

'I'll remember,' she confirmed. 'Not that I'm sure the youngsters today take that much notice of the law. When I was young, we were terrified if a copper came round our house. My parents thought it shameful. I think the kids and parents might just laugh nowadays. It was you that put the scare into them, Freddie. You're a big lad—'

Freddie laughed. 'Well, just you take care of yourself. I'll come and see you when I get back,' he promised.

He left the shop, smiling to himself. He liked Martha Jones and hoped she wouldn't get any trouble while he was away.

* * *

As Freddie cycled to the college, he was thoughtful. He'd taken to leaving his bike a few yards outside the gates of the compound and chaining it to a railing there. So far, he hadn't had any more slashed tyres and he wondered if Henry Simpson had had a word with Crawford, as he'd promised.

Walking into the college grounds, he saw three students standing on the grass, one of whom was Crawford; they appeared to be arguing and then one of them walked off in a temper. He glanced back and saw Freddie and the look in his eyes was furious. What was Crawford upset about *now*?

As his stride took him towards the other two students, he saw Bradley and another of Crawford's friends. They seemed intent on whatever it was they'd been arguing with Crawford over and then

Bradley turned and saw him. Crawford and his crony had walked off, still apparently arguing.

Bradley hesitated and then took a step forward. 'Oh, Ronoscki,' he said. 'I wanted to congratulate you. You've been selected as a reserve to train with the boat race team.' The training for next year's race had already begun in earnest and a lot of students had been hoping to be included.

'Really?' Freddie stared at him, surprised and yet pleased. He hadn't expected to make the team and it was an honour just to be a reserve. It surprised him that Bradley would congratulate him. 'When was the list announced?'

'Just an hour or so ago,' Bradley replied. He hesitated, then, 'I wanted to apologise for my foolish behaviour the other day. Throwing that stone: it was stupid and childish.'

Freddie hesitated, then, 'Apology accepted and the incident forgotten,' he said. He offered his hand. 'Will you shake?'

'Yes.' Bradley stepped forward and they shook hands. 'I should warn you, Ronoscki. Crawford is furious that you've been put on the list.'

'Why?' Freddie asked. 'I know he dislikes me, but I really don't know why.'

'I can't answer that,' Bradley replied. 'If I knew, I wouldn't tell you – but I have nothing against you personally.'

'Thanks.' Freddie wondered at his change of heart but decided to accept it. 'I'm sorry if I offended either of you. I would much prefer to be on good terms.'

Bradley nodded. 'I've been given another chance for the cricket team. I've been warned it is my last chance and told I'll be out if I don't act honourably, and I've given my word. No dirty tricks. Crawford thinks I'm a fool, but I've learned my lesson.'

'Good, I'm glad you've decided to have another go. A friend of mine in London is a good cricketer. I prefer football and I like the rowing – though I know others are stronger at that than me. I'll only make the final team if someone has to drop out and I hope they won't for their sakes.' The next boat race would take place in Freddie's final term at college and he doubted he'd be good enough by then, but to be a reserve was honour enough.

Bradley looked at him long and hard. 'You're a decent sort,' he said. 'It's probably what Crawford doesn't like.' He shrugged. 'I'll see you around...'

Freddie watched him walk away. He still felt surprised at Bradley's change of heart. Something had caused him to fall out with Crawford and because of that he'd decided to make it up with Freddie.

Hearing the ancient wall clock strike brought Freddie out of his reverie. If he didn't get a move on, he would be late for his lecture! He walked swiftly towards the classroom, his thoughts on the wedding he was going home for the next day.

* * *

'Did your tutors mind you coming home and missing a day's training?' Freddie's father asked as he entered the kitchen of the Pig & Whistle. Freddie was eating a large slice of his mother's apple pie with custard; he shook his head vigorously, his mouth full of delicious pastry. Able nodded his satisfaction. 'Good. It was short notice and not at holiday time as we'd hoped. How are you getting on with the rowing team?'

'Great. I really enjoy it.' Freddie had swallowed the last morsel of pie and grinned at his father. 'Simpson is the captain of the team I train with. I've been selected as a reserve for the boat race team next year. Cambridge won it this year, of course...'

'The Cambridge-Oxford race?' Peggy said, looking surprised. 'That's rather good as it's your first year of rowing.'

'More than I'd expected,' Freddie replied. 'I never thought I'd be in the actual team, but I'm chuffed about making the reserves.'

'You are strong,' Able nodded to himself. 'My father was a big strong man, of a similar build to you. I think I was a disappointment to him because I was tall and thin.'

'You're strong, though,' Peggy remarked. 'My father was a big man, too. He worked on the docks but caught a chill that turned to pneumonia. Mum was small-boned, like me. Fay takes after me.'

Freddie smiled at her. It felt good to be at home with his family for a while, away from the rush and tear of student life, where he was always hurrying from one place to another.

'Where is Greta?' Able asked. 'She did come with you?'

'Yes, she is upstairs, unpacking,' Freddie informed. 'She is really looking forward to the wedding.' He frowned. 'I'm not sure it is much fun for her in that lodging house. I don't see her every night. I have training or study, but we go somewhere at the weekends—' He broke off as Greta entered the kitchen a little uncertainly. 'Ah, here she is. I was just about to tell Mum and Dad about our bikes. Greta suggested we get bikes so I could get about easier and we could cycle out somewhere on a Sunday.'

'Freddie gets so little time,' Greta said. 'I'm not sure I was right though – after your tyres got slashed.'

Freddie shook his head at her, but it was too late. His mother was staring at him. 'Your cycle tyres were slashed?'

'Yes. Some idiot at the college. He's a bit of a prankster – been in trouble with the cricket team for dirty tricks, but he apologised yesterday and says he's turned over a new leaf.' He wasn't sure Bradley had slashed the tyres; it might well have been Crawford himself, but just wanted to reassure his mother.

'So I should hope!' Peggy exclaimed. 'What else has he done that you haven't told us?'

'Mum, don't worry,' Freddie told her. 'I sorted it and it doesn't bother me. Crawford and his gang are just idiots. They think they own the place, because they come from rich families. I ignore them.'

Able looked at him then. 'Be careful, Freddie. I met that sort in the Army. They can be vindictive buggers...'

'I know, Dad, but Simpson's father knows Crawford's father and he has dropped a few hints. He thinks that should settle it.'

His father nodded and left it there but still looked thoughtful. Thankfully, from Freddie's point of view, Maggie entered the kitchen and the conversation was dropped.

'I should have thought you'd have the day off to get ready for tomorrow?' Freddie said as Maggie put on her apron. 'You're not going to cook the food for the reception yourself? It will be a desperate dash to the church if you do...' He grinned. 'I can just see you in your plimsoles dashing for your own wedding.'

'Lovely to see you, too, Freddie,' Maggie quipped. 'No, I am not cooking for the wedding, but I've done all my preparation, so I'm doing my share of the restaurant work today. We'll be closed to the public tomorrow, of course.' She looked at Greta and smiled. 'Good to see you, Greta. Fay will be here any time now. Her plane arrived last night and Greg met her at the airport. He is driving her home.'

'I wondered if she would get here,' Greta said, looking pleased. 'Freddie wasn't sure she would make it, because we hadn't heard anything.'

'She got a cancelled ticket at the last minute,' Maggie replied. 'I bought her a dress to match yours, just in case. Sarah's will be the same colour but different, because she is younger – she is Uncle Pip's daughter. You'll all be my bridesmaids... I'll show you your dress when Fay gets here. I think you will like it.'

'I'm sure I will,' Greta gave a little laugh of excitement. 'I've never been a bridesmaid and I couldn't believe it when Freddie said you'd asked for me.'

'I know it was last minute and I wasn't sure if I could find dresses for you both, but I did at Harpers in Oxford Street. I hope you haven't got thinner?' Her gaze went over Greta with a little frown.

'No, I'm just the same, size 36,' Greta said. 'Fay is a little smaller than me. I remember she tried on a size 34 when we went shopping together.'

'Yes, she was always very slim. I teased her about getting fat, but she never did despite all the food she tucked away.' Maggie's smile lit up her face at that minute. 'I think I can hear voices – yes, here they are.'

The door to the kitchen swung open and Greg entered carrying two large and very smart suitcases, followed by Fay. Everyone looked at her, wondering whether she had changed, but she was just the same, her clothes perhaps a little more fashionable and more expensive, her hair beautifully cut in a pageboy style, but everything else was as it always had been.

'Fay!' Peggy was on her feet as her youngest daughter hurled herself at her and they hugged. 'You look wonderful, darling.'

'You, too, Mum.' Fay's gaze travelled round the room. 'You all look great. I have missed you, all of you – but it's such fun.' Her eyes met her father's. 'You were right, Dad, it does suit me. I'm having a fantastic time. Jace knows so many people – in films and things – and we have lots of parties. I cater for some of them, but I'm a guest at most and I get to film premieres and fabulous balls and meet all sorts of people. I even spoke to the President, Mr Kennedy, at one party...' She finally paused for breath and giggled as they all stared at her in amusement.

'Trust you to be having fun while I'm slogging away at college,' Freddie teased his twin and everyone laughed. 'I might have known you'd be living the life of the idle rich...'

'I do not!' Fay said and then burst into laughter. 'Well, yes, I do, a lot of the time. We were planning on making my catering more official but...' She shrugged off her coat. 'I'm having a baby, so we decided I would just do a few parties for friends for now...'

'Fay!' Peggy stared at her. 'Are you sure? You don't look any different.'

'Yes, I'm sure, Mum,' Fay said and looked at her. 'I know you might be disappointed – after all the money you spent on me, letting me take those special culinary courses. I promise you I won't waste it. I will open that restaurant one day.'

Peggy put a hand out towards her. 'How could you think I'd be disappointed, Fay? Of course I'm pleased – but are you?'

Fay's smile lit up her lovely face. 'Yes, I am, Mum. At first, I was shocked. I didn't imagine it would happen so quickly – but Jace is over the moon. He insisted I come over to the wedding to see you all so I can spend some time with you, and apologises because he can't be with us; his busy schedule won't allow it. I'll go back with him when he's finished his next tour. He has been offered a part in a film – a musical – and he wants to take it. We will probably be based out in Hollywood for a few years. I want you to promise you'll come over and visit. When the baby is due if you can. Jace is going to book me into the best maternity home for the birth, but I'd like you to be near when I come out, if you will?'

'We will come,' Peggy said and hugged her again. 'We had already decided to visit after you were settled and, now, we certainly shall.'

'Congratulations,' Maggie said and took her turn to hug her. 'Are you happy, Fay? No, I don't need to ask. I can see that you are, love.' She looked at her speculatively. 'I hope you'll fit into the dress I got – I think you have put on a tiny bit of weight.'

'Fay had better try it on as soon as possible,' Peggy advised. 'We can probably let the seams out if we have to.'

'Let's go and try them now.' Maggie included Greta in her invitation and the three went out together.

'Well,' Peggy said, looking at Able. 'I didn't expect that quite as quickly. It seems we are going to be grandparents – your first time, Able.'

'It's good, isn't it, hon?' Able looked into her face and Peggy nodded.

'Yes. A shock but nice when you get over that...'

'I'm going to be an uncle,' Freddie said, eyes twinkling. 'I think that makes me feel old.'

His father laughed. 'How do you think it makes us feel?' he said but looked like the cat that got the cream. 'My little Fay a mother-to-be. She certainly knows how to keep us on our toes.'

Peggy grunted. 'Well, grandmother for the fifth time or not, I have some cooking to do. You should go and unpack, Freddie – haven't you got any work to do, Able?'

Able laughed. 'I know you want us out of the way. I'll go and see Tom. He was hoping to hear whether we'd got a new contract this morning.'

* * *

It was an hour or so later that Freddie managed to see his twin alone. She smiled at him as he waited for her at the top of the stairs. She'd just come from the bedroom she was sharing with Greta that visit.

'Did the dress fit?' he asked.

'It was lucky,' Fay replied. 'Greta's was a bit loose and it fitted me – and she has the one Maggie bought for me. They were the same except for the sizes, so it makes no difference. We need to take mine up a little, but that is easy.'

'Greta has lost weight?' Freddie nodded. 'I thought she wasn't eating properly. I wish she would stay here until I finish college, even though I enjoy the time I do get to spend with her.'

'She told me she has had some of her articles accepted by a magazine,' Fay said. 'I think she is trying to write a mystery story. She probably forgets to eat when she is writing, Freddie. You'll have to make sure she eats when you see her.'

'I shall,' Freddie agreed. 'So, are you really pleased about the baby – or is it a bit too soon for you?'

'I wasn't sure at first,' Fay said honestly. 'I never expected it to happen so quickly – but then, Jace was so happy. He wants a big family. He never really had one – not like we have.'

'Are you all right with that?' Freddie looked doubtfully at her. 'What about your ambition to be a famous cook?'

'It will happen one day,' Fay replied. 'Having a family won't stop me cooking and learning to get better. I'll do it more slowly perhaps, but I will get there, Freddie.' She gave him a sisterly hug. 'What about you? Are you enjoying college?'

'Some of it,' he said. 'There are elements I don't like – some elitist types who think a bloke from the East End is the pits. I try to ignore them and not let them spoil things.'

'Freddie! That's a shame,' Fay sympathised. She slipped her arm through his as they made their way to the sitting room, which was empty at that moment. 'Come on, tell me all about it. We might not have a chance to chat again before you have to leave.'

9

Maureen looked at her eldest son as he came downstairs that evening. He was dressed smartly and she raised her eyebrows in surprise. 'Where are you off to, Gordy?'

'Freddie is taking me to that sports club he helps out with sometimes,' Gordy said. 'He said to come round at seven, after they've had dinner. You don't mind if I'm a bit late home, do you, Mum?'

'No. As long as you're with Freddie, I know you're all right.'

She smiled as he went out of the front door. Gordy looked up to Freddie Ronoscki and she'd never minded where he went with him.

Her husband came down the stairs just after Gordy had left. He too was looking smart in slacks and a navy blazer, with a pale blue shirt open at the neck.

'Are you ready, love?' he asked. 'Peggy wanted us to go round at about half-past seven for a few drinks. I thought you would have been changed by now.'

'It won't take me a minute,' Maureen said, glancing at the wooden mantel clock. It was later than she'd thought! 'Shirley was on the phone just now. She and Ray aren't coming this evening. He has an emergency surgery and she says she would rather stay home. She'll rest so she's fit for the wedding tomorrow. She is just happy to be home and not still in hospital.' Shirley's stay had been brief, and she'd been told that she was not to work but take gentle exercise and then rest in the afternoons.

'Sensible girl,' Gordon said. 'She is all right – not feeling ill?'

'No, she has been fine since she got home from that maternity clinic. All she needed was rest and she has been very good these past few weeks I'm glad to say.'

'It gave her a bit of a shock when she felt unwell.' Gordon nodded his approval of his daughter changing her routines. 'She had been used to working all hours, but she can't do that until she has had the baby.' He looked at Maureen. 'Did I hear you say Fay is expecting when you were on the phone to Peggy earlier?'

'Yes. It was a big surprise, but they are all pleased. Peggy says you wouldn't know it to look at her, but she has put on a tiny bit of weight.'

'She was always so slim. It will be better for her to flesh out a bit,' Gordon said and squeezed Maureen's waist. 'I like something to get hold of...'

'Are you saying I'm fat?' she said in mock outrage.

'No, just cuddly,' Gordon replied and laughed. 'It's the way I like you, so don't go on a diet, please.'

'No, I shan't,' she said, smiling at him.

'Good...' He looked into her eyes. 'Have you stopped worrying over what might happen to Mulberry Lane?'

'I've accepted it,' Maureen told him and smothered a sigh. 'I don't want it to happen, but if it does – well, we'll find somewhere else to live. Gordy finishes school soon and Matty is away at his, so we don't need to worry about that...' Matty hadn't wanted to come back for Maggie's wedding and elected to stay at school, where he was enjoying himself.

'That is the right way to look at it,' Gordon approved. 'Go on up and change, love, or we shall be late.'

* * *

It was like old times in the pub that night, Maureen thought. Every table was filled and men were crowding the bar, the sound of laughter making it noisy. The smell of perfume mingled with hair cream, fresh cooked food, and beer. Peggy was handing out free drinks and little savouries to her regulars. She'd decided to give one of her parties for the regulars, because, as she'd said to Maureen, there might not be another occasion.

'If we do lose the Pig & Whistle, it might be the last – although I might throw another party just to stick two fingers in the air at the authorities who think they know best.'

'Peggy!' Maureen laughed. 'You don't change, thank God. Have you thought any more about what you'll do if it all goes?'

'No. I'm refusing to worry,' Peggy said. 'If the time comes when we have to go, I'll decide then. Fay is going to be living in America for a few years yet and Maggie will spend her time between London and the Cornish countryside – lucky her! I think Janet will find a home in London… I think Pip might make the move to America, but he's not sure when. I'm hoping to hear more of his plans when they get here later this evening.'

'You wouldn't think of living there?' Maureen felt hollow at the idea.

'No. I shan't live there, but I shall visit,' Peggy replied. 'Able thinks that within a year or so travel will get easier and cheaper. He says we will be able to fly wherever we want and Pip says the same. Pip thinks we'll all be having regular holidays in Spain and France before long.'

'Goodness me,' Maureen said. 'That sounds very grand and adventurous to me. I've always been content with two weeks in Devon or Cornwall.'

'I think I might like to go down that way to live,' Peggy said and grinned at her. 'Shall we start a boarding house or a small hotel down there together?'

'Oh, that sounds wonderful,' Maureen laughed. 'I'd say yes in an instant if it were not for Shirley. I promised I'd look after her baby when she is working and I'm looking forward to that…'

'Yes, of course you are,' Peggy said, slightly regretful now. 'I shan't be able to help Fay and Jace that way very often, because we'll be on different sides of the Atlantic, but, hopefully, I shall see them now and then.'

'Yes, of course you will,' Maureen said, but she felt that it wasn't what she would want. She was looking forward to being there when Shirley's baby was tiny right through the school days, until he or she was grown up and perhaps even married.

'I know what you're thinking,' Peggy said and sighed. 'When Janet had Maggie, she was living a long way off. I went down there, but the birth was over by the time I arrived and she didn't really need me. I was there for her when Jon was born...'

Maureen saw the sadness in her eyes. 'You worry about that lad, don't you? I really thought Ryan and Janet were getting on better last year, and he definitely tried to get to know his son more. I realise marriages don't always last, but I don't understand it in their case. I am positive Ryan thinks the world of her...'

'I think I might...' Peggy glanced round to see where Janet was and saw her sitting with a young man laughing. It was the man who was buying her flat. He'd been to the pub a couple of times now to see Janet. 'I think Ryan may be ill – and I mean *very* ill.' She lowered her voice so that only Maureen could hear.

'Surely he wouldn't choose to go all that way off if he was?' Maureen stared at her. 'Wouldn't he want to spend his last months with his family?'

'No one in the family, other than Janet and Jon, has ever seen this place he has bought. We know nothing about it,' Peggy said, nodding thoughtfully. 'Supposing he didn't want Janet to know he was ill – perhaps dying?'

Maureen felt cold all over. 'Is that what you think?' Peggy nodded gravely. 'But why? I don't understand.'

Peggy was reflective, 'It is just a theory as yet, but I have an odd feeling about it. Ryan knows he got Janet on the rebound. He must be aware that she has never forgotten her first husband, Mike. His death was so traumatic for her. I think perhaps Ryan felt he should release her rather than let her see him slowly leave her. And there is Jon too. Ryan knows he is happier with us – so I think that could be the explanation. He didn't want to inflict his illness on his family. Foolish but noble in its way.'

Maureen nodded but looked and felt shocked. 'It makes a strange sort of sense. Janet suffered enough when Mike died. I suppose Ryan might think he was doing her a favour by breaking up their marriage rather than letting her suffer through a long but fatal illness with him.' Her eyes met Peggy's. 'Supposing Janet had chosen to go with him?'

'I think Ryan knew she wouldn't. It was arguments about that idea that caused rows just before Jon ran off. Jon told Able that he hated the place his father was going to buy and that's why he tried to get to us in London – and you know what happened then. Jon's accident caused their marriage to completely break down. They did try to mend it but...' Peggy sighed and shrugged.

'I like Ryan,' Maureen said thoughtfully. 'Is there any way that we could find out if he is really ill and help him?'

'Able is going there after the wedding,' Peggy told her. 'I'd go with him, but I need to be here to oversee things while Maggie is away. It will be for several weeks. They are combining their honeymoon with some meetings Greg has in Italy with a motor racing team.'

'I'm not sure I'd like my husband spending time working on my honeymoon, though she is lucky to go to Italy,' Maureen replied, wrinkling her brow. 'What has she said about it?'

'Maggie is really excited. They will be in Milan some of the time when Greg has to work and he's told her there are fabulous fashion shops – and of course the food will be exciting; she is longing to discover new ideas and recipes. She has been working almost non-stop these past few years, so it will be good for her to have time to just spend doing whatever she likes – and she is very much in love with him. Had they not arranged the wedding so quickly, it might have meant waiting until later in the year.'

Maureen nodded. 'She has worked very hard...' Her gaze travelled across the room to where Maggie was standing with Fay and Greg, her head tilted up to her husband-to-be, face alight with laughter. 'You can see how happy she is...' Her glance settled on Janet. 'Janet looks more relaxed tonight. Who is she with?'

'His name is Lars Stevenson,' Peggy informed her. 'He is in the process of buying Janet's flat – the one she renovated. That's why he's been round to see her a couple of times, at least that is his excuse.'

Maureen looked at her sharply, seeing a look in Peggy's eyes that made her exclaim, 'Do you think there is more to it than that?'

'I think he rather fancies her,' Peggy replied thoughtfully. 'I've noticed him looking at her a few times and it made me think there might be more on his side.'

'Not on hers?'

'I don't know yet,' Peggy admitted.

'He looks to be quite a bit younger than her,' Maureen observed, her gaze returning to the two of them. 'And very attractive.'

'Able is younger than me,' Peggy reminded her.

'Yes, but I think the gap is bigger between those two...'

Peggy's brow furrowed. 'I know – but I can't see that Janet is likely to jump into anything. She probably feels flattered, but I doubt if it's more... It might do her good to have a passionate affair...'

'Peggy! You don't mean that?' Maureen was slightly shocked.

Peggy was silent for a moment. 'I'd rather she did that than fall in love with him. Janet hasn't had the happiest life, Maureen. I think she might be learning to like herself more and in time she'll be able to become the independent woman she needs to be. I'll be glad when Able finds out what is going on with Ryan.'

'Janet did have a rough time during the war,' Maureen agreed. 'But so did we and we've both found a way to have a good life. Maybe her restlessness is inherited from her father?'

'Might be,' Peggy conceded doubtfully. Laurie had been prone to moods but she believed Janet's unhappiness sprang from a different source. 'I feel impatient with her sometimes, but then I see that look in her eyes and I try to understand. She lost her first husband in such tragic circumstances and I know it haunts her. Not everyone can be strong all the time.'

'No, I suppose not.' Maureen watched as Lars stood up, kissed Janet's cheek and walked out of the pub. Janet watched him go and then looked about her, making her way to her daughter and Greg to join in the fun and laughter of Peggy's party. She couldn't see whether Janet was emotionally involved, but she thought Peggy was right. That young man fancied Janet.

* * *

'It was a good party, wasn't it?' Gordon asked as they snuggled into bed later that night. 'Reminded me of the parties we had when the war ended. Greg has a nice singing voice and he can belt out a tune on the piano.'

'Yes. He is a thoroughly decent chap all round,' Maureen agreed. 'I am glad he and Maggie met.' She was silent for a moment, then, 'Did you see the blond-haired man Janet was with earlier?'

'Can't say I noticed,' Gordon replied sleepily. 'Is he someone special?'

'He likes Janet a lot,' she asserted but snuggled up into the warmth of her husband's body. 'I am sure he fancies her.'

'Janet is still married to Ryan – do you think they will divorce?'

'Peggy thinks Ryan might be ill,' Maureen said. 'I hope she isn't right...' she murmured but a gentle snore told her that Gordon had fallen asleep.

Maureen thought about Ryan for a while. She'd felt for him when he'd made the effort to get closer to his son while Janet was in America at her mother's hospital bed. It seemed to her that he'd had a rough deal, too, losing his first family to a bombing raid during the war. He'd married Janet on the rebound and there had always been the shadow of Janet's first husband between them.

Oh, well, it wasn't her business. She couldn't help hoping that Peggy was wrong, though. It would be awful to think of Ryan suffering alone.

10

Maggie looked at herself in the beautiful, simple, white silk gown. It was perfect for a cool but bright spring day. The line was soft and flowing at the hem with long sleeves and had a Medieval look about it. She'd loved it immediately in the shop, though she knew both her mother and Granny Peggy preferred another one that was frothy lace and chiffon. Her veil was short – falling just to her shoulders – and suspended from a coronet of seed pearls and diamanté that framed her face and was all the embellishment she needed, together with the single strand of real pearls Peggy had given her that morning as a wedding gift.

'We wanted you to have something personal you can always keep,' Granny Peggy told her. 'You'll have a ready-made home, Maggie, and you can add to it or change it as you go along.'

Maggie and Greg had received lots of gifts, from his friends and hers, ranging from a magnificent silver tea and coffee set from his uncle to a pair of tea cloths from one of Peggy's elderly regulars. She'd set them all out on a table in the restaurant extension with their cards. Greg had given her a beautiful car as her wedding gift and she looked forward to driving it in the future. Maggie had found a small bronze figure of a horse in a curiosity shop that she knew he would like and he had been delighted with it, saying it would fit beautifully in his collection of bronzes.

Greg knew her so well. She smiled now at the thought that within a few hours he would be her husband. She was so lucky to be marrying the man she loved. A lot of men still thought their wives should give up work when they married, but Greg understood that she wanted to follow her ambition. In fact, he understood everything she'd never told anyone else much about, including her feelings when her father had died and the uncertain times when she'd sensed a certain strain between her mother and Ryan. She felt lucky to have found the perfect man for her.

Maggie's smile deepened at the thought. Just after Christmas, they had gone down to his country home in Cornwall so that she could see where they might spend some of their lives. It was so beautiful, but the thing that she'd loved more than anything was its air of permanence. The building was old, the faded red brick having mellowed over the centuries and its sloping roof of thatch was so romantic, though Greg had laughed and told her it could be far from it when the wind got in and tore part of it away.

'We have to have it rethatched every so many years and I have it checked each autumn to see that the protective wire on the ridge is in place and there are no unwelcome visitors living there,' he'd told her.

He'd looked at her quizzically as she walked from room to room, exclaiming over the twisting staircases, of which there were two, their steps of worn wood testament to the years of service. She loved the beams blackened by smoke from huge fireplaces, and the little windows with their thick grey glass. Only the kitchen showed signs of having been changed into something manageable, with modern appliances like a big shiny range, towering cabinets of light oak and a slate-tiled floor.

'It is beautiful, Greg!' she'd exclaimed.

'I thought you might want something more modern? You can rip the kitchen out and start fresh if you wish?'

'No, I love it,' Maggie had told him excitedly. 'It just looks as if it has always been here – and we never stayed in one place long enough when I was a child. This is a home not just a house.'

He'd nodded and smiled. 'We can live here one day. I've always loved it – it belonged to my grandfather but he left it to me. My father never liked it and nor did my uncle, but I had wonderful holidays here. There is a beach not more than two miles away.' Sadly, Greg's parents were dead, but he had an uncle he cared deeply for and a cousin, of whom he hardly ever spoke.

'It is perfect for us one day,' Maggie had agreed. 'I have to stay at the restaurant for a year or two or until it is sold, and then perhaps?'

'Yes, we can look into starting one down here – should be easy for a top London chef to make a success somewhere around here, Maggie.' His smile had teased her.

'I wish...' she'd said and laughed. 'I am a good cook but not a top chef.'

'I think you are perfect,' he'd told her and then they'd kissed.

It was that night, after a long walk on a secluded beach, that they had made love for the first time. Maggie had given herself to him without reserve and just as she'd expected he was a gentle, wonderful lover. They hadn't planned on making love, intending to wait for marriage, but it had just happened and Maggie was glad. Her wedding night held no anxiety for her and she knew she would be happy as Greg's wife.

'You look wonderful,' her mother's voice interrupted her reverie. Janet had just re-entered the room after changing her own dress. 'I wasn't sure in the shop. I thought it might be too plain, but now you have the veils and Mum's pearls you look beautiful. You always are beautiful, of course.'

'Thank you...' Maggie kissed her mother's cheek. 'I do love you, Mum – and thank you for the gold watch. You can't see it, but it's under the sleeve.'

Janet nodded. 'Your father bought that for me just before he died. We were just getting used to each other again—' Maggie frowned as her mother's voice almost broke. 'I never wore it afterwards... I want you to have it and enjoy it, love. I had it cleaned and checked over. It works perfectly.'

'Thank you. I shall treasure it.' Maggie hesitated then, 'Did Ryan say why he wasn't coming today, Mum?' She'd felt a little disappointed that he'd simply sent her a card with a cheque as a gift, because he had been her father for most of her life.

'Just that he couldn't make it as he had something important to do – work, I suppose,' Janet said, frowning. 'I might go to visit next week. I was so annoyed with him for making a weak excuse, but I didn't want to have another row before your wedding. However, it is time we talked...'

'Did you ever love him?' Maggie asked her. 'I mean romantically and with all your heart?'

'Yes, very much at one time,' Janet replied. 'I suppose I still do in a way – just not in the way I loved your father. I feel sorry about that and I did try, truly I did. We were happy a lot of the time. He couldn't forgive himself for Jon's accident and... well, we've just grown apart. I think the trip to America must have made him think he didn't need me or something. It was strange – but shortly after I came home, he changed... withdrew from me. I have no idea why.' She paused reflectively, then, 'I thought we were getting on better and then he just announced he was leaving me, going to live on that wretched smallholding. He didn't even ask if I would go, just said, "I know you don't want to come, so stay here with Jon," and then walked out.'

'Are you very unhappy about it?' Maggie asked.

Janet looked at her and then shook her head. 'I was upset – but more because I felt I'd failed him and Jon. I thought Jon would miss him and he does ask after his father at times, but he seems to have settled. He loves his Granny Peggy, just like you do.'

'Yes, I do love her very much,' Maggie agreed. 'But I love you and Jon, too – and Ryan. He was like a father to me as I grew up. I just wished that you were happier.' Maggie had been aware of something between them even as a small child; there had been good times but also bad and she privately thought it might be the undercurrent between them that had caused Jon to go off the rails, indulging in some petty theft and culminating in his terrible accident.

'I think I was happy enough then...' Janet frowned. 'I know we quarrelled the night you went off to try to find the Loch Ness monster, but things got better after that, didn't they?'

'Yes, they did for several years – and then you seemed to go away from us a bit, Mum – not physically but emotionally.' Maggie had been older then and able to cope with her mother's silent moods, but Jon had been too young to understand. He'd resented it when she didn't turn up at his school sports day.

'Did I?' Janet met her eyes. 'I'm sorry if you felt that, Maggie. I think I just got a little bored. There simply wasn't enough for me to do up there. I much prefer what I do now. I like to be busy and I enjoy town life – to be able to visit a theatre or a museum or wherever I feel I'd like to go on the spur of the moment.'

'Good. I am glad you are happier now,' Maggie told her and they hugged. 'You will be here when I get back from my honeymoon?'

Janet laughed. 'Where would I go? Of course I'll be here, silly girl. You shouldn't be thinking like this on your wedding day, love. It ought to be the happiest day of your life.'

'It is,' Maggie told her. 'I'm not like you, Mum. I know what I want out of life and I've got it all.'

'You sound like your father. Mike always knew what he wanted – so did I when we were together.' She smiled at Maggie. 'I suppose you hardly remember him?'

'Vaguely, but I know I loved him. He used to pick me up and tell me he loved me.'

'And you recall that? You were so young still when we lost him.'

'Sort of,' Maggie said. 'It's a smell of his soap and hair cream and just a feeling that that's what he did…'

'Yes, he would certainly have loved you and he would have been so proud of you. You take after him more than me,' Janet said, looking sad. She was about to say more when the bedroom door opened and Fay and Peggy walked in.

'We wondered if you were ready,' Fay said. 'You look fantastic, doesn't she, Mum?'

'Beautiful,' Peggy said and smiled at them all. 'I don't know where I got you all from. You all look wonderful – you too, Janet. That blue dress suits you so well. It's not the one you bought when I was with you?'

'No. I decided I liked this better,' Janet said and blushed. 'Blue is my favourite colour and I should wear it more... so I've been told.'

'Well, it suits you.'

'You look lovely, too, Granny Peggy.'

'Thank you, darling. Your flowers are downstairs,' Peggy said, smiling at her. 'Your bouquet is gorgeous, Maggie, and so are the posies for the bridesmaids and we've all got lovely buttonholes to wear. Look, I've got a gorgeous orchid. I've never had one before.'

'Kiss me, Granny, for good luck,' Maggie said and Peggy did as she was bid, careful not to crush the dress. 'Now you, Fay. Where is Greta?' she asked as Fay hugged her.

'Downstairs with Freddie. I think they went to look at the restaurant and make sure everything was as it should be for when we come back... or maybe they just wanted a few minutes alone.'

'I think we'd better go down,' Janet said. Her eyes met Maggie's. 'Everything all right, love?'

'Yes. It couldn't be better,' Maggie told her, and yet she was still a little disappointed that Ryan hadn't come to see her married. She'd always thought of him as her father while knowing her real one had died, but they'd been close for some years. 'Let's go down. I don't want to keep Greg waiting...'

* * *

The ancient church was chilly despite the sunshine peeping in through the stained-glass windows, but the scent of gorgeous flowers was everywhere. Both sides of the aisle were packed, though Greg didn't have much family. His uncle had sent a magnificent gift but wasn't able to make the journey, because of ill health. His cousin was there as his best man and about twenty or so of his friends, but Maggie's friends and family had overflowed their side and filled the empty pews on his. As she walked down the aisle towards him, Greg turned to look at her, the love in his eyes making her feel as if she were floating on air.

It was a little unreal, the service soft and flowing, the sound of hymns filling the echoing walls and touching the ceiling. So many of

Peggy's old customers had come and their singing was loud and lusty. Quite a few hadn't actually been invited, but they'd crowded into the church at the back and she'd been conscious of their smiling faces as she entered. Fay's wedding had been less well attended, but then she'd married at a registry office, her reception mainly for close friends and family. Peggy had invited a lot of people this time because, as she said, their customers were also their friends. Only a certain number would attend the reception because it wouldn't have been possible to invite all of them, but Peggy's party the previous evening had given them all a little celebration. A lot of them had watched Maggie leave her home for the church, but some of the more enterprising were here in church to see her wed.

* * *

Able smiled at Maggie as he gave her hand to Greg and the marriage ceremony came to an end as they followed the vicar to the vestry to sign their names. Greg lifted her lace veil and kissed her lightly on the lips and then they were on their way back through the church as the congregation filed out behind them into the sunshine.

It was pleasant despite some hazy clouds overhead as they gathered on well-cut lawns to have their photographs taken, the line-up being arranged by one of Greg's friends who was a professional photographer and taking the pictures. Maggie couldn't stop smiling. She just felt so warm and happy inside. The uncertainty of her childhood was behind her now and she held onto Greg's arm as he posed for the photographs without the self-conscious air he'd had when they'd met. Like Maggie, he'd found peace in their love and was no longer aware of his scar, which was fading more as time passed.

After the official photographs were taken, they all piled into the various hired cars and private ones and were driven back to the Pig & Whistle.

Maggie and Greg stood to receive their guests into the restaurant – which had been decked with white flowers and silver garlands – and were given more gifts. His cousin Philip kissed Maggie's cheek as he presented her with a beautifully wrapped box and told her that Greg was a lucky so-and-so. Something in his voice and a look he shot at Greg warned her that perhaps he wasn't the smiling, generous young man he appeared to be. However, she was too busy greeting her other friends to take much notice.

Shirley was looking wonderful, glowing and happy on Ray's arm; she hugged Maggie, laughing about her bump as she congratulated her. Fay had gathered a little circle of friends around her and was laughing as she told them stories about her life in Hollywood. Greta was with them, with Freddie, and Rose and Tom Barton, with their children. Jon was talking to his cousin Chris and Uncle Pip, while Maureen and Gordon were with Aunt Sheila and Cousin Sarah, in the midst of a large group of chattering Mulberry Lane residents, all of whom were laughing excitedly. It was a special wedding in the lanes, and everyone was having a wonderful time as the champagne flowed.

The reception was buzzing, everyone amazed and delighted with the delicious buffet meal of lobster in lemon sauce, prawns grilled with garlic, roasted spicy chicken wings, warm crumbly pastries and tarts that melted deliciously in your mouth, quiches, and exotic salads, crusty bread, and jacket potatoes, with butter or cheese; all followed by sherry trifles, melting chocolate desserts, and beautiful meringues filled with fresh cream and fruit.

It was only when all the delicious food had been devoured, and the magnificent three-tier cake was cut, and the speeches made, that Philip sidled up to Maggie. Greg was standing with Able and Peggy, talking to them and laughing when a voice spoke softly beside her.

'I suppose you know you only got him on the rebound, because that bitch Tania couldn't stand the sight of him after the accident…' His voice sounded slurred, as though he'd drunk too much, and she smelled the strong spirits on his breath. He had probably been drinking even before he came to the reception, because he was clearly intoxicated.

Maggie was shocked by the vicious tone in his voice. For a moment, she couldn't speak, but then she said, 'However it happened, we love each other. I feel very lucky to have met Greg.'

'Well, well, she is in love,' Philip drawled and she saw the jealous spite in his eyes. Something was eating at him to make him this nasty. 'Or is it the money you like? I suppose any scar fades if there is enough money to make it worthwhile...'

Maggie was speechless, but after a moment she recovered enough to say, 'I am not sure why you hate us, but it hardly matters. I love Greg and he loves me. Now please excuse me...' What an objectionable young man he was – and why was he so jealous of Greg?

Maggie moved away, but her face must have shown her discomfort because Greg came to her at once. 'What is wrong, darling? Did Philip say something appalling? I invited him to be my best man because my uncle asked me to and I'm fond of Uncle Norris – but he has never been my friend. I think he is a bit jealous because I have a good relationship with his father.'

'He was a bit unpleasant,' Maggie replied and clasped his hand. 'It doesn't matter. I took no notice anyway.'

'Good.' Greg bent to kiss her. 'I'll have a word with him before we leave. Put him straight...'

'Don't bother,' Maggie said. 'I think he just left anyway...'

Greg nodded. 'Just remember that I love you and always will.'

'I know,' Maggie said. She did know and his cousin's spite couldn't touch her when she could see the love in Greg's eyes. She just wondered why Philip disliked Greg so much that he would try to ruin his wedding day.

* * *

'So, tell me,' Greg said when they were alone in their hotel room later that evening. He put his arms around her, kissing her neck as she let down her luxuriant hair from the elegant twist she'd wound it into for their wedding. 'What did my cousin say that upset you?'

'It's nothing,' Maggie said.

'Please, tell me, Maggie.'

'He said that I got you on the rebound because someone named Tania had let you down after the accident – and hinted that I married you for the money.'

To Maggie's surprise, Greg gave a shout of laughter. 'The devil he did! Let me assure you, my dearest one, that Tania was never more than a girlfriend; she came along for the glamour, but when she thought I was finished she ditched me.' Greg kissed her softly. 'Believe me, she can't hold a candle to you, Maggie – and I never felt this way about her.' He looked down at her. 'You are the only woman I have ever truly loved – or ever will.'

'Good, because she doesn't deserve you,' Maggie said. She lifted her face for his kiss, which was warm and sweet and made her cling to him. 'I thought he was pretty horrid to say things like that on our wedding day. Some women would have been very upset over it.'

'He's the kind you ignore,' Greg said and held her close, his breath soft on her face. 'I shall tell him just what I think of him next time we meet, darling. Please promise me you will never believe a word he says. I think he was born with an adder's tongue.'

'I wondered why he was so unpleasant,' Maggie said. 'Is he jealous because you have a better life – or what?'

'Goodness knows, though I think he fancied Tania and she never looked at him – even after she left me. He has always envied me, right from school, but why – who knows?' Greg shrugged. 'He isn't important. Let's forget him?' He tipped her chin. 'You won't brood over what he said – any of it? It is all nonsense.'

'Yes, it is,' Maggie agreed and kissed him. 'I am sorry for him. He must feel so inadequate or have a rotten life...'

'Don't waste your sympathy on him,' Greg said. 'He has had all the same advantages I had, but he let them slip away. Yes, I am lucky, because I have you, my darling. The rest of it – as far as I'm concerned nothing is worth the candle without you.'

'Oh, me too,' she said and clung to him. Greg smiled and then laughed and scooped her up in his arms, heading for the bed. Maggie giggled with delight as he threw her down amongst the sheets and then fell to the bed with her. 'I do love you...' she murmured against his lips, but after that there was no point in talking; they just let their desires and needs take over and Greg's foolish cousin was forgotten in the delight of their love.

11

'Maggie looked gorgeous, didn't she?' Greta said after the bride and groom had left on their honeymoon. Maggie had thrown her bouquet over her shoulder in Greta's direction, but she had missed it and one of Greg's guests had caught it. 'It was a wonderful wedding. Even better than Fay's, I think, though that was lovely too.'

'Yes, Fay's was a bit too rushed,' Freddie agreed. 'She was in so much of a hurry to go off with Jace that she gave up her dream of a white wedding.'

Greta nodded. She had only ever attended the weddings of his family because she had no siblings and no cousins or even close friends. 'It was so nice of Maggie to ask me to be a bridesmaid.'

'Maggie is a nice person,' Freddie said and looked thoughtfully at her. 'Why don't you give up that little room of yours and come back here? You like Maggie and Janet – and Mum, too, don't you?'

'I like all your family.' She looked at him wistfully. 'I do like being here, but I should never see you...' Greta bit her lip. 'Don't you want us to meet at the weekends?'

'Of course I want to see you whenever I can,' he said. 'I just don't like to think of you being alone so much. You don't have any friends in Cambridge...'

'I'd rather be there so I can see you,' Greta said. 'I understand you are busy. You told me you wouldn't get to see me much before I came, but I followed you down there and I like it, so don't worry.'

Freddie nodded. 'It's up to you,' he acknowledged. 'As long as you're happier than you were when we met?'

'You know I am.' She hugged his arm. 'What time is our train tomorrow?'

'Just after three,' Freddie said. 'We'll have lunch a bit earlier so we're in plenty of time. Is there something you want to do?'

'No. I just wondered. Fay said something about having a chat before we leave, but there will be plenty of time in the morning.'

'Yes, of course there will,' he agreed. He glanced at his wristwatch. 'It's not late yet – only half-past seven. Shall we go somewhere? Mum is having a few friends in at eight for drinks and snacks, but we don't need to stay.'

'Can we just go for a walk?' Greta asked, smiling at him.

'Come on then,' Freddie offered his hand to pull her up. The restaurant had almost emptied now, though some people were just sitting around talking. 'If Mum doesn't turf this lot out, they will be here all night…'

Greta laughed. 'Your mum knows so many people and they all want to talk to her. She can't get away.'

'She has known them all so long,' Freddie said. 'I think in the war she opened the cellars up to everyone. It was safer down there than in most of the houses in the district.'

'I was too tiny to remember even the end of the war,' Greta sighed. 'It must have been a terrible time.'

'I don't remember either,' Freddie said as they walked from the restaurant, which was being slowly cleared of the debris of the magnificent feast. 'I just listen to Mum and Dad talk…'

* * *

Greta stroked the pretty dress as she took it off later that evening. Maggie had chosen well, because the full-skirted style could be worn as a special occasion dress at any time. Greta would be able to use it for summer evenings or a dance. She might lift the hem a little, but then it would be perfect as her best dress. Greg had given her and Fay an oval gold locket on a chain as their bridesmaid gift. Greta had never owned much jewellery in the past, but Freddie had bought her a thin gold bangle the previous Christmas and now she had the locket.

Sometimes, she had to pinch herself to make sure she wasn't dreaming and wouldn't be back at her aunt's boarding house when she woke. Freddie worried that she was lonely. Occasionally, she was a little, but most of the time her head was off in her stories. She'd written quite a few since living alone in the boarding house. None had been published yet, but she had now sold several articles, mostly about Cambridge and the colleges. One of the magazines she'd sent her stories to had suggested she might do better if she tried writing something longer. Since then, the idea for a mystery story had been fermenting in her head and she'd actually written a few pages before coming to London for the wedding. She felt quite excited to go on with it when they got back to Cambridge.

Of course, she wished she could see Freddie more. She wished they were married and he came home to her each night, but knew she had to be patient. Freddie had a lot of studying and exams to pass before he could apply for the job he wanted, which meant he wouldn't even think about marriage until then. Greta already knew the man she loved pretty well. Freddie was the strong silent type. A lot of the time when they were together, he hardly spoke more than a few words, but then he would look at her and smile and it didn't matter. When he did talk to her, she knew he cared and she hadn't had that in her life until now. Of course, there were the times when he was in a teasing mood, and then he was entirely different. He teased his sister and cousin unmercifully on occasion, his mother, too, if he could get away with it. Greta liked it when he teased her, but with her, he mostly seemed more serious. She sometimes wondered if he truly wanted to be with her. Had she pushed him into a relationship? Was he just too nice to push her away?

Sometimes, Greta worried that he merely liked her as a good friend and didn't feel the same as she did, but at others she would see a look in his eyes that made her feel loved. When he kissed her, she always clung to him, but Freddie seldom became passionate. Once, as they'd kissed in her room, she'd thought they would make love and she would have given herself to him, but he'd drawn back, just saying, 'Better not, love. We need to be sensible.'

Greta sighed inwardly. Freddie had an iron resolve. He had his eyes firmly fixed on the future and she knew he was right. They couldn't afford to get married. He was living on the money his father had given him for his education and she... well... her wage was barely enough to pay her rent and food and didn't often allow for many luxuries, like a bar of chocolate or a few bottles of beer when Freddie popped round. The money she'd earned from the articles she'd sold had been like winning the pools. Although it wasn't really very much, the surge of pleasure had been just as good as if she'd won a fortune.

Greta's father was still working abroad. Now and then, he sent her a postal order and a cheque on her birthday. He'd given her five pounds for Christmas and she'd saved it, buying a pair of pretty shoes to wear for the wedding.

She longed to be with Freddie, but Greta acknowledged in her heart that they needed to wait. An unwanted pregnancy could ruin all their hopes for the future. Of course, there were ways of being careful, but she wasn't sure what they were, though she was aware that her innocence was also a part of Freddie's reluctance to make love before they were married – or at least engaged.

She had hoped that the atmosphere of the wedding might prompt him to suggest an engagement, but it hadn't. Greta shook her head. There was no point in dwelling on it. Freddie had told her he loved her after Fay's wedding, but he'd also made it clear there would be no wedding until he'd passed his exams, finished his training and reached his goal of becoming a teacher in a secondary modern school.

* * *

Freddie frowned as he undressed that evening. Greta had looked so wistful earlier at the wedding and he'd understood that she must long for their marriage. God knows he wanted it badly enough himself. It was becoming harder to give her a quick kiss and say goodnight and more than once he'd had to clamp down on his rising passion. Yet he knew that, when he married, he wanted to be able to give his wife a decent home and bring his family up properly. Freddie had seen enough of poor conditions in the East End of London. His own family were lucky, but he'd seen the way hunger and poverty turned men and women old before their time and the kids at school with patched clothing and much-mended shoes if they were lucky, rags and bare feet if they had no father or sometimes even no mother.

No, Freddie would never risk his family going short. Yet there was a job waiting for him with Tom Barton whenever he wanted it. He frowned as the thought occurred to him. Should he have taken it when Tom offered it to him the previous year? He could have earned enough to marry then and would rise in the firm as he learned – but it wasn't what Freddie wanted or needed from life. He felt a bit selfish putting his own wishes first, but Greta understood. She knew he loved her – didn't she?

Freddie wasn't one for romance if he was honest. He did love Greta and he believed they would suit one another, but he could never find the words to say the things he supposed girls liked to hear. Freddie's father was so good with making his mother feel loved, giving her little smiles and touching her hand, telling her how lovely she looked. He'd heard his father tell his mother he loved her many times; it seemed to come easily from Able and Freddie wished he could be more like him, but there was something inside that held him back when he was with Greta and he couldn't say the things he wanted to. He just hoped she understood. If he had more money, he would take her flowers and chocolates, buy her pretty things to wear, but he'd had to practise economy to get through as a student. All those things would just have to wait until he had the job he needed.

Freddie had never intended to start courting until he'd done all he needed to – but his feelings for Greta, sympathy at first and then love, had just come out of the blue and caught him. He laughed and shook his head. Greta understood. Of course she did. Besides, she needed time to write those stories of hers...

12

'So what are you doing today then?' Peggy asked as Janet entered the kitchen the next morning just as she was popping the last of her pies into the big shiny ovens they'd had installed when Maggie took over the restaurant. 'You look very smart – are you going somewhere?'

'I am meeting a friend for lunch,' Janet replied. 'I just thought I would pop in and see if you needed any help with Maggie away?'

'I think it is all under control,' Peggy said thoughtfully. She glanced round the large kitchen. The two cooks they employed were hard at work preparing the dishes they could in advance, engrossed in their work but sharing a smile with each other now and then. It was very different from when she'd done most of the cooking for the Pig & Whistle herself with just an occasional helping hand from Maureen or Rose and she felt a flicker of nostalgia for the past; they had been good years, the pub to run, meeting Able and falling in love – if she was honest, for the first time. For a moment, her thoughts went back further to her childhood, but she shut them off quickly. 'Shall we go upstairs and leave the girls to it?'

'Yes, if you've got time,' Janet agreed and looked pleased.

Peggy wiped her hands on a cloth and led the way into the hall and up the steep stairs at the end. She'd sensed that her daughter had something on her mind. Something she might not want to share with others present.

Upstairs, there was a small kitchen, a large sitting room and then bedrooms and more up in what had once, long ago, been an attic. Peggy had asked Tom Barton to paint the old beams white, which made the ceilings look higher. When she'd first come to the pub, it had been very dark, but she'd had more windows put in at the back which made it lighter and the sun was pouring in now, highlighting the warm mellow wood of the antiques she'd been able to collect these past few years. She liked the glow of satinwood and had chosen small pieces that lit up dark corners with their soft yellowish patina.

'This is such a cosy room,' Janet said, sinking into a comfy sofa near the fireplace, which now and for the summer held a collection of scented pine cones and logs. 'I should like furniture like this one day. I have some things in store – but most of it was Ryan's and I believe he took it with him.'

'Are you thinking of finding a place of your own?' Peggy enquired. 'We have plenty of room here, Janet.'

'I know – and no, not yet.' Her daughter hesitated. 'Mum, would you mind if I left Jon with you while I go down to Wales? I think I should talk to Ryan, see if we can sort things out or if it really is over. If it is, I think I'd like a divorce.'

'That's drastic,' Peggy said, looking at her hard. 'Why? You said you never wanted to marry again – has something changed your mind? You haven't met someone else?'

'Not that I want to marry,' Janet replied. 'I meant it when I said I would never marry again – but that doesn't stop me having a friend, does it – not if I am divorced?'

'You mean an affair,' Peggy said. 'Is it that young man you were talking to for ages at Maggie's wedding?'

'Lars – yes,' Janet agreed. 'He more or less said he was interested in getting together that night, well he's hinted before, but I couldn't say yes, not until I've settled things with Ryan. I would feel wrong if I didn't – though why I should after the way he just went off like that, I don't know...'

'Have you considered that Ryan may have had a very good reason – an unselfish reason – for doing that?' Peggy's tone made Janet's head come up.

Janet stared at her. 'What do you mean? It seemed pretty selfish to me...'

'Unless he believed he was very ill and that his suffering would be a trauma too many for you?' Peggy met her startled eyes. 'Ryan knows how much you went through when Mike died, Janet. You also lost your father too soon after the war. He may feel that he can't put you through another prolonged illness and painful death.'

Janet's gaze narrowed. 'Has Ryan spoken to you about this?'

'No, not directly. It is just a feeling I had after he sent me this...' Peggy went to her desk drawer and took out a letter. She returned to where Janet was sitting and handed it to Janet. 'It arrived two days before the wedding. At first, I wasn't sure what to make of it, but then I started putting two and two together. I had wondered before, but this makes it clear, I think.'

Janet snatched the single piece of paper and scanned it, her anger obvious. After a moment or two, she looked at Peggy. 'He is telling you the things he should have told me – where to find bank accounts and things he wants Jon to have should he die...'

'Yes. He says he has made a will, given me the solicitor's address here in London, but also where his personal documents are kept. He placed most things with the bank, but there are some things he needs to keep with him and he's told me where to find them. I suspect that is the action of a man who believes he is dying.' Peggy frowned. 'I suspected as much when I got that letter and then he didn't come to the wedding. He sent Maggie a cheque and card, but that isn't like the Ryan I knew. He loved Maggie like a daughter...'

'Yes, he did. She kept us together when we might have split years ago,' Janet acknowledged and sank back in her chair. 'I was beginning to think something wasn't right, Mum. I thought I might go and see him to sort out... but, if he is really ill...' She closed her eyes. 'I feel awful now. It's my fault he withdrew. I never quite gave Ryan all of myself the way I did Mike, and he knew it.'

'I'm really sorry, Janet. Able was going to go there in a couple of days – but if you're going, we'll stay out of it for now. Unless you'd rather Able went?'

'I'll go myself. I have to,' Janet replied, looking at her sadly. 'Have I been a selfish bitch all my life, Mum?'

'Don't go blaming yourself for this,' Peggy told her. 'It isn't your fault that Ryan is ill, my love – if he is – and we don't know for sure. My intuition could be wrong.' Janet shook her head. 'No, you haven't been selfish, Janet. Sometimes you might be a bit that way but not deep down. Mike's terrible death affected you badly and it took you a long time to get over it. Ryan wanted you and wouldn't leave you alone until you agreed to marry him. I hoped you would be happy together, but perhaps it would have been better if you'd given yourself more time?'

'I don't think I could ever be the same as I was when I married Mike,' Janet said thoughtfully. 'When I woke up and found him dead beside me... blood everywhere...' A shiver of remembrance went through Janet. 'I think a part of me curled up and died right then. I did love Ryan – I still do care for him, but not in the way I did Mike.' Tears trickled down Janet's cheeks and she let them. 'I know it was a long time ago, but I still think of him and then of that morning. It still hurts, Mum.'

'It was an awful thing to happen,' Peggy agreed. 'You've suffered too much.' She hesitated, then, 'If Ryan is very ill... dying... it will surely be too hard for you. Would you like Able to go with you?'

'I would, but this is something I have to face alone, Mum.' Janet looked resolute. 'I know what I have to do now. I'll go to my room and pack.'

'What about your lunch appointment?'

'I'll telephone Lars and let him know I can't make it.' Janet drew a deep sobbing breath. 'I was going to tell him I'd spend some time with him – but that will have to wait, perhaps it won't happen now.'

'If you want it to it will,' Peggy told her.

'You don't think it's shocking of me to consider having an affair with a younger man?'

'Able is younger than me – though not by as many years – but no, I don't mind what you do, Janet. Once I might have been shocked, but things have changed. I just want you to be happy.'

'I'm not miserable, Mum, just restless,' Janet replied with a dry laugh. 'I think I get that from my father. He had you, a good business, and lots of friends, but he was always looking for more. Pip is lucky; he is like you, takes things in his stride. I don't think he's ever looked at anyone but Sheila and he's happy with his life.'

'You are my daughter, too,' Peggy reminded. 'Had Mike survived his war injuries I think you would have been as happy and settled as I am.'

'Yes, I think I would,' Janet said and this time her smile lit her eyes. 'One thing I do know; I am lucky to have you for my mother.'

'I think I am lucky to have you,' Peggy said and gave her a hug. 'I have a wonderful family and I wouldn't change one of you. I love you very much, my darling.'

'Thanks, Mum; I love you, too,' Janet whispered as she kissed her cheek and responded to the hug. 'I feel better now. I don't need to ask, but you will take care of Jon for me? Explain that I can't take him with me this time, please.'

'Naturally. If you feel you need to stay with Ryan for a while, do so. I shall make sure Jon doesn't feel neglected.'

'Thank you. I'll let you know what is happening when I can...'

Peggy gave her another hug and watched her leave with mixed feelings. If her hunch was right, Janet would have another traumatic situation to face. For a moment, she wished she had kept her thoughts from Janet, as she'd first intended, but perhaps this was what she needed. Until she saw Ryan and sorted things out with him, the wound of their parting would fester inside her. In her opinion, Janet had always loved Ryan but been haunted by her first husband's death, perhaps feeling it wrong to give her whole self to him out of a mistaken loyalty to her first husband. Had she felt guilty that she'd slept whilst Mike had died beside her?

* * *

'I'm not sure when I'll be back,' Janet told Lars on the telephone. 'I'll let you know when I am home.'

'Why won't you tell me what is wrong? Perhaps I could help you?'

'Not this time,' Janet said. 'I'll speak to you again soon.' She replaced the receiver before he could try to persuade her to tell him why she couldn't keep their appointment that day.

Janet closed her eyes for a moment. His fleeting resemblance to Mike wasn't enough to explain the way her whole body reacted to his voice on the telephone. She knew a moment of regret that she wouldn't be spending the afternoon in his bed and dismissed it. If Ryan was ill... She shook her head at the thought. Janet had been thinking him selfish these past months, breaking up their marriage for a whim. He'd known neither she nor Jon wanted to live on a smallholding in rural Wales. It had caused trouble between them before and led to Jon's crippling accident.

Lifting her head, Janet looked at herself in the mirror. She wished she could see Jon before she left, but he was at school. Peggy would explain, but Janet had written a hasty, few words, telling him she loved him and would bring him a present when she came home. At least, he was with his beloved granny, who would make sure he didn't brood. Jon had been so much happier living here at Mulberry Lane.

Janet frowned as she heard the taxi to take her to the station arrive outside. She picked up her case and hurried downstairs.

Peggy was waiting at the bottom of the stairs and pressed some money into her hands. 'Just in case you haven't got enough,' she said, closing her fingers over it. 'Take care of yourself, darling, and let me know how things are when you can.'

'Love you, Mum,' Janet said. 'Tell Jon I love him.'

And then she was out in the taxi and on her way to the station, unsure of anything much. She had the money her mother had stuffed in her hand – it looked to be more than a hundred pounds. Surely she wouldn't need all that? Janet could stay with Ryan... unless he wasn't there? If he was in hospital... Coldness touched her spine and she shivered, busy streets just a blur as she was driven to Paddington Station, where she could get a train for Wales. She would get the first train available, which should be in half an hour or so... but what would she find at the end of her journey?

* * *

Able came home about an hour after Janet had left. Peggy told him where she'd gone and he frowned.

'It's a pity she went off on her own, hon. I'm not sure what she will find when she gets there. She hasn't been to that smallholding for a couple of years, not since he first bought it. I've never understood why he went off so suddenly last year.'

'Ryan was going to sell it,' Peggy said thoughtfully. 'He thought he had, but just before it went through, the buyer changed his mind. He let the house out after that and I think the land is still let – but the house became empty and that's why he went down there. He was going to make sure it was all right and see about a new tenant and then he suddenly told Janet he was going to live there... '

Able shook his head. 'I should have known there was more to it at the time,' he said. 'I wish I'd gone down straight after Maggie's wedding, but I didn't think a few days would make much difference. What made you tell Janet about the letter that came from Ryan? You were undecided whether to and that's why I was going, wasn't it?'

'I know – but something she said made me realise she needed to know,' Peggy admitted. 'She was thinking of going soon, but when she saw that letter, she decided to go immediately.'

'I just hope she finds that we're barking up the wrong tree,' Able commented. 'I can't think it will be good for her to walk into something like that, hon. I remember when she was having Jon. I took her down to see Pip in hospital after his car accident. She told me she couldn't have faced it alone, though she desperately wanted to see him.'

'I think actually it might do Janet good to do this alone, Able. Her feelings have been bottled up inside for too long. Perhaps it will help her sort out what she really feels for Ryan.'

'If she discovers how much she loves him, and I'm pretty certain she does despite the way she's tried to show everyone she didn't care that he'd just wrecked what they had by going off to Wales on his own – how is she going to feel if he dies?'

'Do you think you should go down after her?' Peggy asked, looking at him anxiously. Able was fond of Janet and if he was worried for her, it made Peggy feel uneasy.

'Let's wait a couple of days now,' Able said. 'We'll see how she is when she rings. It might all be supposition on our part, hon. If Janet needs us, we could both go – and if you can't manage it, I will.'

'Thank you,' she said. 'I don't know what I would do without you, Able. I was so lucky to find you.'

'You know how I feel about that,' he replied and took her into his embrace. 'Don't worry until we know we have cause. Janet is old enough to look after herself – but if Ryan truly is desperately ill, I wouldn't want her to go through that alone.'

'No, nor would I,' Peggy agreed and sighed. She looked at him then and saw he was still concerned about something. 'What is it, Able? There's more – that council meeting. What happened? I'd forgotten about it after talking to Janet...'

'I'm afraid they have put the proposal forward to the planning stage,' Able said heavily. 'I was assured privately that we shall receive adequate compensation, because of the renovation work we did, and the chance to rent or buy a new property when the rebuilding is complete – but they are resolute. Mulberry Lane is due for clearance and it will be sooner than we expected...'

Peggy felt a pang of something. She wasn't sure if it was regret, disappointment, or anger, but, seeing how concerned Able was for her, she smiled. 'It's all right, love,' she said softly. 'When I lost my memory, this place was my anchor and I did need it then, but I'm fine again now. I shall miss it, naturally, but I think I am ready to start a new chapter of my life. When did they say it would start?'

'Probably another year or two, because the planning and permissions will take that long.' Able swore softly beneath his breath. 'It makes me angry that they imagine financial compensation makes up for losing your home, business, friends and everything you've known. There are a lot of folk it is going to hit hard, Peggy.'

'Yes, I know,' Peggy agreed sadly. 'Once upon a time I would have fought to save it, Able, but I know it has been happening all over London. I can't stand in the way of progress and I shouldn't try. We might not like what is happening, but I noticed rats coming out of one of the boarded-up houses further down the lane yesterday. People need decent homes and much of this area is in terrible condition.'

'Yes, it is a two-sided thing,' he agreed. 'Well, if you can accept it, I guess I can. Tom says we're well established now and the move to his new builders' yard won't make any difference to our business. I think he may start to look for a new house for his family soon. He says the one he has isn't big enough really, but he's stayed on because Rose had friends here.'

'Yes, I expect those that can will move when they find what they want,' Peggy agreed. 'Some will stay to the last moment, but others will move elsewhere.' She sighed. 'When you think about it, the regulars have been getting younger lately – a lot of my older customers have already gone... died or moved to be nearer children, or in a few cases, gone into rest homes.' Once, not too long ago, they would have been called the workhouse, but now they were places of rest for those who had nowhere else to go.

'Have you given our eventual move any thought, hon?'

'I'm not sure,' Peggy said. 'When we moved to the sea before we had that café and it was hard work. The pub and restaurant had just got into a nice routine – and there is Fay's catering business, too. I'll have to ask her what she wants me to do about that...' She looked at him enquiringly. 'What do you feel we should do?'

'I don't think you should bother too much about the catering, hon. That was Fay's dream, not yours – but...' He hesitated, then, 'I believe we should divide our time between the town and the country. Tom doesn't need me here all the time. I don't do much except the paperwork, help him to plan for the future, and attend any meetings that he needs to know about. Perhaps we could find ourselves a nice little flat up here and a cottage in the country. Somewhere not too far away, so we can travel between the two in a couple of hours or so...'

'That sounds like a plan,' Peggy agreed and caught his hand, entwining her fingers with his. 'You've considered it from all angles, haven't you?'

'I want you to be happy when it happens,' Able told her. 'If we start looking now, we shall be ready when the time comes rather than feeling as if we have to buy the first thing available.'

'We'll go house hunting together,' Peggy said, because he was right. They needed to explore several avenues before making the decision that would shape the rest of their lives. 'It will be fun and exciting. Something we've never done.'

'I'll start looking for likely properties and then we can visit them together,' he promised.

'Yes, you do that and I'll tell Maureen what we're planning,' Peggy said. 'It might help her to feel more settled if she knows that we will be spending some of our time here in London. I might be able to hold on to Fay's catering business if I can find somewhere to set up the kitchen...'

'Discuss that with her,' Able suggested. 'You know my feelings – you can't carry everyone's dreams, hon.'

Peggy nodded and then smiled as she thought of something. She reached into her apron and took out a postcard. 'Look what came earlier when you were out. It's from Maggie. She is having a wonderful time and finding lots of new ideas for her cooking.'

'You will enjoy hearing about them when she returns,' Able said with a smile.

'Yes, I shall – and I will talk to Fay about the catering,' Peggy agreed. 'I think she might have different ideas about what she wants now...' She let out a sigh. 'Fay, a mother – it doesn't seem possible...'

Able laughed. 'It happens. She seems happy, so that's all that matters, isn't it?'

'Yes, of course it is.' Peggy smiled and kissed him. 'Am I getting old, Able?'

'You – old? Never!' Able gazed down at her from his superior height, his eyes warm with love. 'You'll always be young, beautiful and sexy as hell to me, hon.'

Peggy giggled her delight. While she had Able's love to warm and protect her, nothing bad could ever really touch her.

13

'I know you've done the best you could to keep the catering business going for me, Mum, but I don't think it's what I want or need any more,' Fay told her when she spoke to her the next morning. 'I shall come back to England to live one day, but not necessarily in London. Jace says we might have a nice place overlooking the sea in Cornwall. Maggie will probably live and work down that way and I might do the same, but for the time being we have to stay where we are. While Jace is in demand, he needs to be where the work is; he says it will last a few years and then his popularity will wane, but he'll have made his fortune and we can come back here to live.'

'Yes, I thought you might say that,' Peggy nodded. 'In that case, I'll decide what I want to do when the time comes. We've decided we might buy a flat in London and a cottage in the country. I'm not as young as I was and I dare say I shall soon begin to feel I've had enough and enjoy taking things easy.'

'You've worked all your life, Mum,' Fay said and reached for her hand, pressing it to her cheek. 'I am hoping you and Dad will find time to come and stay with us for holidays – and I mean long ones.'

Peggy smiled as she responded to Fay's caress. 'Yes, I am sure we shall, my love. Your father and Tom are doing really well. I can't see that changing, because there is always building work to do. I don't need to work any more. I do it because I enjoy it, but the catering business suits me, so I may keep it on. I need only take the jobs I fancy, just for the fun of it really.'

'You've got a big party coming up next week, haven't you?' Peggy nodded. 'I can help you with that, Mum. I'll make all the desserts and cakes and leave the mains to you.'

'Done,' Peggy said promptly. 'I was hoping you might. It will be fun working with you again, love.'

'Yes...' Fay looked wistful. 'That is the one thing I miss, working with you and Maggie. I did love that... but I am making friends out there, Mum. It is really lovely. The sunshine and the swimming pools and the beach. Jace has bought a place for us so we can spend weekends and holidays by the sea.'

'You really are happy, aren't you?'

'Yes.' Fay's smile lit up her face and warmed Peggy's heart. 'It is exactly the life I would have chosen, Mum. I always wanted excitement and something new happening all the time, and that's how it is out there. Of course it helps having so much money. Jace is earning what he calls "silly money" now. He says he is going to milk it for a few years. And in the meantime, he thinks that I should cook for friends and do their parties for them – and write recipe books. Jace says I'll earn far more doing that once I have a reputation. He says he'll get me a contract to do cooking on television, local at first and then maybe all over the country, and then my books will sell the way his records do.' Her lovely face was alight with enthusiasm and it was clear that for Fay life was magical just now.

Peggy nodded but made no comment. Every other sentence was 'Jace says' or 'Jace thinks', which made Peggy smile inwardly. Fay had Hollywood stars in her eyes and had been swept up in the glamour of it all. It wouldn't be the life Peggy would enjoy, but perhaps if she'd been younger... She shook her head mentally. She'd never had the chance. It had been hard work, the trauma of war and rationing and all the stresses and strains of trying to make a living. She didn't think she would want the life her daughter described, but she was glad that Fay had the chance and hoped she would make the most of it.

'It all sounds wonderful,' she told Fay after she had considered. 'Don't forget you have a baby on the way, though.'

Fay placed her hands on the barely noticeable curve of her stomach. 'I couldn't forget that, Mum. We are both so thrilled – but a baby doesn't have to stop me doing what I want. It never did you, did it?'

'No, that is true,' Peggy agreed. 'I am glad you are happy, Fay. It's all we want for you.'

'I am very happy,' Fay told her. She looked thoughtful for a moment. 'What did you think of Freddie, Mum? Is he happy? I felt he had things on his mind. Do you know if he and Greta are all right? They aren't engaged yet...'

'No, they aren't, but they have an understanding,' Peggy agreed. 'He said he was OK, but if you noticed something, I'll write and ask him if needs anything. He might just be short of money. Students usually are.'

'I asked him if he was all right for money. He said he didn't need anything.' Fay frowned. 'I don't think it is money. I might pop down to Cambridge and see him before Jace gets here.'

'I am sure he would like that – but drop him a line and let him know, so he's expecting you. Freddie rushes from one place to another the whole time, so he says – on a bike of all things. Your father is talking about getting him a little car of his own when he passes his final exams.'

'Jace bought me one,' Fay said. 'It is white and very American – very sleek. A Cadillac.'

'Greg bought Maggie a little MG for her wedding gift,' Peggy commented. 'I think he feels she will need a car of her own when they move to the country.'

Fay nodded and smiled. 'Two East End girls that got lucky. You never had much chance for fun when you were our ages, did you?'

'When I got married, we moved to the Pig & Whistle almost straight away. My first husband was fortunate to get the licence and we thought we were in clover having a business to run.' Peggy sighed, remembering. 'It was a good life in many ways, but Laurie... nothing was ever quite enough for him. I don't know why. Whether it was me or just something in him... but after Janet and Pip were born, he got restless. I don't think he had affairs until after Janet was married and he went to Scotland for his war job, but I don't know for sure. I thought we were reasonably happy until then, but looking back I can see it was never ideal—'

'Then you found Dad and he loved you the way you deserved,' Fay said and hugged her. 'I know he adores you, Mum. He makes you happy the way Jace does me...' She laughed confidently. 'I'm enjoying everything out there, Mum, but it's because of Jace. The rest wouldn't make me this content without him. Don't think I've had my head turned by it all, because I'm still me.'

'I know you are,' Peggy said and smiled. 'It's wonderful that you have the chance to see another life, but I'd like to think you could be happy anywhere with Jace.'

'Yes, of course I would,' Fay agreed. 'It's just fun having all the extras for now. Jace says it may not last and he doesn't want to stay there forever, but he'd be mad not to see how far he can go in the film industry.'

'Yes, he would,' Peggy concurred. 'Well, I've got things to do. If you're in the mood, you can whip up a nice coffee and walnut cake for your dad?'

'I will,' Fay said instantly. 'I'll make two and I'll take one down for Freddie when I go. I know you said I should let him know, but he won't care. If I can't find him, I'll take it to Greta and have a chat to her.'

'Yes, I should—' Peggy began and then heard the sound of Maureen's voice in the hall; the next moment, she poked her head through the doorway and Peggy sensed her excitement. 'What is it, Maureen? Is everything all right?'

'It's Shirley,' Maureen told her. 'Ray just rang me to tell me she has gone into the maternity clinic; the baby is on the way!'

'Oh, that's good,' Peggy exclaimed. 'I know she was getting fed up with the waiting and felt uncomfortable... but isn't it rather early?'

'A couple of weeks or so,' Maureen told her. 'Ray said not to worry. He will let us know when it's born, but I couldn't sit still, Peggy. I'm excited and anxious all in one...'

'Get your breath back and come and sit down,' Peggy invited, putting the kettle on. 'No need to worry, love. I was a couple of weeks early with the twins. You handled that beautifully and I didn't even have time to get to the hospital.'

'Oh, Peggy,' Maureen said and laughed with relief. 'That's why Gordon told me to come round. He knows you always make me feel better. If I was with her, I'd be all efficiency and telling everyone else not to worry – but when you're not there and you don't know what is happening...'

'I know. I felt the same when Janet had Maggie. I wasn't around when she gave birth and I felt awful – but she was here when she had Jon. I never turned a hair then...'

Maureen nodded and accepted a piece of Victoria sponge cake from Fay. She smiled at her. 'Peggy tells me you are expecting a baby, love. Are you excited about it?'

'Very much so,' Fay told her. 'I can't wait to hold her – or him. I expect Shirley feels the same.'

'I know I do,' Maureen said. 'Shirley wants children, but I know she isn't too happy about having to give up work for a time. She trained so hard to become a doctor and yet she and Ray really want a family.'

'I didn't train as long or as hard as Shirley,' Fay said, 'but I know she must want to go on working. I love what I do and I intend to carry on as much as I can. I shall probably have a nursemaid to help me so that I can continue my catering.'

Maureen nodded. 'I think Shirley may be contemplating the same thing – though I'll be around if she needs me.' She looked thoughtful. 'So do you like living over there, Fay?'

'I love it,' Fay told her. 'I have lots of fun doing buffets for pool parties and making special birthday cakes, some for children – things like spaceships and Bat Mobiles, from the comic books,' she added as she saw Maureen's blank stare.

'That sounds nice,' Maureen said. 'Is it lovely and warm there, Fay?'

'Most of the time. I don't sit in the sun too much, though. My skin is too fair and it can be very hot. I have a swim early mornings and often at night – there's a pool at the house Jace took for us.'

'I've never swum in a pool, except a few times when I was at school,' Maureen said. 'It's usually a paddle in the sea for us...'

'Me too,' Peggy said and laughed. The faint look of anxiety had eased from Maureen's face. 'I've never been much of a swimmer. The twins were water babies; Able saw to that when we lived near the sea.'

'Gordy likes most sport, but he isn't much interested in swimming, though he learned at school,' Maureen commentated. 'But that certainly sounds a lovely way to spend your life, Fay.' She glanced at her wrist-watch. 'Ray said Shirley went into labour at about six this morning; it could be hours yet, I suppose.'

'Probably,' Peggy agreed just as the telephone rang.

Fay went to answer it and came back a few seconds later.

'It's for you, Maureen. Gordon has some good news—'

Maureen was out into the hall like a shot.

Peggy smiled at her daughter. 'Did Gordon say whether it's a girl or a boy?'

'He didn't say, but he sounded very excited...'

They both turned to look as Maureen came back, looking excited but overcome.

'She's had twins, a girl and a boy!' Maureen said, clearly astounded. 'I can't believe it. No one said a word to me...' She sat down on the chair, looking pleased but dazed, as if the news had swung her off-balance. 'Ray told Gordon he knew but they chose not to tell us in case we worried too much.'

'As you probably would have,' Peggy confirmed with a laugh. 'No wonder they came early. That is wonderful – mother and babies doing well?'

'Absolutely fine, according to Ray. Gordon is over the moon. I still can't quite believe it. No wonder she got so big and felt so tired these past weeks.' Maureen shook her head in wonder. 'Oh, well, they've got their family. I think they wanted two children, so they got lucky.'

'Twins are a lot of fun,' Peggy said, looking fondly at Fay. 'I've always found my two a handful, but I wouldn't have changed that...'

'Freddie never caused you any problems,' Fay chirped. 'I was always the troublesome one, Mum.'

Peggy laughed. 'This calls for a little celebration. Shall we have a sherry?'

'Just one,' Maureen told her. 'You know it always goes to my head, Peggy. More than one small glass and I'm tiddly.'

Peggy smiled and poured them all a small sherry. 'To Shirley and her twins,' she said and drank a little of her drink. Maureen sipped hers and they all talked about the twins and what it would mean for Shirley. Maureen left, saying she'd better get home because Gordon would want to talk about the news.

'That was unexpected,' Peggy remarked after her friend had gone. 'You're not expecting twins, are you?'

Fay laughed and shook her head. 'Not to my knowledge, Mum. Don't worry, if I am I will let you know. I wonder why Shirley didn't tell Maureen...'

'I expect they thought Gordon might fret too much. He does tend to worry about Shirley a lot – perhaps because her mother died young.'

Fay nodded. 'Yes, and he isn't as well as he could be, is he?' She looked at Peggy thoughtfully. 'I wonder how Janet is getting on... She hasn't rung yet, has she?'

14

It was mid-morning when Janet finally arrived at the remote farmhouse. She'd stayed overnight in Cardiff at a small hotel close to the railway station and hired a car to drive herself out to Ryan's home that morning. The car radio was on, playing popular music, and she hummed along to a Cliff Richard record, but then the news came on and an announcer said that according to the latest opinion polls less than half the voters now approved of Harold Macmillan as Prime Minister. Uninterested, Janet frowned and switched the radio off just as she drew to a halt at her destination.

The house looked uninviting; its grey stone walls unadorned by any kind of greenery. A couple of dilapidated barns were behind the house and there was a pasture of several acres with a few trees in the distance, but no real garden, just a few scrubby bushes, cobwebs on the branches sparkling with the rain shower that had just ceased. An old truck was parked out front, and as Janet got out of the hired car, from behind the building, a dog ran towards her barking its head off. It was a Rottweiler and looked fierce, saliva dripping as it bared its teeth at her.

When had Ryan got himself a dog? Janet tensed. He'd never been keen on the children having dogs.

The dog moved nearer to her and then stopped, growling aggressively. She took a step forward, only for it to snarl, showing the whites of its eyes, its throaty growls increasingly alarming.

'Ryan!' Janet called nervously. 'Ryan, call this dog off... It's Janet.'

The dog crouched down low and growled, clearly threatening what it would do if she dared to move. She felt a mixture of fear and anger. What kind of a welcome was this?

Just as she was wondering whether to get back in the car, a man walked from behind the house. 'Sultan! Come here!' He summoned the dog, who ran to him, but didn't approach Janet himself, his expression as forbidding as his dog's. 'Who are you? What do you want? We don't like strangers much round here—'

'I am looking for my husband, Ryan,' Janet said. 'Ryan Hendricks – he owns this farm. Or I thought he did?'

The man's eyes narrowed in suspicion. 'He might own it, but I'm looking after it. I took it over last week.'

'Who are you?' she asked, bewildered. 'Has Ryan let the place to you? Where is he? I've come from London to see him.'

The man stared at her in silence, then frowned. 'You'd better come in for a moment.' He barked an order at the dog, who dropped its head on the ground, never taking its eyes off Janet as she walked cautiously towards its owner. 'My name is John Griggs. I own land next to Ryan's and he asked me to keep an eye on things while he's away.'

'Ryan isn't here?' Janet felt a surge of frustration. She should have rung first, but he hadn't answered the phone the last few times she'd tried and when Peggy told her about his letter, she hadn't waited. 'Where has he gone – will he be long?'

John Griggs led the way inside the big old kitchen. It was a room that some might find charming with its low-hanging beams long blackened by smoke, dark slate floor and a huge range that threw out a lot of heat when it was working. At the moment, the room was chilly. Clearly no one had been living here for a while, because there was an air of desertion about it, as though it had been abandoned.

'What is going on? I don't understand...' Janet said, but a cold lump had settled around her heart. She felt its ice as she looked at the stranger and saw an expression in his eyes that frightened her. 'Is Ryan ill?'

'You really don't know? Gwen, that's my wife, thought you must be a heartless bitch staying up there in London when...' He hesitated then, 'There's no way I can make this easier even if I tried – Ryan is dying. He has cancer of the liver and bowel and he went into hospital last week. He isn't expected to come out again. I wanted to let his family know, but he wouldn't let us...'

'Oh no...' Janet felt as if all the air had been punched out of her and sank down on the nearest chair as her knees went weak. 'I had no idea... why didn't he tell me?' She bent her head as the pent-up emotion poured out of her in noisy sobs and tears trickled down her face. 'Why did he choose to come to a forsaken place like this to spend his last months?'

'Ryan told me he wanted peace and this is where he found it,' John Griggs told her. 'He never mentioned you until a couple of weeks ago. We didn't know he was married. I made him an offer for the place when he asked if I'd see to things, and he said you would sell to me when he was gone.'

'Why didn't he tell me?' Janet asked the question of herself rather than the stranger, but he answered it.

'Ryan told me he didn't want you to suffer the pain of seeing him die. He thought you had suffered enough with the death of your first husband...' His voice softened slightly. 'We misjudged you, Mrs Hendricks. Gwen said any woman would want to be with their husband in his last days unless she was without feelings – and I can see you aren't.'

'I love Ryan. I thought he was being deliberately obstinate by coming here when he knew I didn't like it. I would have come if I'd known, to look after him.' Janet looked up, tears on her lashes. She blinked them away impatiently. 'I should like to see him. Where is he, please?'

'It's a small hospice, at least twenty miles from here – and difficult to find if you don't know.' John Griggs gave a small impatient sigh. 'I will show you the way if you wish?'

'I need to get there,' Janet faltered uncertainly. 'I expect you are busy?'

'You've come down from London. I can spare an hour or two to get you there. I'd take you, but my truck isn't a good ride and you'd have to come back here to rescue that car...' He cast a scathing glance at the smart Vauxhall she'd hired. 'Not very suitable for round here, is it?'

'No, I shall probably change it,' Janet agreed.

'You'll be staying then?'

'For a while, yes,' she confirmed.

'Here or in Cardiff?'

'I'm not sure. It depends on Ryan,' Janet admitted. 'If he feels able to return here with me to care for him, we'll do that, if not, I'll stay in Cardiff.'

John Griggs nodded. 'I'll come back and light the fire. Get a few things in for you. I'll give you my telephone number. If you need help, ring me.'

'Thank you, that is kind,' Janet said. She lifted her head and looked at him. 'I'll follow you then, all right?'

'Best way.' He nodded once. 'I doubt he'll be up to coming back here, but that's for you to ask. I'll get the place warm for you and some fresh milk and tea. Ring me if you need more. Ryan is a friend.'

Janet thanked him and they left the farmhouse. The dog eyed her fiercely but made no move to attack her as she got into her car and started it. John Griggs summoned the dog to get in the truck with him and then set off back down the track she'd used to approach the farmhouse.

* * *

A fine mist was in the air, clinging to the trees and making the day seem colder than it actually was, clouds obscuring a watery sun that was only half-heartedly trying to make an appearance. Janet gave a little shudder. The isolation of this place was what Ryan had liked, but Janet preferred the hustle and bustle of the town. Winter here would have been almost unbearable for her and she knew Jon felt the same. Yet if she'd known

Ryan was so desperately ill, she would have come, of course she would. The knowledge of his sickness had settled inside her like a hard knot and she felt the tears building as she followed the truck as it bounced along narrow country roads. Her car hit every bump and sent jolts through her, making her wish she'd hired something more suitable. She would have to change it if she took Ryan back to the farm – but he might be too ill for that... Janet's heart ached as she thought of the husband she'd always loved in her own way.

It hurt to know that Ryan had kept his illness from her, because it showed her that he cared for her far more than she'd understood. He'd done it to protect her, believing she couldn't bear another traumatic death, but Janet knew she was strong enough to care for him.

Watching the tail lights of the truck ahead as they turned down yet another winding road, Janet sighed with relief as she saw the cluster of buildings set below them, nestling in a little valley. The sun had finally broken through those clouds and it turned the walls of ancient cottages and what had probably once been a grand house golden. If this was the setting of the hospice, she could understand why Ryan had wanted to spend his last days here. The farmhouse was bleak and uninviting, but this place had its own little touch of quiet magic as it nestled amongst the hills.

The descent into the valley was just a gentle slope and as they got nearer, Janet had a sense of peace. At least Ryan had what he wanted here.

* * *

She was too late. Janet stared at the matron of the hospice in disbelief. Ryan had passed away just hours previously. If she'd driven straight here last night, she would have been in time to say goodbye, but she hadn't known he was here.

'May I see him?' she asked when she could master her voice. Inside, she was trembling, but outwardly proud as she looked at the woman who had just told her Ryan was dead. 'I didn't know he was ill – can you tell me more please?'

'You'd better come and have a cup of tea in my office,' Matron said, her tone softening. 'I will give instructions for you to be taken to see him in our chapel of rest. Ryan was at peace when he died, Mrs Hendricks. He left a letter for you. It was dictated because he couldn't manage to write it and something was distressing him. I will give it to you in my room.'

Janet straightened her back. She knew the tears were very close, but she held them back. She would cry when she was alone. There was time enough to grieve. For now, she had to be strong, to see Ryan, beg his forgiveness and say her last goodbye.

It was evening when Janet was able to let the tears fall at last. Even as she'd stood by his cold, still body, she'd not been able to cry. Instead, she'd felt the hard lump of grief in her throat, as she bent her head to kiss his blue lips and touch the marble of his face. This wasn't Ryan; this wasn't the man she'd fought with, laughed with, had a son with, and, yes, loved. Yet he looked peaceful, calm, at rest. It was a bitter irony that she'd swallowed her pride and come to him, too late.

Alone in the hotel room she'd taken for a few days, she finally let go and the tears came, cascading down her cheeks after she'd read Ryan's last letter to her.

My darling Janet,

Forgive me for not telling you the truth. I couldn't bear to witness your grief, knowing how badly Mike's death affected you all those years ago. I thought I knew best, that I was protecting you, but in these last days before I leave this earth, I have realised I was wrong. I know that you loved me in your way – as much as it was possible to give, you gave, my love. I loved you so very much. Forgive me for what happened to Jon, though I can never forgive myself. I have loved you as much as any woman could be loved and I beg you not to hate me for what I did. Please do not feel you failed in any way, for you did not. It was I that failed you, my darling. Do not weep for me. Remember only that I loved you and think kindly of me if you can.

I always loved you.

Ryan

Janet sobbed broken-heartedly. She hadn't known just how much he had cared for and understood her. Why hadn't he told her these things, instead of just heading off on his own to that awful farmhouse? If only he had done so, they could have been together, shared their love until the last.

Ryan had asked the hospice to contact her. Matron had told her that they'd tried to ring her the previous evening – but she'd been on the train down and by the time she got there it was already too late. Too late to tell him that she did love him, too late to mend fences or reach a better understanding... Except that Ryan's letter did seem to understand.

Janet cried for a long time. She cried for the times they'd quarrelled and the times they'd been happy, for the years lost through his premature death and then she cried for Mike, and for the waste of the years when she had felt that guilt inside – guilt that she could be happy when Mike was gone. She'd always harboured a feeling that she had no right to happiness after he'd died. It was his war wound that had killed Mike but he'd died by her side as she slept and she ought to have known – to have held him in his last moments. Now it poured out of her in a torrent of grief and regret.

Afterwards, she felt drained, falling asleep on the bed without undressing, and waking – as the first fingers of a rosy dawn crept through the windows – to feel stiff and achy all over.

* * *

A warm bath and a cooked breakfast helped Janet start to recover, at least physically. After leaving the hotel, she went to change her car for something more suitable and drove out to the farmhouse in a Land Rover. Pale sunlight was shining now, which made the house look more habitable. When she walked in, the range was alight and burning steadily, driving away the sense of cold depression she'd felt the previous day.

She looked in the large cold pantry and discovered a small churn of milk, which was icy cold, some bread that looked home-baked, butter, cheese and a jar of homemade chutney. Janet smiled, because it was thoughtful, especially as her benefactor imagined her to be a heartless wife who had deserted her husband in his time of need. Well, she had in a way, but she hadn't known the facts. She'd thought Ryan had simply got fed up with her and wanted a break. In her heart, Janet had always felt that she and Ryan would eventually get back together – and now it was too late to tell him how much she'd loved him. She'd realised during the long night of sorrow that she had loved Ryan more than she'd thought. It was just a different kind of love to that she'd known for her first husband. What a fool she'd been to let her grief and guilt over Mike's death sour a relationship that ought to have been perfect.

It was no use crying for the moon. Janet made herself a pot of tea and looked around the big kitchen. It looked as if Ryan had done most things in here other than sleep. He didn't have a TV but he had a record player and she knew that was how he would have spent his evenings, reading while soft music played in the background. There was also a large roll-top desk and Ryan had clearly made use of it.

She got up and wandered over to the record player, selecting an LP of country music; it was something they'd both enjoyed. Once it was playing softly in the background, she went to the desk and opened it. The first thing she saw was a letter in Ryan's hand addressed to her, care of Peggy.

Had he thought she wouldn't come herself?

Fighting the bitter tears of regret, Janet opened the letter. It told her of his arrangement with John Griggs, the agreed price and then went on to explain about various bank accounts, things he wanted Jon to have, and then, right at the end.

It is all for Janet. I've left a will with my solicitor in London. Most of it is in this place and some money in the bank but she will find something personal in the secret drawer.

Janet nodded to herself. He'd discovered the secret drawer the first time they'd visited together. It was just a little dummy piece that looked like decoration, but if you pressed it, the door opened and a secret hiding place was revealed. Janet had laughed when he was so thrilled with it, telling him it was easy to find if anyone looked.

She opened it and saw first an envelope addressed to Jon, and beneath it a small black velvet box. Taking it out with a hand that shook slightly, she lifted the lid and gave a gasp of surprise as she saw the beautiful old pendant within. It was an oval gold locket on a heavy chain, embossed with fine gold wire work around a small ruby, and just the kind of thing she loved. As she took it out, she saw a small piece of paper underneath it.

I never told you I loved you enough,

Ryan had written and she could hear his voice saying the words.

I was going to give you this when you got back from America and ask if we could start again. Then I had my appointment with the hospital and realised I couldn't put you through all that rotten stuff. It was already too late to do anything. They told me six months to a year.

Janet gave a choking gasp as the tears came rushing again and she found herself wandering through the rest of the house, crying, and hugging herself. Ryan hadn't bothered with it much. Most of the rooms were closed up, some unfurnished. Only his bedroom showed any sign of use.

She opened the closet and closed it again, leaning her head against the door. She couldn't face this just yet.

Hearing a sound downstairs, she wiped her face and went back to the kitchen. John Griggs was standing there looking about him.

'You came back then,' he said. 'Are you staying here for a while?'

'No, I think I'll stay in Cardiff,' Janet replied. 'I'm not sure when I can face clearing Ryan's things. Not until after the funeral anyway.'

'That is fine. I want the place for my son. He is getting married in August. I shall do it up a bit for him, put in a better bathroom and see if we can get a TV signal here. There is no hurry – but I could clear it for you if you wish? Rory will be pleased to have the furniture if we can agree a price.'

'It is much too soon,' Janet said harshly, then realised he was merely trying to make it easy for her. 'I know you want to help, but I have to sort Ryan's things myself. I doubt I'll want the furniture, but I can't deal with it now. I shall ring my mother. I was too upset to do it last night, but Mum will come for the funeral.'

John Griggs looked at her for a moment and then nodded. 'Just as you like.' He thought for a moment. 'Do you want me to come in and keep the fire going for you? It needs the range to make it cosy, but it's a warm house when that is lit.'

Janet agreed. 'If that isn't too much trouble, I would like you to carry on as you did for Ryan.'

'I banked the fire up for him most days, when he started to feel it was too much for him.'

Janet met his harsh look. 'Was he very ill before he went into that place?'

'Yes. He hung on until almost the last, refusing to seek help. I don't know why.' His brusque words were like a knife thrust to her heart.

Janet closed her eyes for a moment. Ryan had hoped she would come, but he hadn't asked for her until it was too late. Why, why hadn't he told her? She felt the tears choke her again but refused to let them fall.

'I'm sorry, Mrs Hendricks. I shouldn't have intruded on your grief.'

Janet blinked and looked at him. She'd almost forgotten he was there. 'No, you've been kind. I'll be all right now. I'll drive back to Cardiff before it gets dark.'

'Ryan told me to have the phone cut off. I was reluctant to do it, but I did two days ago. You'll need to do your telephoning from Cardiff.'

Janet thanked him. She'd already discovered the phone wasn't connected. 'Yes, I'll do that,' she said.

John Griggs nodded and walked to the door. There he turned to look back at her. 'Gwen told me I should find out where you lived and tell you when he went into the hospice. I'm sorry I didn't.'

'I'm sorry, too,' Janet replied. 'It wasn't your fault. Ryan wouldn't have let you. I don't know what changed his mind, but, apparently, they did try to ring me the other night, but I was on my way down here.'

'Yes – I think it was the reverend at the hospice. I visited Ryan and he said he'd had some long talks with him – Reverend Peters. You might want to talk to him.'

'Yes. I am seeing him tomorrow about the funeral arrangements,' Janet replied.

He nodded and walked out.

Janet sat down at the table. Her tea, which she'd forgotten had gone cold.

She decided to leave things as they were, drive back to Cardiff and ring her mother. That way, perhaps she could face what she needed to do, but alone it was all too much.

* * *

For a moment, Peggy was too stunned to respond, then, 'I am so sorry, darling. We had a call the night you left from the hospice asking for you, but they didn't tell us anything – just said would you ring them. We tried to ring Ryan's number, but there was no answer, just the operator saying it was unavailable... Of course I'll come down tomorrow. Do you want me to bring Jon?'

'No, I don't think so. It would be too upsetting for him. He's lost his dad and it will be hard for him to understand. I think he would be better at home with Able.' Janet suddenly remembered. 'Oh, Mum, can you manage it? I'd forgotten for a moment that Maggie's away.'

'The girls will manage, and I dare say Maureen will pop round and make sure everything is all right – besides, Able will be here. You need me there and that is all that matters for now.'

Janet closed her eyes. It was stupid the way she could cry at the smallest thing. 'Thanks, Mum. I know I should be able to cope but—'

'I understand perfectly,' Peggy said. 'It would have been much better had he told you and let you make up your own mind what you wanted to do.'

'I would have come here if he'd explained,' Janet said. 'I was so angry with Ryan for just walking out on us but I think he realised it was a mistake, but not until it was too late.' She'd thought their marriage was over, been furious with Ryan, and thought she was ready to move on – but now her world had turned upside down. If Ryan had only told her... Janet shook her head as the tears welled once more. 'Why did he do it?'

'So foolish of him, noble in its way but wrong,' Peggy said firmly. 'Try to be brave, love and I'll be there as soon as I can...'

15

Fay stood outside the ancient college in King's Parade and looked at the magnificent building. She'd wondered why her brother wanted to come to Cambridge for university, before going on to a teaching training post, when he could have applied for a similar place nearer home, but having wandered through the town after leaving the bus that brought her from the railway station, she'd felt the peace of the old city. There was less hustle and bustle than in London and the greens were pleasant. Now the peace of this venerated college made her smile. Yes, this would suit her easy-going brother with its slower pace.

Approaching the gates tentatively, she wondered if she ought to have let Freddie know she was coming. Fay realised suddenly that she couldn't just wander in searching for him. She was pondering her problem when a man came out of what she realised was probably the porter's lodge and approached her.

'May I be of help, miss?' he enquired politely. 'Were you looking for someone?'

'Oh – yes, my brother,' Fay said, smiling at him. 'He is a first-year student – Freddie Ronoscki. My mother said I should send him a telegram to let him know I was coming, but I thought I'd find him easily... now, it's so much bigger than I imagined.'

'Yes, lovely but impressive,' the man replied with a little laugh. 'I could ask someone to take a message for you – Miss Ronoscki, is it?'

'No, I'm Mrs Sorrel now,' Fay replied with a little giggle. Jace hated his real name, which was why he only ever used his stage name and she still hadn't got used to it. 'Just say it is his sister Fay, please.'

'Yes, madam,' the porter said a twinkle in his eyes. 'I know Mr Ronoscki well. He's one that always stops to have a word when he sees me...'

He nodded to her and went off, leaving Fay to look about her. The sun was warm on her head and she found a short wall to perch on while she waited, and in fact it was only a few minutes before she saw the porter returning with Freddie in tow. 'That was a bit of luck, miss... he was just leaving his lecture when I spotted him by the hall.'

'Thank you so much,' Fay responded as Freddie demanded anxiously, 'What's wrong? Is it Mum?'

'Nothing is wrong,' Fay told him. 'I just thought I'd come for a quick visit. Can you get away for an hour or two – or shall we wait until this evening?'

'Thank goodness! I thought when Jumbo here said you were at the gate something awful had happened—' It was because of their mother's accident the previous year, of course.

Fay sent him an apologetic look. 'Sorry, Freddie. Mum told me to send you a telegram, but I said I would just come and take my chances. Do you have another lecture you must go to immediately?'

'As a matter of fact, the rest of the day is mine to study as I please,' Freddie replied. He handed the porter a half-crown and thanked him, then reached to give Fay's arm a squeeze. 'I'm really glad you came. We hardly had any time together when I came for the wedding. Is there anything you want to tell me, Fay?' He studied her for a moment. 'You are happy over there?'

'Yes, perfectly!' She grinned. 'I miss my brother and Mum and Dad... and working with Maggie, too, but I love Jace and I'm having fun. No, I just wanted to spend some time with you.'

'I am glad you did,' Freddie told her. 'Shall we go to the river and find somewhere to sit? We could get a few sandwiches or fish and chips?'

'That reminds me, I brought you a coffee and walnut cake.'

'We don't want to take that with us – until we go to Greta this evening. You will stay, won't you, Fay?' Freddie hesitated. 'I don't want to waste time going to my room – we'll leave it with Jumbo.'

'Tell him not to eat it all,' Fay teased as she handed over the tin. 'There are some other bits and pieces in there, too.'

Freddie opened it, took out a sausage roll and offered her the tin, but she shook her head. He took the tin to the porter and asked if he would keep it, explaining what was inside. 'There are some more of these sausage rolls if you fancy one? My sister is a good cook…' He showed him the sausage roll he was munching.

'That is mighty nice of you, Mr Ronoscki,' he replied and took a sausage roll when Freddie lifted the lid and offered it. 'I'll keep the rest safe and sound for you, don't you worry.'

Freddie nodded, biting into his own as he sprinted to Fay, who had wandered over the road to look in the window of a shop selling antiques. He tucked his arm through hers, finished his sausage roll and grinned at her.

'Your porter seems very friendly,' Fay said as they walked off in the direction of the river. 'Why do you call him Jumbo?' He was a small, wiry man with grey hair and a thin face and smiling eyes.

'I have no idea – it's just what everyone calls him. His real name is Alfred Briggs.'

Fay nodded, squeezing his arm. 'This is so nice,' she said. 'Its ages since we went anywhere – just the two of us. Do you remember when you used to take me to the skating rink after school every day?'

'Of course I do. I had to miss football practice, you brat.'

Fay laughed. 'Poor Freddie, but you always did it even if it wasn't what you wanted.'

'You're my twin,' he replied. 'I couldn't let you go alone – and I knew how much it meant to you. It was a pity your ankle let you down, Fay. You were good.'

'Yes – but not good enough,' she replied. 'I did love it – but now I love my cooking and the life I have with Jace.' She looked up at him searchingly. 'What about you, Freddie? Are you happy here? Is it what you wanted?'

'I like the course I'm doing and most of the tutors are great,' Freddie replied. 'Teaching is what I want to do, Fay. I want to help kids and I think it is the best way. If you can help form a child's mind and give them a desire to learn then you've done something good.'

Fay nodded and smiled warmly. 'I sometimes wonder how we can be twins,' she said. 'We're so different in our ways. Dad says I'm like a butterfly, never settling for two minutes – and I know I can be selfish – but you're so steady and so considerate of everyone else.'

'I don't think you're selfish,' Freddie replied, smiling down at her. 'You like to enjoy life and you get your own way most of the time – but if anyone you care for needed help, you'd be there.'

'Perhaps,' she agreed. 'But you would help anyone, Freddie – and that's the difference.' He shrugged and shook his head. 'Is everything all right with you and Greta?'

'Yes, I think so...' He looked thoughtful. 'I do worry about her, Fay. She lives in her bedsit and I see her two or three times a week. She says she is happy that way, but I wish she'd stayed in London, where Mum and Maggie could have looked after her.'

'Yes – but then she wouldn't see you much,' Fay replied. 'If I were in her shoes, I'd rather live the way she does than not see you...'

'Would you?' He met her eyes and she nodded. 'I'd miss seeing her – but sometimes—' He broke off with a sigh. 'I know Greta wants us to get married, but it would be wrong until I can support her. It's hard enough managing as it is...'

'You know I've got money to spare,' Fay said, but he shook his head and looked cross. 'It's not Jace's money. I earned it myself – and you could pay me back when you're ready.'

'Thank you for the offer, but I won't accept it,' Freddie replied. 'I can manage as it is – but I can't get married, unless I take a job.'

'Mum said you were helping out in a sweet shop on Saturday mornings?'

'I don't get paid – the owner's nephew runs the cycle shop and he asked if I would keep an eye on her, sort out some kids who were stealing and causing damage. He put some new tyres for free on my bike when they were slashed.'

'Did someone slash your tyres?' Fay asked so Freddie explained.

'I'd report them if I were you,' she retorted, nettled by the insult to her twin.

'No, you wouldn't – it isn't done,' Freddie laughed at her furious face. 'Honour amongst gentlemen.'

'Be damned to that!' Fay muttered fiercely. 'They don't have much honour if they play tricks like that – so why should you?'

'For one thing I have no proof,' Freddie told her. 'In any case, I just wouldn't.'

'I told you, you are better-natured than me,' Fay retorted. 'Have they got any tyres you could slash?'

Freddie laughed. 'One of them has a car, but I've no intention of damaging it – just makes me as bad as them. No point, Fay. I really don't care – and one of them apologised, though I doubt he slashed the tyres. I think that was Crawford or another of his cronies at his instruction.'

'You're too easy-going,' she said and then hugged his arm. 'I suppose that is why we all love you. Don't change, Freddie, don't be like me.'

'I couldn't if I tried. You've got more talent in your little finger than I could aspire to in a million years.'

'Daft!' she said but hugged his arm. 'No wonder you're my best friend as well as my brother – besides, Jace, of course.'

Freddie made a face at her. 'Flattery will get you nowhere, little sister. There's a pub just here where Greta and I get a ham roll or a salad sometimes. It's not as good as Mum makes, but it is OK.'

'I'm not hungry for the moment. I'd like to go on the river and eat later – unless you're starving?'

He shook his head. 'It's a bit chilly despite the sun, but we'll go on a punt if you like and I'll show you the backs of the colleges?'

Fay expressed her agreement with his plan. Freddie seemed much like his normal self, yet she sensed something more was on his mind. Whatever it was, he didn't seem inclined to talk about it.

'Greta finishes work at three-thirty today,' Freddie told her. 'When we're ready, we'll meet her and we'll all have something to eat.'

* * *

Greta's landlady had agreed that Fay could stay for a few nights and Freddie had left them laughing and planning a shopping expedition the next day. He was pleased that they got on so well and was feeling cheerful as he went back to his room that evening. Jumbo had delivered the tin of home-cooked goodies to his room and as Freddie cut himself a slice of the delicious cake Fay had made for him, he was pleased that Greta would have some fun while he was studying. It wasn't possible for him to take another day off and he was intending to spend the night making up for the time lost when a knock came at his door. He opened it to discover one of the tutors standing there.

'Ah, you're back, Ronoscki. I've been asked to tell you that the police were here looking for you today…'

'Looking for me?' Freddie asked, puzzled. 'Is it my home – has something happened to one of my family?'

'I don't think it is anything like that – it was to do with a serious incident last Saturday.' Mr Hinks looked at him oddly. 'I was told that you sometimes help an elderly woman with her sweet shop on a Saturday morning?'

'Yes, yes, her nephew asked me to see if I could stop some kids behaving badly – Miss Martha Jones.'

'That's right,' Mr Hinks said, looking slightly relieved. 'Well, it appears that she was attacked last Saturday as she was locking up for the night. She deposits her takings in the night-safe at the bank on the market square every Saturday night – and this time she was attacked and robbed.'

'Is she badly hurt?' Freddie asked, immediately concerned.

'I believe she is in hospital and unconscious,' Mr Hinks replied heavily. He cleared his throat. 'Did you know it was her habit to bank the whole week's takings on Saturday evening, Ronoscki?'

'Yes, I did know she did that,' Freddie began and then stared at the tutor in shock. 'You don't think I had anything to do with that? Good grief! Is that why the police asked to see me?'

'I think the officer said they needed to eliminate you from their inquiries.'

Freddie frowned. It was most unpleasant to be told you were even vaguely suspected of such a despicable thing and he felt a surge of anger. 'In this case, it is easily done,' he said in an icy tone, unlike his normal voice. 'As it happens, I was in London, attending a family wedding.'

'Excellent,' Mr Hinks said, looking relieved. 'I am very glad to hear that this rather sordid affair can be swiftly closed as far as you are concerned, Mr Ronoscki. If you go down to the police station in the morning, you will be able to settle it.'

Freddie looked at the clock. It was nine-thirty. 'I think I might go this evening, sir. The sooner I explain, the better – and they might be able to tell me how Miss Jones is getting on. I feel partly responsible. I did tell her she should vary the times she took her money to the bank – and if I'd been there—'

'You can't change people's habits,' Mr Hinks said. 'You would hardly have been there had you been in Cambridge, since you only assisted on Saturday mornings... isn't that what you said just now?'

Freddie nodded. 'It's just that I like her...' he said. 'I feel that I ought to have been there... if you understand what I mean, sir?'

'Yes, well, we all feel that way when something like this happens,' he said. 'Don't be too late back, Ronoscki. You have an important lecture in the morning.'

'Yes, sir. I know,' Freddie replied, frowning. 'I can't understand how anyone could harm a lady like that...'

'No? There are plenty who would do it for a few pounds,' his tutor said cynically. 'I didn't believe you were one of them – and I informed a rather bumptious police officer of my opinion, but I'm glad to hear you confirm it with a story they cannot question. We can't afford to have one of our students under a shadow of doubt.'

'Thank you, sir,' Freddie said, shrugging on his jacket, a twinkle in his eye. 'If I'm not on time for my lecture in the morning, you will know why.'

'Not funny, Ronoscki,' Mr Hinks said wryly. 'However, I shall bear it in mind – should you not arrive. I do believe we have your home telephone number should the need arise.'

'I hope to God it doesn't,' Freddie said, sobered. 'Surely, it should only take a couple of calls to confirm that I was in London all weekend?'

'One would think so,' Mr Hinks said dryly. 'However, if my visitor is anything to go by, you might find yourself spending a night in the cells while they make their inquiries...'

* * *

It was late when Freddie returned to the college and to his own room. Too late, he thought, to telephone his father and tell him what had occurred. He didn't know Billy Jones' home number so he couldn't ring him and he knew that the hospital wouldn't give him personal details about an old lady who wasn't his relative.

Freddie went to bed with a heavy heart. He liked Martha Jones and it saddened him that she had been harmed, also he was frustrated and angry that the police had suspected him. The only reason he knew Martha Jones was because he'd wanted to help her and repay Billy for repairing his tyres. He hoped Billy wouldn't think he could possibly have done such an evil thing.

After a night spent trying to sleep without much success, Freddie was up early and went for a long run by the river. On his return, he showered, ate breakfast and then took his bike round to the cycle shop.

Billy looked up as he saw him and nodded. 'I thought you would come,' he said. 'She has recovered consciousness at last, bless her, and the hospital said she was doing well and would make a full recovery.'

'Thank goodness for that,' Freddie said. 'I was anxious for her. Does she know who attacked her?'

'I was told that she didn't see anything because they hit her from behind, but she is sure there were at least three of them – and she thinks it was teenage boys.'

Freddie nodded, because it was what he'd thought himself. 'I saw some of them outside the shop the other Saturday afternoon and scared them off. I was in London for Maggie's wedding, as I told you, Billy – but I don't suppose I could have stopped it.'

'It was my fault,' Billy replied. 'I told her I would go round and take the money to the night-safe for her, but I was busy in the shop and didn't get there before she left.'

'She can't keep doing it,' Freddie said seriously. 'I'd go and fetch it if you can't, Billy.'

'It's time she gave up the shop,' he replied gruffly, clearly feeling upset. 'I couldn't believe it when the police came and saw me. I think they thought I might have done it.'

Freddie gave a short laugh. 'They definitely thought it was me until I told them I had a hundred witnesses to prove that I was in London – loads of people saw me in church and at the reception on Saturday afternoon.'

'I told the idiots it wasn't you,' Billy said. 'They never listen – always look for the obvious. I'm her nephew, so stands to reason I'd benefit if anything happened to her – or that's what they thought – and because I was here in the shop and had a witness, they looked for another easy victim and that was you.'

'Well, now they have to do some proper investigating,' Freddie said and heard a clock striking. 'Damn, I am going to be late for my lecture if I don't go...'

'Come and see me this evening,' Billy invited. 'I shall visit Aunt Martha this afternoon. I'll tell you how she is.'

Freddie agreed and left. He pedalled like mad through streets just beginning to feel the rush of feet as the city awakened to another day. It was five minutes past the half-hour when he finally entered the lecture room, several minutes late.

Mr Hinks glanced at him but said nothing and went on with his discourse on the benefits of proper diet and exercise for those wishing to be good sportsmen. He spoke of the splendid record of rowers who had come through the portals of King's College and recommend the practice of early-morning running.

'An active body makes for an active mind,' he told his students. 'As teachers, you will be responsible for moulding the minds of your pupils, and as sports experts, you must be prepared to practise what you preach. Even if you go into another area of teaching, the same principles will stand you in good stead. I want to congratulate all of you that have made the various sporting teams to represent the college, and now we'll open our books and study the theory of physical awareness and fitness.'

Freddie did as he was bid, his mind only half on the lecture about the theory of psychology in sport – or mind over matter, as his father would call it. Freddie smiled grimly as he thought of his father's probable reaction when the police called to ask him his son's whereabouts on the previous Saturday afternoon.

16

'I'm so dreadfully sorry,' Maureen said when Peggy rang her to tell her about Ryan. 'That is rotten luck for Janet. I'm glad you're going down to be with her. She shouldn't be alone. Of course I'll pop in to see how things are.'

'I wouldn't have asked, but Fay has gone to Cambridge. I'd forgotten that when Janet rang. I know the chefs can cope with the restaurant and Carla will take my shift in the bar, and, of course, Able will be here – he'll come for the funeral but not before.'

'It is a horrible shock for Janet,' Maureen said. 'You know I'll be glad to pop in and see things are running smoothly.'

'Yes, thankfully.' Peggy sighed deeply. 'How are Shirley and the twins – and Ray?'

'All fine. The twins are gorgeous,' Maureen told her, a note of delight in her voice then. 'The little boy has dark hair and the girl's hair looks as if it will be red. They are both beautiful.'

'Oh, lovely,' Peggy said. 'And Shirley feels well?'

'She can't wait to get home. Ray is having a private nurse in to look after her for a few days – and help her with the children. They haven't actually named them yet. I think the boy feeds well, but the girl isn't quite as keen. Shirley may have to bottle-feed her – but she will have an experienced nurse to help her get the hang of things, so that's good. I offered to go, but Ray said it was all arranged…'

'I expect he didn't want to put too much on you… and it's early days yet. I expect they are still getting used to the reality of twins.'

'That's what he said, about me having enough to do, but I felt a bit disappointed. I'd have liked to look after them for a while.'

'Ray is a doctor. I suppose he thinks of the clinical side.'

'I was a nurse – I know I didn't complete my training…' Maureen sighed. 'No, I am being daft. I felt a bit shut out though…'

'Yes, I know how you feel,' Peggy agreed. 'It was like that when Janet had Maggie. Her friend , Rosemary, seemed to take over and I felt shut out – but later on it was all right and she came home to her mum.'

'I know I'm being daft…' Maureen laughed. 'It was fine when we visited them. Shirley says I've got enough to do looking after Gordon…'

'Well, she is right in a way,' Peggy told her. 'Give them my love the next time you visit and I'll see you when I get back.'

'Tell Janet… well… just give her my love,' Maureen said. 'I am just so sorry, Peggy. Janet didn't need this.'

'No, she didn't,' Peggy said and sighed. 'If it isn't one thing, it is another. I just thank God for Able and Freddie; I know they are always stable and I don't have to worry about either of them. I'll ring when I can…'

* * *

Maureen shook her head when she replaced the receiver. It seemed that troubles never came singly and she wondered what would be next. Her heart ached for Janet and Ryan too. She'd got to know him well when Janet was in America and she'd looked after Jon for a few days to help Ryan out.

'Mum…' Maureen turned to look as she heard Gordy's voice and then gave a little gasp as she saw the state of his face. He looked as if he'd been in a fight, his lip cut and what she thought might be the start of a black eye. 'Don't worry – it was just one of the lads at school. We got in an argument. He looks as bad as I do.'

'Oh, Gordy,' Maureen said. 'Come here, love, and let me bathe your face for you.' She shook her head as he sat at the kitchen table and let her bathe his cuts with a little warm water and Dettol. 'Whyever did you get in a fight?'

'One of the lads made a rude remark about Matty – said only poofs go to boarding schools, so he must be queer. I just lost my temper and hit him—'

'You should just ignore that sort – they crop up in all areas of life, love. It isn't worth the trouble it causes hitting them. They are just spiteful idiots.'

'Matty isn't queer,' Gordy said, clearly still incensed by the remark. 'He is just sensitive and he likes different things, that's all.'

'I know that and so do you,' Maureen said. 'But if he was different, and some boys and men are – well, that's their affair. The best thing really is just to ignore spiteful jibes, Gordy.'

He nodded at her. 'I'll be glad when we move away, Mum. There's a rough crowd at my school now. They are always picking on someone.'

'Where would you like to live if we did move?' she asked and he shrugged.

'I dunno – just not round here...'

Maureen nodded and patted his cheek dry with the towel. 'Well, that's done. I don't think you need to see a doctor, but you'll have a black eye for sure.'

'He'll have two,' Gordy muttered with satisfaction and Maureen sighed.

'Do you want me to speak to your headmaster about these bullies?'

'Nah, I can handle them. They'd be worse than ever if you interfered, Mum.'

'I suppose so,' she said with a sigh. 'I don't know what is happening to the lanes. They never used to be like this...'

* * *

Gordon listened when she told him her news later and nodded. 'You get bullies wherever,' he told her. 'I wouldn't worry, unless Gordy gets set on by a gang of them. I don't think it is much to worry about, love.'

'It never happened when I was at school – or to Shirley either.'

'She got her hair pulled a few times,' Gordon reminded her. 'Times have changed, Maureen. When I was a lad, if youths got to fighting, the local bobby knocked their heads together and sorted it. Nowadays, they don't seem to bother. Or maybe they're not allowed these days.'

'I haven't seen a bobby on the beat in years,' Maureen observed. 'There was always one around when I was young, nowadays you hardly see one.'

'I suppose that's what happens when an area goes downhill a bit,' Gordon said. 'Maybe it will improve if they pull it all down and start again...'

Maureen's reply was lost as the telephone rang. She answered it and discovered it was Shirley, her face lighting up with pleasure. 'I just wanted to tell you I feel fine now – and to thank you and Dad for all the presents. It was a good thing you made so much in white, because it suits both of them.'

'Oh, Shirley love,' Maureen said. 'How are they?'

'Both fine. Amelia has started to take her feed better and Anthony is full of life, screaming the place down until he gets his feed. I think he didn't leave enough for her, so she's better on the bottle. Young master is a greedy little devil.' Shirley laughed. 'Ray feeds Amelia and you should see his face, Mum... besotted...'

Maureen laughed. 'I'll bet. Your dad was just the same over you and the boys.'

'Ray has to work tomorrow,' Shirley told her. 'Can you come and spend some time with us? I have the nurse coming, but I'd like you to come for a while if you can.'

'Of course I will, my love,' Maureen agreed instantly. What an idiot she'd been to feel shut out! 'Your dad is here – shall I put him on? He wants a word...'

Maureen handed the receiver to her husband and returned to the sitting room.

Gordy came in then and picked up his satchel. 'Got some homework,' he explained and went out again. She heard him walk up the stairs and smiled. He was none the worse for his fight – but she and Gordon would have to give more thought to the move. Perhaps it might be as well to go sooner rather than wait until the last.

17

Fay and Greta had clearly enjoyed their time together. Fay had decided to stay for two nights before she went back to London so she was still there when Freddie went to see Greta the following evening. She listened in silence as Freddie told them about the attack on the elderly lady and the way one police officer had behaved, as if Freddie was guilty before they'd even heard his story.

'Oh, how could anyone think that of you?' Greta demanded, clearly affronted on his behalf. 'I hope he apologises when he knows he was wrong.'

'I doubt he'll do that,' Freddie said and grinned. 'I was pretty annoyed at first, I can tell you – but upset too that she'd been attacked like that. Fortunately, she was too tough to kill and has now given the police to understand it was some teenage boys. Billy said she was indignant when they suggested it might have been me and told them they were fools.' His smile had gone as he thought of the old lady's suffering but returned as he thought how feisty she was despite what had happened.

'Well, so they were,' Fay said. 'Mum will be livid when she knows...'

Freddie nodded, then, 'I don't suppose you've phoned home today, Fay?' She shook her head. 'Mum has gone to Wales. Ryan has died in hospital – apparently, it is why he didn't come to Maggie's wedding. He was very ill but didn't tell anyone and Janet got there too late. She has to sort things out and Mum has gone to help her.'

'Oh no! Poor Ryan,' Fay said. 'I liked him – and he thought the world of Janet. Why on earth didn't he tell her he was ill? I am sure she would have wanted to be with him...' A little shiver went through her. 'I couldn't bear to think of Jace being alone at such a time.' She frowned. 'I ought to go back – they might need me in the restaurant...'

'Dad said to tell you it is fine. Maureen and Rose have both offered to help; he insisted you stay here and enjoy yourself – at least until he goes for the funeral.'

Greta nodded her agreement. 'I expect they can manage, Fay,' she said, not knowing what else to say because she didn't know Ryan, then, 'Janet must be upset. It's awful when anyone dies, especially your husband.'

'Dad says she was devastated.' Freddie gave her a reassuring smile, understanding her uncertainty. 'But he didn't see any reason for Fay to go home – he only needs to manage for a couple of days.'

'They would have to manage if I was in America,' Fay said, 'but I'll phone Dad later and make sure.'

Greta glanced at Freddie. 'What did your father say about the lady who was attacked?'

'He asked how she was and told me to take her some flowers when I get the chance. Told me not to worry about the bumptious police officer, said he was just doing his job – even if he could have done it in a more considerate way.'

'That's Dad,' Fay said, smiling fondly at her brother. 'He doesn't flare up the way I do. I think I am more like Mum in that respect.'

'Yes, Mum sometimes acts first and thinks afterwards,' Freddie agreed. 'She would come charging to the rescue if either of us were in trouble, but Dad would be talking quietly to the lawyer in the background and sort the whole thing out in a trice.'

'We're lucky to have them,' Fay replied. 'Janet lost her father and her first husband – and now Ryan. I dread to think how she feels; it must be awful for her.'

'I imagine she is inconsolable,' Freddie said. 'Dad was quite cross over it and that isn't like him. He said it was stupid of Ryan to just go off like that; Dad understands why he did it – as he thought, to save Janet the grief of seeing him suffer – but thinks he was wrong. Dad says she would have come to terms with it had she known but will now blame herself for not being there.'

'Of course she will,' Fay agreed. 'Mum says she can't forgive herself for sleeping while Mike died beside her. It wasn't her fault she didn't know until she woke and found him, and he probably died very quickly without knowing much himself – but Janet felt she should have been conscious of it.'

'She has never quite gotten over it.' Freddie nodded gravely. 'Now she has another tragedy to cope with. Poor Janet. She was getting on so well with her renovating, too.'

'Perhaps that was another reason Ryan didn't tell her,' Greta put in. 'He must have known she was happier living in London but didn't want to be there himself. London is a busy place and if you're ill, I suppose you want peace and quiet.'

Fay nodded her agreement and Freddie looked at Greta in silence for a moment and then inclined his head. 'I don't suppose London suits everyone,' he said, making a mental note to ask Greta a few questions when they were alone.

'As Mum is away with Janet, Dad suggested you might like to stay on a bit longer here,' he said. 'I'm sure Greta would enjoy your company.'

'Yes, I might do that,' Fay agreed. 'If Dad is OK on his own there until the funeral? I'll talk to him later, after the pub closes.'

'He says the restaurant runs itself and if he can fix up for someone to help in the pub, he is probably going down there for a few days at the weekend; he thinks Rose will go in for a few evenings. Tom doesn't need him for the building work so they will sort something out, I dare say.'

'Then I shall definitely stay here. Greta's lovely landlady says I can stop as long as I like. I just pay her for any meals she prepares – same as Greta.'

'Good. I shan't see much of you until Saturday afternoon, well evening really. Billy has asked me if I will go into the sweet shop all day and I said yes. He is trying to find an assistant full time but isn't sure whether the shop earns enough to pay more than part-time wages.'

'I wonder if they would let me look after it for her?' Greta suggested, surprising Freddie. 'I only do part-time work where I am – and my hands are getting sore, because all I've done for the past four shifts is wash up. I'd far rather work in a sweet shop. In fact, I would enjoy it.'

'I'll write a note for you to take into Billy,' Freddie told her. 'How much notice do you have to give at the restaurant?'

'A week, I think, but they haven't been that busy recently, so they might be pleased to let me go sooner. I'll ask tomorrow and then I'll start next week or as soon as I can if Billy agrees.'

'I think that is a good idea,' Freddie said and smiled at her. 'Do you think you can deal with those lads that caused damage if they come back?'

'Yes, I am sure I can,' Greta said confidently. 'I'll simply blow that police whistle. Even if the police don't come, someone will – and I doubt they will return to the shop if they are the ones who attacked Miss Jones.'

'Let's hope you get the job,' Fay told her, glancing at her hands, which were a bit red. 'I've got some good cream you should use, Greta. Maggie and I always use it at night to stop our hands getting rough. They are in and out of water all day when we're cooking.'

'You've got lovely hands,' Greta said and smiled at her. 'I missed you when you went to America, Fay. I like Maggie very much, but she is always so busy...'

Freddie watched and listened, then he went off to fetch fish and chips and mushy peas for their supper, which they were allowed to eat sitting in the back garden under a small rose pergola with a rustic table and bench. It was a mild night and nice to sit there eating with their fingers and drinking fizzy pop from a bottle.

* * *

Just after nine Freddie left them because he had studying still to do. He had a thesis to write and his head was filled with other things. Greta had opened up more with Fay staying with her and had let him see something he hadn't been aware of before. She didn't much like London, thought it too busy and noisy; it seemed that she much preferred Cambridge or a smaller town – even a village.

Would he be happy teaching at a village school? Freddie didn't think it would be enough for him; he needed a busy school with an active sports programme. He could settle in Cambridge, though. His mother had a friend living here. Anne had lived in London for some years but moved to Cambridge when she married. It wasn't that far on a train, so he'd still be able to get to London often to see his family, especially when he was settled in a job and had the weekends free.

He decided he would talk to Greta about it seriously. If she found herself a full-time job in Miss Jones' sweet shop, she would really begin to put down roots. Miss Jones had lots of regular customers and Greta would soon get to know them. He thought that if he could be sure she was happy here, he might decide to finish his training here and look for a teaching post in the area.

Freddie chained his bicycle to the railings and went into the college courtyard. It was almost dark now, but he heard the sounds of fighting and loud voices almost at once. Directing his gaze in the direction of the source of the noise, he strode towards it, and then paused as the light from windows above showed him what was happening. Bradley was putting up a fight, but there were three of them attacking him, and a fourth – Crawford – watching and encouraging the bullies to beat him.

Even if Bradley hadn't apologised to him, Freddie could never have stood by while he was attacked by three others. He strode forward, grabbed the two nearest by their jacket collars and knocked their heads together. It stunned them and they fell to their knees at his feet. He glanced towards Bradley just in time to see him land a hard stomach punch that had his opponent bending double.

'Bastard!' Crawford said viciously, glaring at Freddie. 'What the hell do you think you're doing, East End boy?'

'Just evening the odds,' Freddie said coolly. 'I don't know what your quarrel with Bradley is – it isn't my affair – but I won't stand by and see an unfair fight.'

'Oh yes, you are the choir boy, aren't you? Didn't stop you attacking an old lady, though...'

'Your information is incorrect, Crawford,' Freddie said, holding his temper on a thread. 'Yes, the police did question me, but I was in London at a wedding and Miss Jones has now told the police she knows her attackers were teenage boys.'

Crawford stared at him strangely and then did something out of character and tried to throw a punch at Freddie. He caught Crawford's wrist and then twisted his arm around his back, leaning in to whisper in his ear.

'I could break your arm in an instant,' he informed the fuming but powerless student. 'I'm not going to, but let this be a lesson to you – stay out of my way.' He thrust Crawford towards the two students who were just struggling to their feet and he crashed into them, sending them all back down to the floor.

'You will pay for this...' Crawford hissed as he was helped to his feet by his cronies. 'You – and that thief...' He spat the word at Bradley, who glared at him but said nothing. 'It belonged to me. I paid to get it – and I know you took it.'

'I've told you; I haven't seen it. And you're the cheat – forcing others to steal an exam paper for you, just so that you can be sure of being the top in results!'

'You're a liar,' Crawford spat at him.

'Why don't you take yourself off to the cesspit you climbed out of?' Freddie asked in an icy voice.

'You attacked us and we shall be putting in a complaint to the—'

He was interrupted by the voice of authority in the guise of one of the masters. 'Indeed, you will not, Crawford. I saw the whole affair and was coming to break up the fight, but Ronoscki did it for me. I saw you try to attack him, after instigating the attack on Bradley, and I watched Ronoscki's very correct response in restraining you despite provocation. You do not attack a fellow student and I will be reporting your conduct myself. I expect to see you sent down for this breach of conduct. Now, return to your chambers at once.'

Crawford glared at Freddie maliciously but signalled to his three friends and they slunk off, rubbing at their heads.

'I saw you were set upon, Bradley,' Mr Hinks said, looking at him. 'I won't enquire into the reason you've fallen out with Crawford but simply ask if you are hurt.'

'It was a private matter, sir. And no, I am all right – thanks to Ronoscki.'

'As I expected.' Mr Hinks nodded. 'I suggest you both go to your rooms and try to avoid Crawford as much as you can – hopefully he and his friends will be sent down for the rest of the term, though I doubt they will be expelled. If it were up to me... But Crawford's father made a handsome donation to the college fund.'

'Yes, sir,' Freddie walked away, but the next minute, Bradley had caught up with him.

'I wanted a word.'

Freddie paused and looked at him.

Bradley flushed. 'You may wonder why Crawford called me a thief? I haven't stolen anything, but he thinks I did...' Bradley hesitated, then, 'An exam paper. He had got it from someone and was using it to cram the questions they'd asked. I didn't take it, but someone did and he's furious, thinks it was me. His father expects him to come first in everything and he can't beat you in mathematics... You came first in the last two mock exams, Ronoscki...'

'Is that why he hates me? Because I beat him in a maths test?'

'That and a few other things. You're everything he wants to be and isn't,' Bradley told him. 'A sportsman, clever too in your own subjects, and everyone likes you. No one likes him. He has made too many enemies.'

Freddie shrugged it off. 'I don't do anything to make myself liked.'

'You don't have to,' Bradley laughed. 'You really don't get it, do you? The way you look, your air of confidence. Crawford tries to rule by bullying. You would only have to ask and most of us would be happy to do whatever you needed.'

Freddie laughed and shook his head. 'Tell that to my twin,' he said. 'I'm sorry he had those idiots set on you, but be careful, Bradley. He could be dangerous. Especially now he is in trouble with the college. If he worries about his exam results to the extent that he has to cheat, what happens if he is sent down?'

'He will be in big trouble with his father,' Bradley replied, frowning. 'It is my last term, so I shan't have to put up with him much longer even if he lies his way into the Dean's good books, but you have another term at least to go, I think.'

'I've chosen to come in for extra lectures and rowing practice some days until the end of spring term next year,' Freddie informed him. 'Though I go for pupil-teacher training in a school this autumn if I can find a place. I'm thinking of looking for a post here in Cambridge.'

'You should go into the law,' Bradley advised. 'I think my father would welcome you in chambers. You have the right temperament for it – would make a good barrister.'

'Is that what you intend to aim for?'

'No – I'll probably stick to conveyancing or writing wills, leave the drama of the courtroom to others, for a few years anyway. My father is a barrister himself and a good one if you ever need one. He wants me in chambers doing all the boring stuff for a few years – and then maybe I'll go on to do defence-attorney work; it's what I'd like... I think.' He smiled ruefully.

'Thanks, I'll remember,' Freddie said. 'Hopefully I never shall need him – though I might have, had I not been at a family wedding last Saturday.'

'I heard about that but didn't believe it was anything to do with you,' Bradley said. They had reached the top of the stairs. 'Goodnight then – and thank you for coming to the rescue, Ronoscki.'

Freddie hesitated and then smiled. 'I'm Freddie to my friends,' he said.

'Ah, I'm Henry, after my father,' Bradley reciprocated. 'I hope we'll meet as friends one day when neither of us are students.'

'I'll look for you when I need to buy a house,' Freddie replied and they parted on a laugh.

Freddie walked on to his own room and went in, closing and then locking the door after him. So Crawford wasn't quite as brilliant as he'd thought. It explained why he disliked Freddie, because he'd held the top place in most subjects until the last couple of tests – and perhaps that was because, in the past, he'd seen the test papers in advance.

His loss, if he sought to gain advantage by cheating. Freddie shrugged. He couldn't see the point in cheating just to deceive his father. Whatever honours or merit you achieved should be genuine or they would find you out one day. What a fool Crawford was – and to fall out with Bradley because one of the papers went missing. Freddie wondered idly as he got his books out what had happened to it; he smiled as he thought that probably one of Crawford's cronies had done it to get even for some slight. Anyway, it mattered not one jot. Freddie's results depended on hard work and if he wanted to get a credible mark in most of his exams, he needed to make up for lost time...

18

Fay decided to return to London at the weekend. She'd helped Greta get to know where things were in the sweet shop when Billy had taken them there, he'd been only too pleased to employ her. He'd needed someone he could trust to look after the shop as his aunt was likely to be in hospital for a while, and liked her immediately. Fay had stayed with her in the shop on the Saturday morning in case of trouble, but nothing untoward had occurred.

'I'll go home tomorrow,' Fay told Freddie when he came that evening to take them both out for a meal at a nice restaurant near the river. The evenings were lighter now and they were having a period of settled warm weather. It was pleasant sitting outside in the sunshine watching the flow of the water and some swans gliding by. 'Greta is happy in her new job and I think Mum and Janet will be back soon, probably on Monday after the funeral. I'll do some cooking to welcome them home.'

Freddie nodded. 'I spoke to Dad on the phone, before he went to join them. He says Janet is grieving hard but bearing up. Mum says she has coped far better than she'd expected.'

'I dare say she is stronger than anyone knows,' Greta said, making the twins look at her. 'I thought she was very decisive about things when

I spoke to her.' She flushed as the twins remained silent, and then Freddie nodded agreement.

'Perhaps that is what she really needs, to make her own decisions, and it may suit her to be single once she is over this... Mum always makes allowances for her, but Janet is strong when you think about it, even though she gets restless,' he said, nodding as he turned it over in his mind. 'Janet doesn't really show what she is thinking.'

'Well, I've been known to change my mind a bit,' Fay said, her eyes sparkling at her twin. 'But when I want something, I go all out for it – and so does Mum. So why shouldn't Janet? It's rotten for her that she's lost two husbands like that, but I think she'll be OK.'

'Has Able taken Jon to Wales with him?' Greta asked. 'And what about Maggie – does she know?'

'Yes, to the first and no to the second,' Freddie supplied the answers. 'Jon wanted to go to his father's funeral, and Dad didn't feel he should leave him behind, even though Maureen offered to have him. He cried but seemed to accept he wouldn't see his father again. Dad thinks it was because Ryan had been living apart from them.' He paused, then, 'Janet didn't want Maggie told, because she would have felt she must come home and that would spoil her lovely long honeymoon. Dad says they've had six postcards from her and she is having a wonderful time. There's one for you, too, and I got one yesterday. Says she has found a recipe for a special ice cream she thinks I'll like... very sweet and delicious.' He laughed and Greta smiled, because she knew his sweet tooth, but Fay was thoughtful.

'I'm not sure Maggie will like that, not being told about Ryan,' Fay said, wrinkling her brow. 'I didn't go to the funeral, because Dad said it wasn't necessary, but I know Maggie would have gone. Janet wanted it to be a quiet ceremony at a nearby church. Apparently, that's what Ryan asked for, so she carried out his wishes.'

'He much preferred the countryside,' Freddie agreed. 'Ryan told me once that he'd learned to hate big cities during the carnage in the war – he lost his first family in the Blitz, as you know – and wanted nothing more than the peace of a beautiful rural setting. It was unfortunate that both Janet and Jon hated the idea of living on a remote farm.'

'What do you think Janet will do now?' Greta asked.

Fay shrugged but Freddie considered for a moment, then, 'I think she will continue with her renovation work. She did well with the flat she restored, so she can probably make a living that way.'

They sat by the river until it began to get a little chilly, and then walked slowly back to Greta's lodgings.

'I ought to leave you now,' Freddie said regretfully. 'I need to do some work tonight, I'm afraid, and I have rowing in the morning, so I shan't see you before you leave, Fay. I'm pleased you came down for a nice visit.'

'I'm glad I did, too,' Fay told him and they hugged. She went into the house then and left Greta and Freddie to have a few words alone.

Freddie smiled at Greta. 'You will miss her when she leaves?'

'Yes, I shall. We get on well.' Greta put her hand in his. 'She's your twin, so I love her – but I do like my new job. It's lovely talking to people and especially the children. Most of them are friendly little charmers, a bit cheeky sometimes, but funny. I completely understand why Miss Jones keeps the shop going.'

'It is a better job for you.' He nodded, touching his fingers to her cheek. 'As long as you're happy, darling. I do love you, Greta...' He sighed. 'I wish we didn't have so long to wait before we can marry.'

'So do I,' she said, lifting her face for his kiss and feeling the little shudder of need go through him as he held her tight. 'I want to be yours, Freddie – truly yours—'

'Oh God, don't.' He smiled ruefully and kissed her nose. 'You will be one day...' Tearing himself away, he walked off before he weakened.

Greta watched him go with a little smile. There was a little idea forming in her mind, but she wasn't sure yet if she could make it work. Nodding to herself, she went in and joined Fay in the room they had shared for the past week.

'It's a pity Freddie has to study so hard,' Fay said. 'But he is dedicated to the idea of teaching. I think it is a kind of vocation for him.'

'Freddie is a very caring person,' Greta replied. 'I understand why he needs to work so hard.'

'You don't mind that you have to wait to get married? I'm not sure I could have waited so long. Dad intended to make me wait for a while, but then he decided Jace was all right after all and let me have my way.'

Greta laughed. 'I don't think your dad is capable of saying no to you, Fay.'

'He does now and then,' she replied with a naughty look. 'Not often, though. Freddie never asks for anything. He just gets on and does what he needs to do...'

'Yes, I know,' Greta said and sighed. 'I think we could get married sooner if we could find somewhere cheap to live. Freddie could carry on with his studies. I wouldn't mind. I'll have my work in the shop and my writing... and we can try not to start a family until he is working.'

Fay met her gaze. 'You're up to something. I know it!'

'I might be.' Greta replied, a little smile playing about her mouth.

'I know you can't be earning much – even this bedsit must be as much as you can afford?'

'It is – *was*...' Greta confessed. 'You know when I went to see Mr Jones about the job...?' Fay inclined her head, face alight with curiosity. 'Well, he says there is a flat above the shop that hasn't been used in years. It needs decorating and there's some rubbish to clear out...'

'Go on,' Fay said, eyes twinkling with mischief.

'He says I can have it rent-free as part of my wages. His aunt can't afford to pay me a full wage, but he doesn't want her to be left alone there in future... so if I decorate it myself, I can have it. He will clear the rubbish – tomorrow, he said – and then I can decorate and furnish it. I have to pay a peppercorn rent of a shilling a year to make it legal, but that's nothing.'

'Oh, Greta! That's wonderful – and so good of him,' Fay said and hugged her. 'What does Freddie say?'

'Haven't told him yet,' Greta replied. 'If he finished his college course and perhaps took his in-school training here in Cambridge or nearby, we could get married then.' She hesitated, then, 'This week, I've sold three more articles and a short story, Fay. I could buy some second-hand furniture and make things and...' A little sigh broke from her. 'I'm not sure what Freddie will say.'

'Don't tell him until it is finished,' Fay said decisively. 'Then, when it is ready to live in, take him there and cook him something nice to eat...' She checked as she remembered Greta wasn't much of a cook. 'You'll have to practise something simple, Greta.'

'Oh, I've got better at cooking since you went to America,' Greta told her cheerily. 'Your mum showed me how to make some of Freddie's favourites... but do you think he might be cross if I just do it and don't tell him?'

'He might be shocked, but Freddie doesn't often get angry,' Fay replied. 'If he does look miffed, tell him it was my idea to surprise him.'

Greta smiled shyly at her. 'I shan't blame you, Fay. I think it would be so much better for us – even before we get married, Freddie could stay over sometimes. It would be peaceful for him to study there when I was working too.'

'I think it sounds perfect and you're very lucky to have the chance, Greta.'

'I couldn't believe it when Mr Jones offered me the flat,' Greta told her. 'He really likes Freddie, you see. He said he loved his two daughters, but if he'd had a son, he would've liked him to be just like Freddie – and he wants us to go to lunch one Sunday with him and his family.' She hesitated, then, 'It's like putting down roots, Fay. We would have friends here... Oh, Freddie has made some at the college and I'm getting to know people who pop in the shop regularly but...'

'Yes, I understand what you mean,' Fay agreed. 'We moved to the coast for a while when I was young and it takes time to make real friends. You go for it, Greta. It's a good thing to do...'

'I'll have a place I can type as long as I like,' Greta said. 'I don't like to type all night here in case it disturbs the others... but the flat would be a home...'

'You didn't really have a home with your aunt, did you?'

'No. I was very unhappy living there,' Greta said. 'It changed my life when I met Freddie.'

Fay gave her a little squeeze. 'Freddie and I were so lucky with our parents. I know he is my brother, but he's rather special, Greta. Let him come to you, don't try to rush things...' She faltered. 'I shouldn't preach, sorry.'

'No, you're right,' Greta replied, smiling easily. 'Freddie is special and I wasn't sure that he could love me – I'm very ordinary – but he does. It took a while for me to be sure, but I am now.'

'I know he loves you – and you're not ordinary, Greta. You're *you* and talented,' Fay declared. 'I also know he's stubborn and moves at his own pace. We couldn't be more different, but I love him to bits.'

'I know,' Greta said. 'He thinks the world of you...' She hesitated, then, 'Do you think you will come back to England to live?'

'Yes, in time,' Fay replied. 'We'll visit in the meantime – and maybe Dad will treat you both to a trip out to see us occasionally.'

'That's a lot of money,' Greta objected and then laughed. 'Maybe I'll write a best-selling novel and earn a lot of money...'

'Yes, you do that,' Fay said and yawned. 'I think it must be sitting in the open air. I'm going to bed, if you don't mind?'

'Course not,' Greta said. 'I've got some work to do but I shan't be long.'

* * *

In the event, Greta wasn't given the chance to keep her secret, because Billy told Freddie about his idea when he went into the shop a few days later and he was so pleased that Greta would have a home of her own that she couldn't help throwing her arms around him in excitement.

'We'll be able to do as we like,' she said. 'Cook a meal or bring in chips, whatever we feel like. I can work in the evenings – and you too. We could work together Freddie... if you liked?'

'It will be nice to spend more time together,' Freddie agreed. He looked at her thoughtfully. 'Mum might let us have some furniture if we ask her. She doesn't need all the beds she has and that would save us buying one. I think she has a few nice things stored in the attics, too.'

'The bedroom stuff would be nice,' Greta agreed. 'I can buy some second-hand things gradually, Freddie.'

'Yes, you can,' he agreed. 'If you keep selling your articles and stories, you'll manage well...' He was thoughtful, then, 'I'm going to apply to do my year of pupil-teaching in a school here, Greta. I might try for a teaching post this way too. It makes sense and I think you like it here – don't you? I was worried about you for a while – but you seem happier now?'

'I am happy. I love it here,' she said and smiled shyly. 'We will be very comfortable in our own little home, don't you think?'

'Yes, we will,' he said and reached for her, drawing her into his arms. 'We can't get married while I am at college, Greta; I don't think my tutors would be pleased with that – but perhaps when I'm working in a school as a trainee, we might... if you can put up with being short of money for a while?'

'You know I can,' she exclaimed with a gurgle of joy and hugged him, lifting her face for his kiss. 'All I want is to be with you, Freddie.'

'Oh, Greta,' he admitted, letting himself relax as he drew her in tight. 'You don't know how much I want it too, my love.' He hadn't planned or wanted to get married this early in his career, but love alters everything and his growing frustration had been hard to control, though he'd used an iron will to control it.

'When we have the flat...' Greta hesitated, then, 'I've been to the doctor and asked if I could take that new contraception pill...' She blushed as Freddie stared incredulously. 'Oh, don't think me too forward...'

'Not at all, just brave,' he said, holding her as she would have drawn back. 'I did wonder about it, Greta – but I wasn't sure it was safe for you.'

'I'm young and fit and the doctor says it is so much better than getting... pregnant too soon.' Her face was on fire, but Freddie laughed.

'How sensible you are, my love. I've been fretting over how long we have to wait and you've done something about it. Don't you know it's what I want, too? I was trying to be noble and wait for our wedding night – but am I old-fashioned?'

Greta laughed. 'You might be, but I love you the way you are – but I do think if we have our own home, we might—' Again, she blushed and hesitated, but Freddie grabbed her and kissed her hard.

'How soon can we move in?' he asked huskily and she giggled, because he was letting his need show at last.

'As soon as I can get it looking clean and nice – and we have a bed and a table and chairs...'

'I'll ask Mum if I can have my stuff when I ring her later,' Freddie said and grinned. 'I might even give you a hand with the painting on Sunday.'

19

'How did you get on?' Maureen asked when Peggy popped round to see her the morning after they got back. 'How is Janet bearing up now?'

'She is better than I expected,' Peggy said, looking thoughtful. 'When she asked me to go down, I thought she would be all over the place, but, although she was upset, she just got on with things. Ryan had asked to be buried in Wales and we did it all as he'd wanted.' Peggy sipped the tea Maureen placed in front of her. 'She is selling the house and land to the man Ryan had agreed a price with and there wasn't really much else to sort out – Ryan had left everything in order.'

'He was that kind of man, wasn't he?' Maureen said and sighed. 'Such a shame he went off on his own like that – I suppose he thought it was for the best but...'

'I think in one way it was,' Peggy replied. 'It might have been too hard for Janet if she'd been with him throughout, but now she feels angry. She is grieving but she is also very angry that he didn't tell her the truth.'

'Yes, I can understand that,' Maureen agreed. 'I would be angry if Gordon hid himself from me because he was ill.'

'They didn't have the best marriage and I think it was mostly Janet's fault,' Peggy said thoughtfully. 'I love her dearly, but she isn't always the easiest person to be with or to understand. She has moods... I know she has suffered, but sometimes I feel like giving her a kick up the backside.'

Maureen laughed. 'Of course you would,' she cried in amusement. 'You've always been so positive, Peggy – but Janet has a lot of her father in her. He was moody too.'

'You're right, Maureen. Laurie was just the same, up one minute, down the next – but with him, bad temper took over when he was out of sorts. Janet just gets broody...' Peggy sighed. 'She is back with us now and concentrating on making Jon happy, so perhaps that will be her way out of it.' She thought for a moment, then brightened, giving a little laugh, 'What do you think? Freddie is moving into a flat with Greta...'

'No!' Maureen was astounded. 'Are they getting married?'

'Not while he is still at college, but when he goes for the second part of his teacher training, then they will. Freddie says they will get engaged, but she doesn't know about that yet; it's a surprise. He wants me to let him have his bedroom furniture and anything else I don't need, as long as it is small. The flat is only tiny apparently, just one bedroom, a living room, kitchen and bathroom.' Peggy laughed again as she saw Maureen's astonishment. 'Yes, I know. You could've knocked me down with a feather when he told me. I thought he was set on waiting until they got married.'

'He was so sure about waiting for a few years to finish his training,' Maureen said, still incredulous. 'What made him change his mind?'

'It's because Greta was offered the flat as a part of her wages,' Peggy explained. 'She is now working for an elderly lady who owns a sweet shop. Freddie says Miss Jones, the owner, was attacked as she took her takings to the bank one Saturday evening and is in a nursing home recuperating. Her nephew gets on well with Freddie and so he took Greta on to help his aunt and offered her the flat rent-free, because they couldn't afford to pay a full wage.'

Maureen nodded. 'Well, that is nice, Peggy.' She hesitated, then, 'You don't mind, do you?'

'No – except that it means Freddie will settle there,' Peggy told her.

'He is going to apply to finish his training there and then probably for a full-time job when that is over...'

'You'd hoped he would return to London?' Maureen asked, watching her expression.

'Yes, in a way,' Peggy smiled wryly. 'My family is so scattered these days. I have Fay home with me for now; but she'll go back to America after Jace finishes his tour here.'

'You will miss her.' Maureen nodded as Peggy agreed. 'Has Pip decided what he'll do about that new job offer in America?'

'Yes; he has decided to take it when his contract finishes, so he will be off in the autumn as well – and it is a five-year contract out there so he will not be coming back for a while, if ever.'

'How do Sheila and the children feel about that?' Maureen questioned.

'I talked to them on the phone,' Peggy said. 'They are all excited and happy about the move. You know Chris is talented with the guitar and he thinks America is the best place to live for the music industry – and, at the moment, Sarah wants to be an actress or a model...' She laughed, because Sarah was at that stage in her teens when she changed her mind every few weeks or days. 'That may change, of course.'

Maureen smiled her understanding. 'If Freddie settles in Cambridge – might you go and live there?'

'I haven't had time to think about it yet, though I believe we shall soon have to,' Peggy said and a shadow passed across her face. 'Able says the motion to pull down and rebuild the lanes has passed its first planning meeting and now they will start valuing the houses. People will be moving away, so even if they don't start on the project for a couple of years, it won't be the same around here.'

'Oh, damn!' Maureen said, startling Peggy with the anger in her voice. 'I knew it was coming, but I kept hoping it wouldn't...'

'Yes, so did I,' Peggy agreed. 'To be honest, I am not sure what I want to do, Maureen. I'm not sure what Janet will do if we no longer have the Pig & Whistle.' She hesitated, then, 'I'm toying with the idea of investing in a small hotel – perhaps in Cambridge...'

Maureen stared at her. 'Where did that come from?'

'You remember Anne – she was a school teacher but went to live in Cambridge when she married?'

'Yes, of course I remember her. She sends a card at Christmas. I visited her a couple of times, but not for a while now...'

'She rings me every so often,' Peggy said and smiled reflectively. 'She rang me last night. Her husband has recently retired and they've bought a large house at the sea; they are going to run it as a boarding house...' She paused, then, 'Anne said they had toyed with the idea of buying a small hotel that is now up for sale or rent in Cambridge – but her husband preferred the option of retiring to the coast. She thought the hotel was a better idea but went along with his wishes...'

'Would you think of buying it?' Maureen asked curiously.

'Anne told me that the owner is willing to rent it on a two-year lease with the option of buying it or extending the lease at the end of that period. I think I'd do that, Maureen. I'd know if it was profitable by then and we would have the money from property before that, I imagine.'

'Wouldn't that be a lot of work for you, Peggy? I know you've always worked but...'

'Not too much if it was run by family and friends together,' Peggy said and met her wide-eyed look. 'You, me, Janet, and perhaps even Jon when he grows up. I know he'll want to go on living with us for a few years anyway.'

Maureen stared at her for a moment and then nodded. 'Yes, I'd like that, Peggy. Not just yet, because I've promised to help Shirley with the babies for a while – but...' She hesitated, then, 'Ray told me that he may be changing his job next year. His contract here will be over and he isn't sure whether to go back up north or apply for another job here in London. I asked Shirley what she wanted and she said she would do whatever Ray decides.'

'What about the babies – if she still wants to work?'

'That is just it...' Maureen's face relaxed into a smile. 'She was determined to go on with her work until she had the twins, but as soon as she looked into her daughter's beautiful blue eyes and her son's grey ones, her heart was captured. She says now that she will take a few years off work – until Amelia and Anthony are ready to go to school and then retrain if she has to. She could probably do part-time as a GP, which was her first intention.'

'Well, that is a turnabout,' Peggy said and laughed. 'I think that is exactly as it should be – but what will Gordon say?'

'He thinks we should take longer holidays,' Maureen told her. 'But I think he would quite like the idea of a small hotel – and he might like to spend a few hours a week in the reception, or the bar if the hotel has one...'

'So would you like to be my partner in the hotel – should I get it?'

'Yes, I think so,' Maureen decided. 'I'll talk to Gordon and Shirley and then let you know if we can go ahead. When were you thinking of taking it over, if you decide to go for it?'

'I think it will be at least three months before I could be ready to take it over, perhaps longer. I will go into details more and let you know – but I wanted to hear what you had to say before I got involved. I knew you were hesitating because of Shirley and the babies, but... if they are thinking of moving away, you won't see them as often, unless you follow them? Have you considered that?'

'I wouldn't go up north,' Maureen said firmly. 'I like Cambridge. I've only been a couple of times, but it was pleasant. I think I'd enjoy living in the area and it would be nearer Matty. It does need some thinking and planning, Peggy – but if we are going to be made to move out anyway...'

'We might as well make plans on our terms, not the council's,' Peggy agreed. 'It isn't like starting from scratch. I expect the hotel has staff and it could just carry on for a while, give us all plenty of time to sort things out before we shake it all up.'

'You handed the boarding house over to Pearl to run before she bought you out,' Maureen agreed. 'I suppose someone would manage the hotel for you if you wanted...'

'I am going to suggest that Janet does that for a while,' Peggy said. 'She needs something to occupy her, keep her mind off things – and once I have more time to sort things out, she can go back to her renovating. The hotel probably needs refurbishing and Janet has a good eye.'

'Yes, she does,' Maureen agreed. She smiled at Peggy. 'You always have good ideas. You talk to the agents and hear what they have to say. If it sounds all right, we might go down and have a look one day...'

'That sounds nice,' Peggy said. 'It is ages since we went out together, Maureen. We could make a day of it, perhaps meet Greta and Freddie for lunch if they can get away.'

'It would have to be a Sunday for that, I imagine,' Maureen nodded to herself. 'We could just go down, perhaps on a Saturday and stay there overnight, spy out the land, as it were.' She chuckled mischievously. 'That's the way you see all the faults...'

'That's a good idea,' Peggy said, looking thoughtful. 'We want to be sure the hotel has a good reputation. I know we can put things right once we get going – but if it is doing poorly, we don't want to pay too much for it.'

'We'd be working together again,' Maureen said, smiling. 'I often think of the early days, when I was first married and I started to help you out in the pub sometimes. It was fun.'

'Yes, it was,' Peggy agreed. 'I let Maggie take over the Pig & Whistle, because she had such plans for it, but I missed the way things were before.' She wrinkled her brow. 'I did think for a while that I would just stop working or do a bit of private catering – but when Anne told me about the hotel, it made me think.'

'I didn't expect I'd be able to do anything like that,' Maureen agreed. 'Shirley asked if I'd have the baby when she was ready to return to work and I said yes – but if she looks after them herself or they are moving away, I might as well do what suits us best.'

'Yes, that makes a big difference,' Peggy replied. 'It depends what Gordon thinks, of course – and Gordy, too.'

'He will leave school next term and he knows what he wants to do – he could probably stay in London with his friends if he wants to take up the plumbing apprenticeship he was offered here, but he said the other day that he'd like to move. We could see what the prospects are in Cambridge anyway...'

'Yes, well, it's all *what ifs* at the moment,' Peggy agreed. 'The hotel may have been sold or leased when I ring, but if it has, I'll look round for something else.'

* * *

Maureen spoke to her husband that evening. Gordon was thoughtful for a moment and then inclined his head in agreement. 'I think you would enjoy that,' he said. 'I don't mind much what we do, but we need to hear what the rest of the family wants first.'

'Yes, we must,' Maureen agreed. Her youngest son would be at boarding school for a couple of years yet, so it was only a matter of where he came home for his holidays, but Gordy had more or less settled his future here in London before he'd had the trouble at school – and Maureen wasn't sure what Shirley was intending just yet. 'I'll talk to Gordy – and to Shirley when they come for lunch this Sunday. Peggy isn't even sure she can get it yet, or if it is feasible and worth the effort.'

'I think if this particular idea doesn't work, you might still want to stay close to Peggy,' Gordon suggested. 'I know the children are important, love – but Peggy has been closer than a sister and I think you will miss her if she goes away again. You were younger when she went to the coast before, and I was a lot fitter. We had a business to build – if anything should happen… I'd like you to be close to Peggy.'

'Oh, don't talk like that,' Maureen said. She hated it when Gordon spoke negatively of the future. 'You're still young and should have years yet, love.'

Gordon nodded, but didn't answer. Maureen bit her lip and turned away to pick up her knitting. She was making a dress for Shirley's little girl and the pattern was intricate. It would take her mind away from things that might happen and concentrate them on here and now.

* * *

Maureen felt happier again when Gordy came home from his football practice. He was hungry and devoured the plate of beans on toast she made for him in double-quick time.

'What would you think if we moved to Cambridge?' she asked her son as he took his empty plate to the sink.

'Why?' Gordy asked, looking up curiously. 'Because they are going to knock a lot of houses down?'

'Yes, it seems certain the project will go ahead now,' Maureen answered. 'Would it affect you very much, Gordy? I know all your friends are here – but their families will probably move away soon.'

He nodded and accepted the glass of Vimto she offered him. 'Thanks, Mum. Is there any cake?'

'I made some coconut tarts this afternoon,' she said and produced the tin. He grinned and took two, eating one hungrily before answering her question.

'I don't mind if you want to go,' he said, surprising her. 'Freddie is living there, isn't he? I like him – and I could probably get an apprenticeship there. Mr Toft said that he's going to have to move his business too and wasn't sure if he would be taking on new apprentices next year. He suggested I do another year at school and then ask him...' Mr Toft was the plumber who had first got him interested in the job and promised him a place with his firm.

'I thought it was a certain thing?' His father looked up sharply. 'When we talked to him, he said he would be delighted to take you on, Gordy.'

'I know – but he didn't know about the clearance then,' Gordy said. 'Most of his work is around here, Dad. He will have to find another yard and work up a new round of clients.'

Gordon swore softly, then apologised as Maureen glanced at him. 'Sorry, Maureen – but that doesn't suit my notion of what is right, to tell the lad he can come and then change his mind. I know circumstances have changed, but we could have arranged somewhere for Gordy to stay and carry on with his apprenticeship, if the promise held good.'

'It doesn't matter, Dad,' Gordy said and grinned. 'Freddie was telling me about all the sports he does up there when we spoke at the wedding.

I could probably help him with stuff. I'm sure he will try to get a football team going once he is a teacher – and I'd love to be a part of all that. I think we'd be quite close to Matty, too.'

'Yes, we would,' Maureen agreed. 'Matty could come home more often and you could meet him and take him out sometimes; he would like that. Matty is a gentle soul.'

'He likes being in the choir,' Gordy said. 'If he'd joined a choir here, he would have been constantly bullied. He was bullied, you know – that's why he begged you to let him go to boarding school.'

'Yes, I know – or I suspected it, though he wouldn't tell me,' Maureen said. 'How did you know – did he tell you?'

'No, but I intervened a few times when he was being jeered at and guessed. When I asked him, he just nodded. He told me he wanted to go to a different school, away from London. He will be much happier if you move away, Mum.'

'Yes, perhaps he would – and if you don't mind...'

That only left Shirley.

* * *

Shirley looked at Maureen quizzically as she explained what Peggy had suggested when she and Ray came to lunch on the Sunday with the twins. She sat rocking her little girl in her arms by the grate, which was empty since it was a very warm day. Maureen had Anthony on her lap; he was gurgling up at her.

'Is it what *you* want to do, Mum?' Shirley asked. 'I thought you and Dad intended to take longer holidays in future?'

'Yes, we shall,' Maureen said. 'Peggy and Janet – if she wants to help out, and I'm not sure she will – will all take time off as and when we need to. We shall have staff to do a lot of the work.'

'If you're sure,' Shirley said a little doubtful. 'I know Peggy intends to have long holidays in America. I wouldn't want you and Dad to be stuck with all that work, Mum.'

'I don't think we shall,' Maureen said. 'We haven't decided on anything yet – but it seems as if we shall need to move from here.'

Shirley nodded, hesitating, then glanced at her husband, 'Ray hasn't applied for anything yet. We weren't sure what you intended to do... but, if you are moving out of London, we might too.' She sighed. 'I wanted to work here in the East End, but things are different now. I have to think of what is best for these two.' She bent her head and kissed her daughter's forehead. 'I want the best for them both.' She glanced at Anthony.

'Of course you do, love,' her father agreed, smiling fondly at her. 'We didn't have the luxury of choice at your age. There was a war and we had to work hard to recover from it, but life is much easier now. I think you should do whatever suits you. I agree with whatever your mum wants to do – but she doesn't want to go too far from you if you need her.'

Shirley nodded. 'Well, I've decided to take time off with the twins, so don't feel tied because of me, Mum,' she said. 'I want to be able to see you often, but it isn't hard to get on a train.'

'I could apply for a post at Addenbrooke's,' Ray said as silence fell. 'It is a teaching hospital, after all – and a nice place to bring up children. Either in Cambridge or one of the villages close by.'

'Ray, you wouldn't?' Shirley gasped. 'I thought you had your heart set on going back to the university hospital?'

'I think I could give a few years to a surgical post in Cambridge,' Ray said, his eyes warm with love as he looked at her. 'You'd be close to your mum and dad then and they'd get to see Amelia and Anthony.'

'You mustn't sacrifice your ambitions for my sake,' Maureen said quickly. 'I know the pioneering work you do is important, Ray. Please don't give it up for me.'

'It isn't just for you,' Ray said. 'I may do another research course in the future, but I want some time to spend with my family.' He glanced at Shirley. 'I believe we might be happier living somewhere quieter for a few years, love.'

Shirley met his gaze and then nodded.

* * *

'I'd hoped they might be further advanced with the treatment Dad needs,' she told Maureen later when the men had gone off to watch a cricket match and they were washing up together. 'Ray says it is a very invasive technique and still some way from being perfected.'

'Your dad hasn't been as well as he'd like recently,' Maureen told her. 'He wants to make sure I'm happily settled and thinks I'd be best near Peggy.' She sighed. 'It is all in the melting pot at the moment. Peggy isn't even sure it is what she wants, but we need to start looking.'

'I agree,' Shirley told her. 'I wouldn't mind if we followed you down to Cambridge for a while, Mum, if you go that way – but I don't want Ray to feel obliged. He is a clever man and his work saves lives. If he needs to take up a post in the north, then I'll go with him. I don't like the idea of being too far from Dad, though.'

'You know I would be in touch if I thought—' Maureen's throat caught. 'I can't even say it, Shirley. I try to keep his diet right and not let him overwork. If we can get decent compensation for the shop – and Able says he has found us a good lawyer to make sure we do – then there's no need for Gordon to work. He might answer the phone in reception at this hotel if we get it, or serve a few drinks – but it wouldn't be like trying to keep the shop running. I do think it might be better for him.'

'Yes, I see it would be best for you both.' Shirley smiled at her. 'Don't worry about babysitting, Mum. I know I asked before the twins were born, but I thought I'd want to go back to work as soon as I could then.'

'Are you sure you don't?' Maureen asked her.

Shirley hesitated, then, 'I do hope to return to my job one day,' she said. 'I still want to help people who are ill – but I'm just a doctor. Ray is so much more than I could ever be. He needs me to be there for the children and he would like more, if I can manage it... I want to be with them at least until they are at junior school. If we need a babysitter, we'll find a professional one. I could have a full-time nanny, and I might in a year or two be able to do part-time as a GP, but I'm not sure yet.'

'Would you be happy in Cambridge?' Maureen asked her.

'Yes, if Ray is,' Shirley replied, looking thoughtful. 'I need a little more time to be certain, Mum – but please don't move to somewhere you hate in London just for me.'

'I've looked at a few places, just the brochures in agents' windows. I brought a few home, but I hate those high-rise places, Shirley. I couldn't live in a small flat. I would prefer a bigger garden than we've ever had here.'

'It sounds as if Cambridge might be a good move for you – what do Gordy and Matty think of the idea?'

'Gordy thinks it is OK. I haven't spoken to Matty yet, but I'll see him when he comes home next weekend.'

20

'Janet, there is a phone call for you,' Peggy said, going through to their private kitchen upstairs where Janet was encouraging Jon with his homework. Three weeks had passed since their return from Wales and Janet had spent much of it either with Jon or lying on her bed, though she'd been persuaded to help in the restaurant a few times. 'I think it is Lars.'

Janet looked up quickly. 'I don't want to talk to him, Mum. Can you tell him I am not here?'

'I just told him you were...' Peggy looked at her steadily. 'It's the third time this week that he has called, Janet. You should speak to the poor man. If you don't want to see him again, tell him so.'

Janet frowned and then sighed. 'All right, I suppose I should. It might be something to do with the flat. I thought the contracts had been exchanged by now, but perhaps not.' She got up and went through into the hall.

Peggy sat down at the kitchen table next to her grandson. 'Having a problem with those sums, love?'

Jon nodded and she pulled the exercise book towards her and took a look.

'Logarithms,' she said. 'I was hopeless at those. I can add up the price of a round of drinks in a trice and all in my head – but these things drive me nuts.'

'Me too,' Jon said and giggled. He snuggled up next to her. 'I love you, Gran. Can I stay with you forever?'

'How would you feel if I bought a hotel in Cambridge? We might go and live there when they pull the houses down in Mulberry Lane.'

'Is it far away in the country like... like where Dad died?' Jon asked, his eyes dark with anxiety. 'I didn't like it there – did you?'

'Not much,' Peggy admitted truthfully. 'No, Cambridge is smaller than London, but still a town – or a city. There are shops and schools, colleges, a swimming lido, and cinemas – oh, lots of things. A river that Freddie goes rowing on...'

'Is it where Freddie goes to his college?' Jon asked, looking interested. 'Freddie plays football with me when he's home. He took me ice skating and to the Science Museum.'

'Yes, he is at college there. He is learning to be a teacher now, but I'm sure he would help you to become involved with clubs and things in the evenings or weekends, if you wanted.'

'Yes, I think I should...' Jon looked up as his mother came into the room.

'Lars wanted to take me to dinner this evening,' Janet told them. 'I said I was too busy – well I am, helping Jon with his sums.'

Peggy nodded. She ruffled Jon's hair. 'How about I make us some nice pancakes. What's your favourite?'

'Strawberry jam and cream,' Jon said promptly.

'Don't you mean strawberries and cream?' his mother asked and he shook his head.

'Granny knows,' he said. 'It's jam, isn't it, Gran?'

'Yes, a sort of jam,' Peggy agreed. 'My special strawberry conserves. You have a sweet tooth, Jon. Your dad did, too, as I remember.'

Jon looked at her solemnly. 'We had them together when you went to America – Maggie made them for us.'

Peggy nodded. 'You had a nice time with him then, didn't you?'

'He took me to the zoo and lots of places,' Jon said. 'He wasn't ill then, or he didn't seem ill...' He looked at Peggy hard. 'Why did he get sick and die, Gran? Was it because I wouldn't go to that place and live with him? Was it my fault?'

'Where did you get that idea from?' Peggy said as Janet shot her an agonised look. 'Of course it wasn't, Jon. Your dad was ill with cancer – that's a very nasty illness and people sometimes die with it. You had *nothing* to do with it, love.'

'Why did he go away then?' Jon persisted. 'I thought I'd done something wrong – that he was cross with me... like last time when I ran away.' He bit his lip, the tears hovering in his eyes.

'No, he wasn't cross with anyone,' Janet said, blinking back her own tears. 'He just felt very unwell and wanted to be quiet by himself, that's all.'

'Like you do when you get a headache?' Jon asked her.

'Something like that...' She saw his eyes widen and hastened to reassure him. 'That doesn't mean I'm going to die, love. I just get something called migraine headaches that is all. I shan't die of them, I promise.'

Jon stared at her intensely for moment and then nodded. 'Can I go and play football in the yard? I've finished my homework, apart from those daft sums I can't do.'

'Yes – but don't tire yourself,' Janet said and then shook her head. 'I'm not fussing, Jon. You're getting stronger, but you still have those unsteady moments.'

'I'm all right,' he said and got up. 'I'll have the pancakes when I come back, Gran – if that's all right?'

'Of course it is, love. Half an hour or so?'

Jon nodded and went rushing out. The sound of his clattering footsteps down the stairs made Janet bite her lip.

'He hates to be reminded of his weakness,' she said. 'Perhaps I worry too much.'

'Of course you worry, he's your son,' Peggy replied calmly. 'Jon is fine, Janet. He sometimes gets a few strange ideas but usually listens to what I say.'

'He is happiest with you,' Janet admitted. She sighed deeply. 'Lars asked me to move in with him, Mum. I was angry. He knew Ryan had died but he still said it...'

'You knew he was interested,' Peggy said. 'I thought you rather liked him? You were thinking about an affair, I think?'

'I did – but not now...' Janet tossed her long dark hair back from her face. She looked pale but still attractive, despite faint shadows beneath her eyes. 'How could I even think of it when Ryan—' She broke off as the emotion rose in her throat. 'I feel so guilty, Mum. I was thinking of having an affair with Lars before I knew about Ryan's illness... I should've guessed something was wrong, gone down there long before...' She choked, her eyes wet. 'What sort of a person am I that I didn't know?'

'A very normal one as far as I can see. You were angry with Ryan for going off like that and he wasn't blameless in this, Janet. He ought to have told you...'

Janet sighed and rubbed the heel of her hand across her wet cheeks. 'So what do I do with my life now, Mum?'

'Whatever you want to do,' Peggy replied. 'If you spend your whole life in regret, it makes Ryan's sacrifice rather pointless. He wanted to save you pain – and he would definitely want you to be happy.'

'It was pointless,' Janet said angrily and then shook her head. 'No, that's not fair. I know he wanted to spare me, but it was wrong...' She gave a little sob. 'I don't know what to do...'

'Tell Lars the truth when you're ready,' Peggy advised her. 'Why don't you go away for a holiday for a while, love? Go and stay with Pip. Once he leaves for America you won't get much chance to spend time with him. Jon will be fine with me for a few weeks – and when school breaks up for the summer, I'll bring him for a visit and stay myself for a week or so if you're still there.'

Janet nodded. 'I know Jon would be fine with you, Mum.' She took a sobbing breath. 'To be honest, I don't know what I want. It was just such a shock when I discovered the truth. I should've tried to reconcile, gone down there months ago. I was angry with Ryan for just going off and doing what he wanted, instead of trying to find somewhere we could all be happy.'

'I think Ryan was mistaken to do what he did,' Peggy told her. 'It was both wrong and foolish – but he meant to save you pain, love. He knew how badly it affected you when Mike died. It took you years before you got over it – if you are even now.'

'I know why he did it,' Janet replied, tears glimmering in her eyes. 'I feel selfish and mean. He couldn't have known how much I loved him or he'd have let me be with him...'

'You loved him – but were you in love with him?' Peggy asked, watching her face.

'Oh, Mum, I don't know,' Janet said with a little wail. 'I think I was when we married, but Ryan was always working, always travelling, and then in Scotland it got better, but I had nothing to do and I was bored on my own.' She caught back a sob. 'I just know it hurts now. I did love him – I must have done...'

'Perhaps he understood more than you thought and loved you too much to see you suffer with him,' Peggy suggested. The tears were running down Janet's cheeks now as she broke down. Peggy put her arms about her and held her as she sobbed. 'I know how much it hurts, darling. I loved your father once and it hurt terribly when we drifted apart. By the time we broke up, I'd begun to heal and that was because I had found Able. Don't shut yourself off the way you did when Mike died. You are loved and you're not to blame for what happened to Ryan, any more than you were for Mike's death.'

'I know,' Janet hiccupped, accepting Peggy's handkerchief to dry her face. 'It just hurts so bad, Mum.'

'Why don't you go down and stay with Pip and Sheila for a while?' Peggy said again. 'You've always got on so well with him.'

'Yes, I do,' Janet agreed and raised her head. 'I think I shall. I'll ask Jon if he wants to come and take him out of school if he does – but I think he would prefer to stay with you until you can come down in the holidays...'

* * *

Jon hugged his mother when he came back from kicking a ball against the wall at the back of the pub kitchen. When she told him he could join her for a long holiday with his uncle or come down for a couple of weeks with his granny later in the year, he chose the latter.

'I think you need a rest, Mum,' Jon told her, suddenly showing signs of a new maturity. 'You are upset over Dad. Granny told me how much it hurt you when she came to fetch me in just now. I am sorry if I made you cry.'

'You didn't,' Janet assured him and hugged him, kissing the top of his head. 'Granny thinks she might like to go and live in Cambridge or somewhere nearby, when they decide to start pulling the houses down in the lanes. Should you like it if we both went to live there?'

He smiled and nodded. 'Granny told me. I think it would be nice. If Freddie is a teacher there, I might be in his class at the new school.'

'He might take you for sport or maths and maybe he can explain those logarithms,' Janet agreed. 'I'm going to ring Uncle Pip tonight. Do you want to talk to him?'

'Just to say hello,' Jon said and grinned as Peggy entered and took the pancake mixture from the fridge. 'I'm hungry, Gran.'

'Good, so am I,' she said, smiling. 'Shall I make lots? Do you want to help me?'

'Yes, please!' he said and went to stand by her at the cooker to watch as she poured the batter into the hot butter sizzling in the pan. 'Will you teach me to cook, Gran? I could be a chef then when I leave school.'

'I thought you wanted to be a train driver?' Peggy said, gently teasing.

'That was last week,' Able said from the doorway. 'That smells good, hon. Are we having pancakes?'

'Yes, lots of them,' Jon said and walked across the room to hug his grandfather. 'What sort is your favourite?'

'I like blueberries and cream,' Able said, laughing as his hand reached into his jacket pocket. 'I've got some liquorice allsorts for you – but don't open then until after tea or I'll be in big trouble.'

Janet laughed. 'No wonder he likes being with you two,' she said. 'You spoil him rotten, the pair of you.'

'He's worth a bit of spoiling,' Able said and ruffled Jon's hair. His gaze travelled on to Peggy, regarding her with love and affection. 'Want a hand with those, hon?'

'You can make some more batter,' Peggy said over her shoulder. 'The sooner they are all made, the sooner we can eat them.'

Janet stood up. 'I'll be back in a minute,' she said and left the room.

* * *

In the hallway, Janet picked up the phone receiver and dialled the number she needed. A man's deep voice answered and she took a deep breath.

'I think we need to talk,' Janet said. 'Come to the pub this evening and we'll go somewhere quiet and discuss a few things, Lars.'

'I'll be round at eight,' Lars told her and replaced the receiver.

Janet stood for a moment staring into space, then replaced her own receiver and went back to join the others in the kitchen. She would telephone her brother later, after she had spoken to Lars.

21

'You've got paint on your nose,' Freddie said and kissed Greta. She laughed and dabbed at him with her brush, but he darted back out of her way. He looked around at the room they had finished painting with satisfaction. Greta had covered most of it with her big brush, but he'd done the fiddly bits and it looked good. 'Mum says she is sending the bedroom stuff down by the carrier's van at the weekend. There are also some sheets and towels and a few bits in boxes, plus a couple of small armchairs and a coffee table we can have.'

'That's wonderful,' Greta said, and switched off her radio which had been playing an Elvis Presley song. 'We shan't need too much more. Just a desk and chair we can work on and some crockery.'

'I should wait and see what Mum sends,' Freddie told her. 'We've got most of the flat cleaned up now, so shall we have the afternoon on the river tomorrow? The forecast is for a lovely day.' They were well into May now and were enjoying bright breezy weather with occasional summer-like days.

'Oh yes, that will be lovely,' Greta agreed. 'I love Sunday afternoons on the river.'

'We'll take a boat out and have a picnic somewhere nice,' Freddie suggested. 'You've worked so hard on this these past weeks, Greta. It is beginning to look like a home.' It had taken her some weeks to complete the work, because she looked after the sweet shop during the day and also did some writing when she could. Freddie believed she was working on something special but she'd told him he couldn't read it until it was finished.

'I hope Mr Jones will be pleased with it. He said we could use any colours we liked – but his aunt is coming home from the nursing home soon and I wonder if she will be happy that we're moving in...' Miss Martha Jones had been told she needed a rest and Billy had insisted that she spend a few weeks in a nursing home, to build up her strength before returning to her home.

'She ought to be,' Freddie replied seriously. 'She has never lived over the shop, but it was a waste just leaving it empty. One day, if we get our own house, she will be able to let it now.'

'Mr Jones said they had always meant to have it done up, but kept making excuses, because they were both too busy to sort it out.'

'Don't you worry,' Freddie told her. 'Billy says he wouldn't have agreed that she could return to the shop at all if you hadn't come along. She was becoming quite fragile and the incident with the boys who attacked her has really shaken her, and she shouldn't have the worry of running the shop on her own.'

'I don't think she agrees with him,' Greta replied with a wry look. 'He told me she was cross with him when he visited her the other day, said he took too much on himself and that she would be fine once the stupid doctors said she could go home.'

Freddie laughed. 'Yes, that sounds very much like Miss Jones,' he confirmed. 'She was grumpy with me when I first started helping her, but she mellowed after I scared off some unruly lads.'

Greta nodded. 'I just hope she doesn't come back and decide she doesn't need me to help her after all.'

'I don't think she will, and I don't think Billy will let her,' Freddie said. 'He looks after her – and I think he owns the property. I doubt she pays much rent and so she will probably give in, even if she grumbles.'

'I thought she had been here for years?' Greta was curious.

'She has – since her sister was killed during the war. They were bombed and Martha's sister was trapped beneath the rubble in the sweet shop they owned in Coventry. Her youngest brother was killed abroad during the war, fighting for his country, so his son Billy brought her down here to live, found her a nice little cottage and set her up in the sweet shop. She'd lost everything, except for a few savings in the post office – and she never had a husband nor family.'

'Poor Martha,' Greta said. 'No wonder she gets a bit grumpy. She's never had anyone to love her.'

'We don't know that,' Freddie replied thoughtfully. 'Perhaps she loved and lost and has remained faithful all her life.'

'Freddie!' Greta giggled. 'I never knew you were so romantic...'

He laughed and grabbed her around the waist, swinging her high and then bringing her level with his face to kiss her. 'I might surprise you one of these days,' he said with a wicked look. 'Just because I don't say much, it doesn't mean I don't think or feel...'

His hands moved down over her hips, pulling her in close to his body. Greta snuggled into him, as he caressed her and kissed her, before reluctantly letting her go.

'I don't fancy the floor and I'm determined to make it right when it happens,' he murmured as she sighed with regret. 'I'd best go. It's getting late and you've been working hard, Greta. We'll be together soon, I promise.'

* * *

It was a beautiful afternoon the following Saturday and the van that was bringing their stuff wasn't due to arrive until about six in the evening. Freddie called for Greta at her lodgings and they cycled down to the river, setting themselves down on the grassy bank to relax in the warm sunshine. The river looked cool and inviting, but neither of them was tempted to go in, even though they both wore swimming suits under their shorts and shirts, just in case. For Freddie and Greta, it was enough to just stretch out on the blanket they'd brought and watch as a family of swans passed gracefully by. Greta was sleepy after working so hard every evening to get the flat ready for them and she closed her eyes, falling asleep, before being wakened suddenly by the sound of laughter and yelling.

She sat up, staring at the river. Freddie was on his feet. He was watching two punts on the water. It was obvious that the occupants of both punts, mixed young men and young women, were larking about, probably showing off. One of them had a bottle of wine in his hand and was drinking from it. As she watched, it became clear to Greta that they had all been drinking and were behaving stupidly, and even as she began to speak to Freddie about it, remarking that they looked as if they would collide, they did. She gave a little cry as several of the occupants went into the river and there was a lot of splashing and screaming as they felt the chill of the water. Some of them started swimming to the shore, but just as Greta realised that one of them was in real trouble, Freddie had kicked off his plimsoles and was running towards the river-bank. He jumped straight in and swam strongly towards the man who was clearly drowning, his head going under for the third time. Greta swallowed the scream that built inside her, curling her nails into the palms of her hands as she watched.

The man had not come up this time and Freddie was searching for a sign of him. He dived beneath the water while Greta held her breath and watched. In a moment, Freddie was up but dived almost instantly back down as soon as he'd taken breath. He came up, drew breath again and went back under. After what seemed to Greta an eternity, he came up and this time he had the man with him. She could scarcely breathe as he towed the man to the bank and then dragged him up the grassy incline.

Several of the occupants of the punts had gathered to watch, shivering from their dip in water that was still cold despite the sunshine. None of them moved or did anything as Freddie bent over the half-drowned man. He felt for a pulse, then opened his mouth, removed something that looked like a weed and began compressions on his chest. He breathed into his mouth a couple of times, then did a few more chest compressions, and moved the man into the recovery position, on his side, bringing his legs up to his chest. He smacked him hard on the back and suddenly a shudder went through him and he vomited.

Freddie knelt by him and rubbed his arms and legs and then turned him on his back again.

For a moment, the man just lay still and then he opened his eyes and stared up at Freddie. He groaned and closed them again, shivering and shuddering.

Freddie looked towards Greta, calling out that she should bring their blanket. She picked it up and ran to him and Freddie wrapped it around the man he'd rescued.

'My God,' one of the young women said, awestruck. 'I've never seen anything like that before. You saved his life.'

'Freddie did a life-saving course last summer,' Greta said proudly. 'He was a lifeguard and saved more than one person from the sea.'

'Well done, young man,' someone said from behind them and Greta turned to see a police officer watching them. 'I saw it all and you did more than I could have done.' He shook his head. 'I know it's the swinging sixties, and I don't mind the young ones having a lark – but sometimes they seem to leave commonsense behind.'

Freddie looked at him. 'I think Crawford may need to go to hospital just for a check-up.'

'You know him?' the officer asked.

'We're both students—'

'Damn you.' The man sat up and looked at Freddie. 'I suppose you think I should thank you... well, I do, but that doesn't change anything – and I'm not going to hospital. I'll be fine if you just leave me alone.'

'Fine by me,' Freddie replied calmly. He walked to Greta, who offered him the towel she'd brought in her cycle basket.

'I've called for an ambulance,' the policeman said behind him, his voice stern as he addressed Crawford. 'I'll have to ask you to go, sir – and anyone else who fell in the river. I'd be failing in my duty if I didn't.'

'Do you want to go home and change?' Greta asked Freddie as he dried himself as much as he could on the towel.

'No, I'll just take my shorts and top off and let them dry when we get settled.'

'I need to take some names...' the police officer said as they walked to their bikes.

'His name is Crawford,' Freddie called back. 'I'm Ronoscki. We're both students at King's.'

They picked up their bikes and cycled off down the riverbank, leaving the police officer and the crowd of swiftly sobered young men and women to give their version of events.

* * *

Greta looked at Freddie as they found a quiet spot further down the river and he stripped off his soaking-wet shorts and top, spreading them out on the grass to dry. She had brought a cardigan in case the weather turned as it so often does in early summer and offered it to him, but he shook his head so she spread it on the ground and they sat on it. She took out their picnic and they ate sandwiches and sausage rolls and drank fizzy pop.

'Did you know it was him when you went in to get him?' she asked. 'He's the one that has caused trouble for you at college, isn't it?'

'Yes, I knew,' Freddie replied and smiled. 'I know I've done myself no favours. Crawford already hates me. Goodness knows what he feels now – humiliated, I imagine.' He saw Greta's brows rise and grinned wryly. 'Think about it, love. He nearly drowns and I'm the one to save him – what a fool he is going to feel when the story spreads.'

Greta nodded. 'Quite a poignant revenge if you felt that way – but you don't, do you?'

'Not in the least,' Freddie said cheerfully. 'Any more sausage rolls? I'm starving.' She handed him the last. He ate it, clearly deep in thought. 'I would've kept it quiet if I could, but that police officer will report it and he will tell the Dean. They were all drunk and Crawford was arguing with someone in the other punt. If any of them had drowned, he might have been in serious trouble.'

'If someone else had been in danger of drowning, would you have rescued them first?'

Freddie frowned and then inclined his head. 'That's too profound for me, Greta. If it had been a girl I probably would – but then I'd have tried to get him, too, if I could. Luckily, the others could all swim.'

'He was a bit stupid larking about on a river if he can't swim.'

'Yes. Or arrogant.' Freddie grinned as he leaned over to kiss her. 'Stop worrying, Greta. It is over. Dad is driving down with Tom Barton in the van to help us settle in. Tonight we'll be in our first home together...'

Greta smiled and they clasped hands. The sun was shining; they were young, and life was good.

* * *

Able looked around the small flat as Tom and Freddie finished bringing in the last of the bits and pieces Peggy had sent them. It smelled of fresh paint and Sunlight soap. He nodded with approval to Greta. 'You've made this place look nice,' he said. 'Peggy sent some curtains in one of the boxes. They should fit – perhaps a bit on the long side, but they might do until you can alter them or get some made to measure.'

'I can probably hand-stitch the hems,' Greta replied. 'It was so kind of Peggy to send all this stuff – and of you and Tom to drive down.'

'We're killing two birds with one stone,' Able said. 'Peggy wants me to check out a hotel while I'm here – see what I think of it. She might want to invest in it. When they start knocking Mulberry Lane down, we might come this way for a few years.'

'That would be lovely,' Greta exclaimed. 'Freddie and I want to settle here for a while. Perhaps in Cambridge, perhaps one of the villages. He says he might not get a school in the city – but we'll live here until we get a house with a garden.'

'Yes, this is just right for you two, until you have a family.'

'We can't for a year or so anyway,' Greta said. 'Freddie needs to get a job when he finishes training – and we have to save...' She laughed. 'Besides, I want to finish my book.'

'Ah, yes,' Able smiled with her. 'How far have you got?'

'Only a few chapters, because I work in the sweet shop most days and then I've been painting, but once we are settled here, I'll get on with it again.'

'Good.' He nodded as Tom and Freddie came back into the room. 'All finished here?' he asked Tom.

'Yes, nice little place,' Tom said. 'Just right for a first home in town – or I suppose this is a city. Do you know if there are more flats around here not in use?'

'I'm not sure,' Greta said. 'A lot of the older houses in Mill Road and the centre of the town have rooms to let or bedsitting rooms. I think there are some in need of renovation, but not too many empty flats. We were lucky to get this right in the centre.'

'Yes, very lucky,' Tom said and handed her a pretty plant in a pot. 'Rose sent this for you, housewarming gift. Is there anything you need fixing while I'm here?'

'No, thanks,' Freddie supplied the answer. 'Billy Jones owns the property. He had a few small jobs done and we've cleaned it up and Greta painted it herself.'

'You did the fiddly bits,' Greta said, smiling at him. She looked at Tom. 'If you were thinking of property you could renovate and sell, you should speak to Billy at the cycle shop. He owns a few here and may know if there are any opportunities for investment locally.'

'I expect he's closed by now...' Tom said.

'He will open for an hour or so in the morning. Not officially, but he's usually there working just in case the students need anything.'

'I'll make sure to pop in and see him,' Tom said, smiling at them. 'Might be something for us. If Peggy and Able move down, we could start up a business here – not that Rose wants to move from London, but Able could oversee it and I'll be around when needed, on the end of the phone and in person at the start, middle and end of a job.'

Able gave a snort of laughter. 'Might have known that's why you offered to bring the stuff,' he said. 'Never knew anyone with such a nose for business.' He slapped Tom on the shoulder. 'Let's leave them to settle in – go see what this hotel is like.'

They said their goodbyes and departed, leaving Greta to look at Freddie, eyebrows lifted. 'Not one word of what you did by the river today...'

'Dad doesn't need to know that,' Freddie said. 'Come here, you.'

Greta went and he put his arms around her, kissing her and hugging her. He reached into his trouser pocket and brought out a small box. She gave a squeal of pleasure and opened it to reveal a little pearl and garnet ring, looking up at him.

'This isn't what I'd like to give you – but will it do? I love you, Greta. Will you be my wife – when we can?'

'It's beautiful, I love it – and you know I will.' It hadn't been the most romantic of proposals, but it was Freddie.

Freddie took it and slid it on her left finger; it fit perfectly. 'Good guess,' he murmured. 'It's just for now, my dearest love,' he told her as he kissed her softly. 'When I'm the head of a big school and earning lots of money, I'll buy you diamonds and rubies.'

'I'll never want them,' she said simply and put her arms around him, her head against his chest. 'Nothing could mean as much to me as this ring, Freddie. I love it – and I adore my strong silent giant.'

Freddie chuckled. 'Do you want to get some fish and chips before we start unpacking – or finish up and eat some of the food we brought with us?'

'Let's get straight,' Greta said. 'We can eat later...' Her eyes met his in shared pleasure at all the fun and laughter that would be theirs from now on in their own little home. 'We can eat biscuits in bed. Fay sent a big tin of her cooking for us and there are some of your favourites...'

'Oh yes, I love biscuits in bed,' Freddie said and squeezed her in a bear hug that told her far more than words. 'Come on, I'll help you make the bed.'

22

Peggy wanted to know all about the flat where Greta and Freddie had set up home when Able returned. She smiled when he told her it was exactly right for them, nodding as he described how pleased Greta had been with the bits and pieces she'd sent for them.

'She said they wouldn't need to buy much, because of your generosity, hon,' Able told her. 'In all honesty, they don't have room for much, but I don't think that matters. It is an adventure for them and they are happy, so what else matters?'

'Nothing – though it would be better if they could have married,' Peggy replied with a wry look. 'If we'd moved into together back in the forties, it would've caused a scandal...' She sighed. 'I know things are a bit different now but... anyway, they are engaged now. Freddie told me when he rang that he'd bought her a ring, and I know they will get married as soon as they can manage it.'

'I wish you'd seen how happy they are,' Able said. 'I think they will be sensible and make sure they don't have children too soon.'

Peggy nodded and then smiled. 'I know. This is the swinging sixties – rock 'n' roll, drugs, short skirts, and excitement. Youngsters behave in a different way, and it's good that they have more fun than we did, as long as it doesn't go too far. I have to be happy that none of my children ever had a drugs problem. Janet has had her ups and downs, but she didn't start drinking or taking drugs, thank goodness.'

'Has she rung?' Able asked as she offered him a cup of tea and his favourite apple pie.

'No, but Pip did,' Peggy replied and smiled again. 'He said she is helping Sheila sort stuff out that she doesn't want to take with her to America; they are taking it to some kind of charity shop apparently. They are getting on well together and she seems fine.' Peggy was thoughtful for a moment and then looked at him enquiringly. 'Well, what did you think of the hotel then?'

'Not much,' Able was honest. 'It's a bit on the shabby side, hon, and the breakfast was terrible. I'm glad we ate out that evening – we bought fish and chips and sat on the green near the river. It's a nice place, but it would take a lot of work and money to put it right, Peggy. I'd look for something else if I were you.'

'Oh, that's disappointing,' she said, her face falling. 'I was getting excited about it...' It seemed at times as if nothing would ever be settled again.

'Good thing Freddie wanted his stuff,' Able stated. 'At least you haven't wasted your time going there, hon. I'm sure we can find something that suits us – perhaps in one of the villages near Cambridge. Tom and I did a bit of a detour round the area and I saw an advert for a nice-looking pub that had a lease for sale sign—'

'A pub?' Peggy looked at him and nodded. 'Where – in Cambridge or somewhere else?'

'It was in Ely,' Able said. 'That's where Maureen's boy goes to boarding school. It is down near the river and an oldy-worldly sort of place, wisteria growing over the door and oak beams.'

'What made you thinking of looking there?' Peggy was surprised. 'It must have taken you a couple of hours longer to get back to London if you went that far afield.'

'Tom wanted to explore the area a bit,' Able said. 'He thought there might be opportunities for us – building new homes or renovating.'

Peggy was startled. 'He isn't thinking of leaving town? I know Rose wants to stay in London.'

'No. He says if we go through with it, he'll come and get things started and then leave it to me to oversee – and a foreman, of course. Building is much the same everywhere, hon. Tom would hire the workmen in, as he does here. He'd visit now and then to make sure it was all fine – but I dare say I could manage most things.'

Peggy stared at him. 'I thought you wanted to spend more time travelling?'

'We could still do that, once it was all up and running – but I'm hopeful Fay and Jace will come back to live here one day. I know he has this film coming up soon, but that kind of thing doesn't last forever. He's popular right now, but fashions change and so does music. When all the fuss settles down, he will probably have enough to retire on. Fay says he doesn't know what to do with it all at the moment, though they enjoy life.'

'Yes, I think you may be right. Fay says Jace wants to exploit it while he can, but he doesn't expect it to go on forever.' Peggy laughed. 'I didn't like him much when we first met, but he seems to be making her happy.'

'You can't judge a book by its cover,' Able said with a grin. 'Any more pie, hon? I'm starving.'

'I'll make you a ham sandwich if you like – but we'll have dinner soon in the restaurant.'

He glanced around the room. 'Where is Fay – and Jace? I thought he was due to arrive last week?'

'He did and Fay went with him to a pop concert up in Birmingham… I told you but you've had a lot on your mind.'

'So all your chicks have flown,' Able teased. 'Why did you decide to book the restaurant this evening?'

'I thought it would be nice. Besides, some of their regular customers are away on holiday, so there were empty tables; I've noticed a drop off in the pub's takings too,' Peggy told him. 'I don't know if it is just a seasonal lull – or whether it's because rumours of the clearance have begun to spread.' She sighed. 'Things are changing, Able. Two of my oldest pub customers have decided to move out. Mr James from Number 16 and Mrs Adie Bell from opposite us; they've lived here as long as I can remember, but they're leaving. They both had letters offering them modern flats and have accepted them. Adie was crying when she told me, but she said her drains have started to stink and she was thinking she might have to move anyway.'

'If she'd told us sooner, Tom would've sorted them for her.' Able nodded, understanding her unease at the changes. 'Maggie gets back next weekend,' he said. 'We could take a few days off and go property hunting in the Cambridgeshire area. If you like what you see, we could start to make plans.' Maggie's honeymoon trip had extended weeks longer than first planned, because of Greg's work. Maggie had written to say he'd wanted to spend more time with her so they'd hired a car and driven all over the place.

'I thought Maureen might like to help me run the hotel,' Peggy frowned. 'I shall have to tell her it was no good. I think she was quite looking forward to it...'

'She could still help run the pub – it would be more like you used to do here,' Able suggested. 'I doubt either of you would really want the full-time tie of a busy hotel in a university town. It would mean more work than you have now, hon.'

'I'll talk to her,' Peggy said. 'See what she thinks...'

'The pub I saw would be a nice home for us, Janet too, if she wants to come,' Able told her. 'It's a tied pub. We wouldn't own it, just the business – the property belongs to the Brewery. Maureen could have her own home and just help out. She would be close to her youngest son... I suppose it depends what Shirley decides.'

'It sounds nice,' Peggy agreed. 'Thinking about it, I might prefer the pub. I've run a pub most of my life.' She shook her head. It was so difficult to know what to do for the best.

Able nodded in agreement. 'I think it would suit us – and because we only need to purchase the lease, we could take it on as soon as we like, rather than wait for compensation here. Maggie will carry on with the restaurant here in London until it is all settled, and I'll deal with the council when it comes to it.'

'The pub would be less work than the hotel,' Peggy said thoughtfully. 'It was lucky you spotted it, Able. Otherwise I'd have been thinking maybe I could rescue the hotel.'

'Perhaps you could,' Able agreed, 'But I believe we want a slower pace of life in the next few years. You've worked hard for a long time, hon. We need more time for ourselves. Not complete retirement yet, because that wouldn't suit us, but something we can enjoy.'

Peggy agreed. 'I suppose when Anne told me about the hotel, I got excited – but the pub sounds more like me. I could do easy lunches and someone would look after it when we go away – either Maureen or Janet...'

'Yes – or we could find someone local,' Able said. 'I dare say the people who run it now employ help – or could name someone trustworthy. There are always options, hon.'

She smiled at him. His easy-going manner was comforting. Over the years, Peggy had learned to lean on Able and trust his judgement. His calm steadiness was a match for her impulsive, energetic nature and they made a good team.

'I'll talk to Maureen,' she told him. 'Perhaps she and Gordon would like to come down with us when we go to view it?'

* * *

'Able didn't think the hotel worth the bother then?' Maureen said, looking slightly disappointed. 'That's a shame, Peggy. It sounded such a good idea.'

'Yes. I was disappointed too – but he found something that looks really nice in Ely.' Maureen looked at her in surprise. 'Yes, I know – that's where Matty is boarding, isn't it?'

'Well, I never...' Maureen looked at her. 'It's funny, but Gordon said we might look for a house between Cambridge and Ely. Somewhere I could drive to and fro in less than half an hour. I could take him out for tea sometimes or he might even go as a day pupil...' Her eyes glowed at the thought. 'What's the new idea then?'

'It's a pub,' Peggy told her. 'An old-fashioned pub that does lunches – at least I think they do. I could start anyway...' Maureen smiled and nodded. 'A pub is less work than a hotel. You're closed part of the day and shut for the night. Much less responsibility that having guests all the time.'

'It's what I feel most comfortable with...'

Maureen agreed. 'It would be almost like old times, Peggy. You could manage if I went on holiday and I'd do the same for you.' And she and Gordon would see more of Matty.

'That is what Able thinks,' Peggy told her. 'He thought the hotel might be too much in a few years and he's right. The pub... well, it is what I've always liked best.'

Maureen met her gaze. 'You gave up a lot for Maggie, didn't you?'

'She is my granddaughter and Fay wanted it, too.' Peggy sighed. 'I have to admit that I haven't enjoyed it as much since they took over. It was pleasant working with them, but I'm not in charge of my kitchen any longer, Maureen.'

'You would be at the pub...'

'Yes, I would,' Peggy agreed. 'Anyway, I am glad you don't mind too much about the hotel.'

'I was excited when you told me, but when Gordon and I talked, we realised it might be a lot of work. He says we should get compensation both for the property and the business, because, like you, we've spent money on improvements. We can buy ourselves a house – and Gordon thinks that when Gordy has finished training, we might set him up in his own small plumbing firm. Neither of us wants to work full-time, but Gordon could answer a phone and help get the work in for him.'

Peggy nodded. 'How is Gordon now?'

'Good days and bad days,' Maureen admitted. She sighed deeply. 'He says if anything happened to him, I need to be near you, because we're like sisters.'

'I'd feel the same if anything happened to Able,' Peggy told her. 'Neither of us was truly happy when I went away before. Mulberry Lane was my home – but now they are going to destroy it, we shall have to leave anyway.'

Maureen sighed and agreed. 'It is a shame it has come to this, Peggy, but I suppose it is progress.'

'Of a kind,' Peggy said. 'Personally, I feel they could have renovated some of the buildings and there are worse areas – but it seems they want to build shopping centres and flats and this is the area they've chosen.' She gave a little shudder. 'When I think of what all the folks round here went through in the war and now it will all be gone within a couple of years.'

Maureen frowned. 'I think we should start looking for a new house, even if we rent something for a start... I don't want to leave it until everyone is boarded up and the streets are empty – like a ghost town.'

'I suppose it will be pretty desolate,' Peggy agreed. 'We're going down next weekend to look at that pub and a few other places. Able has been on the phone to some of the estate agents and I think he has three options, so it would be good if we all went together.'

* * *

Gordon agreed to the trip and Gordy said he could stay with a friend for a couple of days. However, when Maureen told him they might be living closer to his brother's school, he looked pleased and said he thought it was a great idea and decided to go with them.

'I might have to go to Cambridge for my apprenticeship,' he said thoughtfully. 'But I should be able to get a train from Ely...'

'You can drive my van if you pass your test,' Maureen said. 'You could apply for a licence next birthday. You'll need to drive if you're going to be a plumber, Gordy. You have to get from one home to another.'

'Yes, I know. I was going to ask about lessons, Mum.'

'I'll give you a few myself,' Maureen told him. 'Once you've got the hang of it, you can take a course and then apply for a test.'

Gordy grinned. 'You're a right one, Mum,' he said and pecked her on the cheek before running off to join some friends for a game of football in the street.

Shirley was non-committal when Maureen rang her and told her the new development. In fact, she sounded so odd that Maureen asked her if she was all right.

'Yes, of course. Why wouldn't I be?' Shirley said in a harsh tone that made Maureen look at the phone.

'Are the little ones well?'

'Amelia has been screaming her head off half the day and the nurse is off sick,' Shirley told her. 'I think she has a bit of tummy ache, Mum. I am giving her something for it – but, oh, you know...' Shirley sighed. 'I love them both dearly but sometimes it is tiring.'

'Would you like me to have them for a day, so that you can get some rest?' Maureen asked.

'No, it's all right, I can manage.' Shirley hesitated. 'I have to go, Mum. Amelia is screaming again. I'll give you a call when I can.'

'All right. If you're sure...?' Maureen stared at the receiver as the phone was put down at the other end. Shirley hadn't sounded like herself at all. Either she was desperately tired or something else was wrong.

Maureen shook her head. Was Shirley angry that Maureen and her father were thinking of moving from London? She'd seemed to think it a good idea, but perhaps with her daughter playing up, she'd decided she could really do with some help – but if that was the case, why hadn't she agreed to let Maureen look after her twins for a day?

* * *

An hour later, Shirley rang her. 'I'm sorry if I was short, Mum, but it was all a bit hectic... and there's something else...' She hesitated, took a deep breath, then, 'Ray has been offered a research project in Edinburgh and I know he wants to take it. He says he'll turn it down, but I can't let him, Mum. I know we told you we'd move to Cambridge if you wanted to go that way... but I think we have to take this post. There is a house and I can find someone to help with the children. I can manage most of the time – it's just when Amelia kicks off...' Shirley laughed. 'Was Gordy ever a screamer?'

'All babies scream sometimes,' Maureen said with a laugh. 'You mustn't worry about going where Ray's work is, love. Your dad will understand – and it isn't the other side of the world. You drive and there are trains. We shall spend time together when we can.'

'I'm sorry, Mum. I know you were looking forward to spending time with the children...' Shirley hesitated, then, 'Would you come over and help tomorrow? I don't think their nurse will be well enough and it would be a big help.'

'Of course I will,' Maureen said. 'We are going to see something in Ely at the weekend with Peggy and Able – but I can come tomorrow. I think we might all have a nice holiday at the sea next month when the schools break up. We could hire a cottage together and spend some time together until Ray takes up his new post.'

'Oh Mum, I do love you,' Shirley said with relief. 'I've been worrying myself to death over telling you. I feel better already.' She gave a little gurgle of pleasure. 'You always take things in your stride.'

'That is what mums are for, love,' she said. 'I'll be over in the morning. You ask Ray about the holiday and then we'll look for somewhere nice together.'

23

'What are you going to do with the house and furniture when you move?' Janet asked her brother that evening as they dined. She had been staying with them in their beautiful cottage in Devon for two weeks now. 'Are you hoping to sell?'

'No, we don't want to do that,' Pip said, glancing at his wife. 'As a matter of fact, we wondered whether you and Jon would like to move in – you can have it for a low rent, just to keep it aired and looked after.'

'I— I'm not sure.' Janet was taken aback by the suggestion. 'I hadn't thought of moving from London.'

'You'll have to give it some thought if Mum's going, and she won't have much choice if the demolition goes ahead.'

'I know...' Janet sighed. 'I was thinking I might buy something – preferably a cottage that needs renovation – and then live in it for a while.'

Pip nodded, looking at her consideringly. 'That is what you really like doing, isn't it?'

'Yes.' Janet smiled. 'It gives me a feeling of satisfaction to buy a place that looks a mess and bring it back to sparkling life. Mum likes cooking and I can cook, but I prefer building work.' She glanced at Sheila. 'What does your father think about you going to America?'

'He says he will visit when we get settled...' A little laugh escaped her. 'I didn't tell you, Janet – Dad has a lady friend. She helps him keep his cottage tidy and cooks food for them both, and I think she stays the night sometimes, though he hasn't confirmed it.'

'Good for him,' Janet said, smiling. 'I like your dad, Sheila. I am glad he has a nice friend to share his life. It is far better than a lonely old age.'

'Dad has changed since he came here to live,' Sheila said, her eyes bright with affection. 'He belongs to several clubs; he goes dancing and has a large circle of friends, but Norma is his *special* friend.'

'Why don't you ask him if he'd like to move in here while you're away?'

Sheila looked at Pip. 'We have thought of it, but if we want to come home, it might not suit him to move back to his cottage and it's an upheaval for him. I think he is better off where he is. Pip said you've moved around a lot and wouldn't mind if we wanted it back.'

Janet laughed. 'Well, I shouldn't, of course. I've never stayed in one place long enough to put down roots – except London; I suppose that is my home, if anywhere is,' Janet said thoughtfully. 'I don't think I can commit at the moment, Sheila. Why don't you just leave it empty and ask your father to pop in and look after it for you?'

'I'll ask about letting it, perhaps for holidays,' Pip said. 'I just thought you and Jon might enjoy living here for a while. I know of some properties you could work on down here.'

'I'll think about it,' Janet told him. 'Mum wants me to relocate with her, and Jon wants to go wherever she goes – but I'm not sure what I want to do yet, Pip.'

'It doesn't matter,' he told her. 'We can sort it out before we leave, Janet love. I was thinking about you really – if you fancied a new start...'

Janet bit her lip. 'I wish I knew what I wanted to do... There's something I need to settle in my mind before I can move on.'

'Well, the offer is there if it seems right for you, but don't worry about it.'

'I never do worry about you,' Janet said and laughed. She looked round as Chris arrived. Her nephew, and Pip's eldest son, was a handsome lad with dark curling hair and blue eyes. He'd been to a music session and came in carrying his guitar case.

'I put some dinner aside for you,' Sheila told her son. 'It's cottage pie.'

'Thanks, Mum, but I had some chips on the way home, maybe later?' He looked round for his sister. 'Where is Sarah?'

'She is staying with a friend this evening,' Sheila said. 'I think a group of them are going to a pop concert and it made sense for them all to go together.'

Chris nodded, went to the fridge, and took out a can of fizzy drink, pouring it into a tall glass. 'It won't disturb you if I practise this evening?'

'Not too loud, Chris,' his father said. 'How did it go this evening?'

'Pretty good,' Chris replied, smiling. 'We've been asked to play at a wedding next weekend – and, this guy, maybe wants us to do the backing on a record he's making. We have to go to a recording studio with him and see if it works.' He hesitated, then, 'If we do get the contract, I might not come out to America with you straight away, Dad. It could be the beginning of something for us.' Pip frowned and Chris went on, 'Grandad says he'll move in here with me for a while so I'm not on my own, if I want—'

Janet burst out laughing. 'There you are – problem solved,' she said to Pip, causing Chris to look at her enquiringly. 'Your father was wondering if I wanted to move in for a while.'

Chris's face lit up. 'That would be great, Aunt Janet,' he said. 'Grandad likes you – and Dad couldn't possibly object to my staying here then, if both of you were around.'

Janet gave him an amused look. 'I suppose I could for a while,' she agreed. 'It wouldn't be for long, but you know I like your music, Chris. I hope it works out for you.'

'I'm not sure how long the contract would be for,' Chris told them. 'It is an album of country songs and this chap is looking for a backing group. If he chooses us and it's a success, it will probably mean we'll all go to America. So I'll be able to spend some time with you then, Mum...? Dad...?' He looked at them for approval.

'Well, you're old enough to look after yourself,' Sheila told him sensibly. 'Just make sure you don't get in with a bad crowd and start taking drugs, that's all.'

'Yes, Mum,' Chris said and sent her a cheeky grin before leaving the kitchen.

'I suppose he would have gone off once we got out there,' Pip said. 'He's mad on his music and that's his world, so we were never going to hold on to him for long. He needs to be ready to move wherever the work is...'

'You should talk to Jace about it,' Janet said and he nodded. 'He knows people in America. If this doesn't work out for Chris, he'll be able to point him in the right direction.'

'He said he might be able to take him on when he was over here before,' Pip said thoughtfully. 'I didn't mention it to Chris because he was still taking his exams. He's finished now so he has to find a job – and I know he wants to play that guitar.'

* * *

They heard the sound of Chris beginning to play up in his bedroom as Sheila started to clear the used dishes. It was a plaintive sound and they all smiled as he sang a sad country song. Janet got up to help Sheila, and Pip went out of the room, saying he had some work to finish.

'It isn't easy to let go. Pip is cautious about Chris becoming a professional musician,' Sheila said as she began to wash the crockery and Janet wiped, placing the dried pieces on the beautiful old oak dresser. 'But they grow up and you have to. You let Maggie go to London when she wanted to become a cook.'

'I knew she would be all right with Mum,' Janet told her. 'I wanted to live there as well. Ryan was making vague noises about retiring – but I never expected him to want to go off to that isolated smallholding... or what happened afterwards.'

'No, of course not.'

'We hadn't been really happy for a while...' Janet sighed. 'But he was getting on with Jon better and I thought... I never dreamed he was so ill.'

'I was so sorry when I heard.' Sheila looked compassionate.

'I didn't ask anyone but Mum to come for the funeral, but Able brought Jon. He said he should say goodbye to his dad – and he was right.'

'It was so upsetting for you both when Jon had the accident,' Sheila said sympathising. 'How is Jon now?'

'Much better physically, though he will always have a limp and occasionally has an off-balance moment – that's what Mum calls them. She makes nothing of it and I think that is why Jon loves to be with her. I make too much fuss, or so he says.'

'Peggy takes most things in her stride,' Sheila nodded her agreement. 'Have you spoken to Maggie yet since she got home from Italy?' she asked, changing the subject in the hope of easing the pain in Janet's eyes.

'She rang this morning,' Janet confirmed. 'You were out shopping. She had a wonderful time in Italy, says she's brought lots of recipes home.'

'Yes, of course, she would,' Sheila agreed. 'I believe real Italian food is wonderful.'

'I've been to restaurants here, but Maggie says it tastes entirely different out there – much fresher and more delicate in flavour. I think she persuaded some women she made friends with to give her their family secrets. She says that is the kind of food people like – not the fancy dishes they do in London.'

'Yes, that sounds like Maggie. You are very lucky in your daughter, Janet. She is a lovely girl and has her head screwed on the right way. She will make a success of her life.'

'I hope she'll do better than me,' Janet replied. 'I seem to have made a mess of things. I'm sure Mum finds me a disappointment, even though she loves me.'

'No, how could she?' Sheila stared at her in astonishment. 'You've had a lot of grief and upset in your life, but you have two beautiful children and my dad never stops singing your praises over the way you did his cottage for him. How could you think yourself a failure?'

Janet looked at her for a moment. 'I did make a nice job of that, didn't I?' she said and smiled. 'I do enjoy that sort of work and I made a decent profit on the last flat I renovated.' She hesitated, then, 'Ryan left me quite a bit of money. Some things are for Jon and there's a small bequest for Maggie – but I shall have enough to buy myself a house and another property, one that I can do up and sell.' Janet was thoughtful. 'There is something I have to sort out in London – but I think I'll come back here just before you leave for America, bring Jon for a holiday, if he wants. He likes being with his granny best. I'll look after things here and perhaps renovate something locally...' She nodded to herself. 'It has helped me a lot being with you and Pip, given me time to think about my life.'

'I'm glad,' Sheila said and they moved together, hugging each other. 'You must come for a holiday over there when we're settled. Dad will make sure everything is all right here.'

Janet looked wistful for a moment. 'It's all change these days. Maggie married and Fay living in America, you going off there very soon – and Mum doesn't know what to do. She feels as if her family is spreading all over the place.'

'Oh, she will cope just fine,' Sheila said confidently. 'Peggy always does.'

'Yes,' Janet laughed. 'She always does.'

24

Freddie chained his bike to the railings and walked into the sunny courtyard, smiling at the porter as he passed him. He was crossing the green, aware as always of the peace of the ancient grounds, when he was hailed in a loud voice and turned to see one of the dons signalling to him. He sprinted up to him, sensing that he was in some kind of trouble.

'You were not in your room this morning, Ronoscki?'

'No, sir. I stayed overnight with a friend. I'd been helping her move into new accommodation.'

'Did you get permission to stay out all night?'

'No, sir. I didn't think it was necessary. I am going to move out of college rooms, sir, if there is no objection?' He met the disapproving stare without flinching.

'The Dean wants to see you. He asked for you to see him an hour ago.'

'Sorry, sir. I'll go at once,' Freddie said. 'Am I in trouble for something?'

'I shall have to report you were not in rooms last night, but I have no idea why the Dean has requested you go to his room.'

Freddie nodded, feeling chagrined that his absence had been noted. It was probably the first time anyone had looked for him so early in the morning and he knew that other students often stayed out all night. He ought, of course, to have let someone know and he would need to give notice on his rooms, but other students lived in accommodation that did not belong to the college, so there was no rule against it. Mr Owen was one of the stricter masters and would undoubtedly report him, whereas some of the others would simply have ticked him off.

Feeling slightly anxious about what he might have done wrong, Freddie made his way to the Dean's study and knocked at the door. There was silence for a moment and then he was bid to enter and did so. Very little sunlight penetrated the old glass of tiny windows and the dark mahogany antique furniture gave the room a sombre air. The Dean sat behind a large desk and a chair was placed to the front and side.

'Ah, Ronoscki,' the Dean said, glancing up at him. 'I am glad you could spare me a little of your time.' The sarcasm in his words stung like a needlepoint.

'Sorry, sir. I wasn't in my rooms.'

'Why would that be?'

'I helped a friend move into new accommodation and it got late, so I stayed,' Freddie replied. 'I shall be giving up my college rooms and moving once I've given notice.'

'Hmm.' The Dean's gaze narrowed thoughtfully. 'We must hope your studies do not suffer for it, Ronoscki.'

'I think I shall have more time for study, sir.'

'That remains to be seen… don't waste your time here, Ronoscki. I have had reasonable reports of you as far as your exam results go, but that is what we expect from our gentlemen.' He folded his hands in a steeple, elbows on the leather-topped desk, staring at Freddie for so long that he became hot under the collar. What was behind that look?

'Have I done something wrong, sir?'

'Have you?' The Dean's expression suddenly changed, lightened. 'It seems you saved Crawford's life last Saturday afternoon? Is that correct?'

Freddie stared at him, taken by surprise. 'Well, yes, I suppose I did.'

'I do not think there is any doubt about it. I have been told that you jumped in, grabbed him and towed him out. You then began compressions and did all that was necessary to ensure he was breathing, before leaving the scene.'

'There was a police officer there, sir. He saw it all and took over, calling an ambulance. I left because—'

'—Because Crawford resents you.' The Dean nodded his head. 'Crawford's father is a good friend to the college. He was an honours student himself and expected his son to do as well.'

'Yes, sir. So I have been told,' Freddie said. 'We... we don't get on, I'm afraid.'

'You mean Crawford has done his best to make life difficult for you?'

Freddie didn't answer and the Dean nodded. 'You may be interested to know that Crawford money has helped to sustain this college over the years as far back as his great-grandfather.' Freddie said nothing. 'However, certain things have come to my notice. I have, therefore, advised Crawford's father that his son might be better suited studying for his last exams with a private tutor at home – and, after the incident on Saturday, Mr Crawford senior has agreed.'

'I— I see...' Freddie replied uncertainly. 'I am sorry, sir.'

'Why, pray, should you be sorry? Not for saving his life?'

'Good grief, no, sir!' Freddie exclaimed. 'I thought it might have been a difficult decision for you and the college, sir.'

'Ah yes, I have been told you are a deep thinker. You are perfectly correct. I feared that the college would lose a certain sum of money that had been promised for repairs to the roof. Our hallowed halls need constant repair, unfortunately. However, on learning that one of our students had saved his son's life, Mr Crawford made the donation.'

'I am glad of that,' Freddie murmured and got a sharp look from the Dean.

'I imagine it will be the last from that source. Crawford minor will not be well disposed towards us – but our traditions of honesty and fair play, as befits men of honour, hold good, and we shall no doubt find other supporters.'

Freddie held his tongue.

The Dean inclined his head, perhaps in approval. Then he rose to his feet, came round the desk, and offered his hand. Freddie took the proffered hand and felt it grip so tightly that he hardly stopped himself crying out. 'Well done, Ronoscki.'

'Thank you, sir.'

'You may go.'

'Thank you.' Freddie turned but was stopped as he reached the door by a question.

'Where did you learn to save lives?'

'I took a holiday training and working as a lifeguard on a beach last summer. It was fun and I thought it might come in useful...' Freddie smiled and went out.

On the other side of the door, he paused to take a deep breath. The interview had left him feeling like a wrung-out dishcloth. It was obvious the Dean had acted properly on whatever had come to his notice, but he hadn't enjoyed the experience. However, he was a man of honour and he'd done what he thought right.

Freddie didn't bother wondering what the Dean had learned; he was aware of Crawford's cheating at exams and other things, perhaps more than he'd guessed. It wasn't his business and he wasn't even pleased that the contemptuous student wouldn't be around to sneer at him. He wouldn't tell anyone what the Dean had told him.

Hearing the clock strike the hour, Freddie was jerked into action. If he didn't move fast, he was going to be late again for an important lecture...

* * *

Freddie took spit-roasted chicken and chips home that evening to celebrate. He'd come top in his latest test results and he was feeling happy as he walked in the door. Greta was polishing furniture, her hair tied up in a ponytail. She turned as he entered, her face alight with pleasure.

'Look at this lovely desk,' she said. 'Billy brought it round for us. He said it had been in a shed for years, but all it wanted was a little polish – it is oak and it goes well with the things your mum sent.'

'It looks good,' Freddie said, placing the packet of delicious-smelling food on the kitchen table and going through to the living room to take her in his arms and kiss her. 'You have dirt on your nose...' He used a finger. 'Cobwebs...'

'From the desk,' Greta told him and hugged him. 'You look pleased with yourself?'

'I came top in the latest maths test – and the Dean shook my hand and said, "Well done" – for saving Crawford's life.'

'So he should,' Greta said. 'How did he know? You didn't tell him?'

'No fear,' Freddie said. 'I wouldn't dare approach him...' He laughed. 'It was a bit odd; I thought I was going to be hauled over the coals, but he just said well done and wanted to know where I learned to save lives.'

Greta nodded. 'Is Crawford back at college?'

'I think he has gone home to recuperate,' Freddie said vaguely. 'I dare say the police told the Dean – and his family. He is going to finish his studies at home with a private tutor and return to take his exams, I suppose.'

'Oh, well, it doesn't matter. Let's hope he doesn't take it out on you when he gets back.'

'I expect he will just ignore me,' Freddie said. 'I'm hungry. Let's eat before the chips get cold...'

25

Peggy looked at her daughter when she walked in the following Friday afternoon and felt relieved as she saw the desperation had gone from Janet's eyes. She met her gaze and smiled. 'Feeling better, love?'

'Yes, I'm feeling better, Mum,' she admitted. 'Pip and I talked for ages and Sheila, too. I've promised I'll go and stay at the cottage for a while when they leave for America. Chris may have a chance as part of a backing group on a record, so if it happens, he wants to stay. His grandfather will move in for a while if they want, but Pip would like me there to keep an eye on him. It would probably be for three to six months if it happens.'

'Are you happy to do that?' Peggy asked her and Janet nodded. 'What about Jon?'

'Yes, I think so. I said no at first, but then when Chris asked, I decided I might as well. I've already seen a property I can renovate and either let or sell.'

Peggy was silent for a moment, then, 'What about Lars? I thought he might be a part of your plans.'

'He might – but only a small part,' Janet replied with a wry smile. 'I might have a fling with him, Mum – but the last thing I need at the moment is a serious relationship. I shall never marry again.'

'And what about Jon?' Peggy repeated quietly, feeling a little sad. Why couldn't this daughter of hers find happiness? 'Where does he enter into your future plans?'

'I'm going to talk to him this evening when he gets home from school. He likes Chris and I suppose I can find a school for him there, if he wants to come – but he may prefer to stay with you. I'll come back for visits while you're here – but you're thinking of moving soon, aren't you?'

'Yes.' Peggy turned away to take something from the oven. 'Are you hungry? Would you like some of this apple pie?'

'I'd like a cup of tea – and pie,' Janet replied, moving to pick up the kettle and fill it. She put it on the hob and turned to her mother. 'Do you think I am being too casual over Jon or selfish?'

'No. I think you need some time to sort yourself out,' Peggy said. 'I don't think you are selfish, Janet. Careless sometimes, but I know you love Jon. He is welcome to stay with me, but he has the choice and it's up to him.'

'Have you been to look at that pub in Ely yet?' Janet asked, changing the subject.

'No, we had to delay it for a week because Gordy had an important football match, but we're going on Sunday,' Peggy said. 'Maureen and Gordon are coming with Gordy and we'll take Jon – and after we've all seen the pub, they will visit Matty. Then we can all see what we think of the possibilities there for our families.'

Janet nodded. 'You need to think about it carefully, Mum. I know you did all right when you lived at the sea for a few years, but you always said your home was here in London.'

'It is and I suppose it always will be,' Peggy agreed. 'I should have liked to stay right here at the Pig & Whistle until I'm ready to retire, but I don't have the choice.'

The kettle boiled before either of them spoke again, whistling loudly. Janet made tea and they sat down at the old pine table that had seen so many family gatherings. 'I thought you would fight to save it,' she observed as she poured a cup of steaming-hot liquid into their cups. 'Or at the very least find somewhere else in London...'

'If I thought there was a chance, I might have done, but the area is due for clearance, Janet. Too many neglectful landlords have let these old houses run down for years. It's fine for us, because we've kept the pub modernised, but some of the terraces are infested with cockroaches and rats.'

Janet shuddered. 'I suppose it is time then,' she agreed with a sigh. 'After Chris finally goes to join his family in America, I'll come to Ely for a while if that's where you are. I suppose I could find property to renovate there.'

'Able and Tom certainly think so,' she said. 'They've seen a few possibilities already. There are plenty of older houses in the area – so they might think it worthwhile to set up a branch of the business there.'

Janet nodded. 'I'll see how I feel when it happens. You've mentioned me working with you, Mum. Of course I'd help out if you wanted a holiday – but not as my main job. To be honest, I find cooking boring...'

Peggy chuckled. 'Good thing Maggie doesn't,' she said as her granddaughter entered the kitchen, bearing bags of shopping.

'Maggie doesn't what?' she asked and kissed her mother on the cheek. 'Sorry about Ryan, Mum.' She gave her a hug and Janet returned it. 'But what were you saying when I came in, Granny?'

'That you don't find cooking boring – your mum says she does.'

'Oh, I know. How are you, Mum? How was Uncle Pip and Aunty Sheila and the kids?'

'They are all well – and I'm feeling a bit better. I might go and stay down there for a few weeks if Chris gets his record contract.'

'Oh, that sounds exciting,' Maggie said, smiling. 'Is there a chance of it?'

'An American singer wants a new backing group and he has asked Chris and his friends to audition. He heard them at a jazz session they took part in and asked them to try out at a recording studio, so he has his fingers crossed.'

'That's good,' Maggie said. 'But what is it that I don't like?'

'Oh, I told Mum I find cooking boring and she said it was a good thing you didn't.'

'I know you never truly enjoyed it.' Maggie looked at her consideringly. 'You're happy making things look nice – that's what you do best. My school friends always said our house looked posher than theirs. It's your thing, Mum. You should do it professionally.'

'Well, I've done a couple of properties up and I'm going to try to do another if I stay down there for a few months.'

'What about interior designing?' Maggie said. Her mother stared at her, puzzled, and Maggie laughed. 'It's making a room a home, Mum – exactly what you did for us, only you show other people who haven't got your talent how to do it.'

'Surely people want to furnish their own homes?' Peggy objected. It was a new idea for her and she wasn't sure of the point of it.

'Not everyone has the time or the flair for it,' Maggie told her. 'It's becoming more the fashion now for wealthy people to have someone decorate and furnish their homes. Fay and I were talking about it last night – a lot of her friends in Hollywood do that sort of thing.'

'Americans,' Janet said dismissively. 'I don't think it would work here, Maggie.'

'You don't know unless you try,' Maggie said and laughed. 'Did you know that Able and Tom have a contract to build several new houses? Fay told Tom he should furnish one as a show home – and he thinks it is a wonderful idea. Why don't you ask him if he will let you furnish the show house? You could find stuff cheap in junk shops, strip it back to the wood and polish or paint it white – and make curtains and cushions. You might get a furniture manufacturer to loan beds, if you promise to have a label advertising their brand.'

Janet stared at her for a long moment. 'Where did I get you from, Maggie?' she asked, laughing. 'You're certainly full of ideas.'

'That's a great plan,' Peggy said. 'Tom won't have a clue what to do and if you did one for him, you might be asked to do others. You could take photos for brochures and see if a magazine would do an article, Janet.'

Peggy met Maggie's gaze and their eyes twinkled knowingly. Janet was looking interested, her face brighter than it had been in a long while. Maggie was such a thoughtful girl and she understood her mother well. Janet always needed to be doing something new and different, looking to the future. A job such as Maggie had described would always be fresh and exciting.

'It doesn't stop you renovating a house when you can,' Peggy said. 'You could furnish it to help sell it – and you can store or sell the contents when you've finished.'

'Yes – and you might sell property better that way. You could give them the option of buying some or all of the furniture. You make lovely curtains and a lot of people can't – I'd ask you to make mine if I needed new ones.'

'If you use old furniture, you can find it cheaply and it looks warm and homely if you polish it well,' Peggy added her mite.

'I think I would need to be based in London for all that—' Janet said.

'Why? A lot of wealthy people live in large country houses,' Maggie asserted. 'You can find customers locally through advertising and you drive, so you can go anywhere you have a commission. Besides, if you combine it with the house renovating, you'll only need a few – unless you want to be rich and famous, and I'm sure you could if you tried.'

Janet laughed suddenly. 'You seem very sure, Maggie. I'm only an amateur…'

'That's daft,' her daughter said. 'You've always had style, Mum. It's just an attitude. Make up your mind to something and you can do it.'

'I'll ask Tom if he's interested,' Janet said and stood up to hug her daughter. 'I love you, Maggie.'

'Love you, too, Mum,' Maggie said and hugged her. She glanced at Peggy. 'Have you seen Fay, Granny? Has she gone out?'

'Had you forgotten Jace was arriving back from tour this afternoon? She went to meet his train. They're staying at a private flat he has rented until he goes on tour again next week – I'm not sure if she will go with him or stay in London.'

'No, she wasn't sure whether he would want her to do that,' Maggie said. 'I had forgotten that Jace was back. I bought something for her, for the baby really – but I'll give it to her when I next see her.' She picked up her bags. 'I'd best go and get ready. We're busy this evening and I'm trying a new dish.'

Janet looked at Peggy as she went out. 'That girl is a whirlwind.

Where did she come from? She is so clever and beautiful.'

'Mike was intelligent,' Peggy said. 'You're beautiful – and you know it.'

Janet laughed. 'I'd almost forgotten what it was like to be young and beautiful.'

She looked round as Able came in, Jon following behind them. Able was eating an ice cream and carrying a large box containing a model aeroplane. On seeing Janet, Jon gave a cry of joy and ran to her, hugging her.

'Look what Grandad bought me,' he said, pushing the box at her. 'We're going to make it together – the way me and Dad used to.'

Janet's eyes stung with tears as she hugged him. 'That's good,' she said. 'It looks like it will be a big one?'

'It's a Spitfire – like they had in the war,' Jon told her. 'Grandad does lots of things with me, Mum.'

'Yes, I know.' Janet sought Able with her eyes, silently thanking him. 'You're a lucky boy, Jon. I hope you thanked Grandad for the present?'

'Of course I did,' Jon said and broke away from her, running to his granny. 'What's for tea, Granny Peggy?'

'Well, let's see,' she said, pretending to think. 'There might be chops or there might be a bacon sandwich—'

'Bacon sandwich,' Jon said instantly and spotted the fresh baked apple pie. 'Can I have some of that now, please?'

'I don't see why not...' Peggy said, knowing he would happily eat it and then his bacon sandwich. She cut him a slice and laughed as Able promptly sat down at the table, so he got some, too. 'You boys...' she teased. 'You're both as bad as each other.'

'We're hungry,' Able said and grinned at Jon.

Janet watched their banter and knew her son would miss it if she took him away from his grandparents. He was happy with them, a responsive, eager boy, all trace of the sullenness he'd once had vanished.

'I might go down to stay with Chris for a while,' she said casually. 'For a few months. You could come with me for a holiday, for as long as you wish, and then, when I can, I'll come back home. Unless you want to stay with me while I do some work there?'

'I'll come for a holiday, Mum,' Jon said, smiling at her. 'I'd like that – but I live with Granny and Grandad now.' His voice was firm and untroubled and Janet felt both relief that he was happy and a pang that he preferred to be with his grandparents.

* * *

Janet rang Lars later that evening and agreed to meet the next day. Peggy, Able and Jon were going to Cambridgeshire to look around the area and view the pub they thought they might take on. Janet was free for the day and so was Lars. It was a good opportunity to talk.

She dressed in a pair of cream linen trousers and a fine lawn blouse with a baby-blue cardigan over her shoulders and her hair tied back off her face. She decided not to use much make-up, just dusting her nose with powder and a dash of lipstick. Janet was still attractive in her forties and decided that Lars should see her as she was, because that was the only way she wanted to be. If they were to have a relationship it would be different to any that Janet had known before as she wasn't prepared to risk her heart a third time.

They met for lunch at a quiet restaurant by the river. Lars looked at her and then took her hand and held it in his, before kissing it. 'You look beautiful, Janet,' he told her and his deep voice sent a tingle down her spine. 'Are you better now?'

'I'm on the mend, I think,' she told him. 'Ryan's death – the way he hid his illness from me – it knocked me for six. I felt so wretched, as though I'd failed him.'

'He wanted to spare you,' Lars said and his voice was softer and caressing. 'I have seen someone I loved die that way – and it is too hard. I understand why he felt it should be private.'

'Not from me.' Janet took her hand from his. 'I did love him. We quarrelled often and things weren't as they should be, but it hurt – too much.'

'Naturally. He was your husband, the father of your child – and your friend,' Lars said. 'My mother died slowly and my father died with her; little by little, I saw the joy of life leave him. They were lovers and friends all their years – it is good while it lasts, but then it leaves a terrible void. My father did not wish to go on after she died; he killed himself by driving his car over a cliff. I was seventeen and, afterwards, I lived alone – have lived alone for much of my life. I have friends, lovers – but I live always alone.'

'Oh, Lars, how awful for you,' Janet said, immediately full of sympathy. He took her hand back into his and this time she did not withdraw it. 'I am so sorry.'

'It was many years ago.' He shrugged. 'One goes on – as you must, Janet. You are young and beautiful, and you hunger for life, don't you? I've seen it in your eyes.' He smiled at her and she felt herself drifting towards him, drawn by something that fascinated her as it soothed her bruised spirit. 'I think you felt constrained for too long, my love. You need to be free – to be allowed to live as you choose, to be an independent woman. Spread your wings and fly, Janet – the world is waiting for you. It is yours to take and hold if you wish.'

Janet looked up at him and it was so natural to be kissed. He did so with a gentleness that made her feel as if she wanted to melt into him, to rest her head on his shoulder. Suddenly, the world seemed a warmer, kinder place.

'Come, we shall eat, and you will tell me your plans for the future – and then we shall go to my home and we shall make love, yes?'

Janet nodded silently. It was why she had come. She had known that Lars would not want to hold her or to own her. The men she had loved before had wanted her to be theirs, to live as they lived, and follow them – Lars was different. She'd felt that instinctively from the beginning. They would be friends and lovers – but not husband and wife. She would come to him when she felt the need; she would not live with him or he with her. They were both free spirits and wanted it that way.

Janet would never marry again. She would stand proud and make her living. She would become successful, just as her wonderful daughter Maggie prophesied, and she would enjoy life. It was the life she wanted and it was how it would be. She had her family and her children, and she would have grandchildren one day. It would be enough.

26

'I love it here, Able,' Peggy said as they all sat on a bench on the quayside in Ely and ate the picnic they'd brought with them. She saw an answering smile in his eyes and turned to look at Maureen. 'What did you think of the pub?'

'I think it is just what we need,' Maureen told her. She took Gordon's hand in hers. 'All we have to do is look for a house that suits us. We'd like one with an annexe – or room to build a little office and workshop for Gordy.'

'Peaceful,' Gordon said and lifted his face to the warm sunshine that had blessed them that day. 'I never knew how good it could be to just sit by a river and relax.'

'I've seen just the house for you,' Able told them and both Maureen and Gordon turned to look at him. 'It isn't far from here – five minutes' walk. I didn't tell you because I wanted you to decide whether you liked the area or not.' He grinned at their looks of surprise. 'Tom found it when we were here last time and we viewed it then. It needs some renovation, but we'll do that – and maybe Janet will advise on the decoration and find the kind of furniture you'd like for it. There are three good bedrooms and a smaller one you could make into a second bathroom if you chose – and room to build that annexe.'

'Is it new—? No, obviously not, if it needs renovation,' Maureen said, laughing in sudden excitement. 'What sort of a house, Able? When can we see it?'

'I asked for a viewing this afternoon,' he said. 'I think we should probably take it on anyway, even if you don't like it – but come and see... if we've all finished eating?'

He stood up, brushing the crumbs from his trousers. A blackbird flew to his feet to gobble them up, and Jon took the rest of his unfinished sandwich to the water's edge and threw it to a crowd of ducks, who proceeded to squabble over it noisily.

Peggy packed the remains of their picnic into the car and they all shook themselves off. Able led the way back up from the quayside and through a narrow lane to where several cottages and terraced houses were arranged in a sort of quadrangle. He walked past the row of terraces to a lovely old cottage at the end. It had had a tiled roof to replace the original thatch at some period in its history, but the windows were small-paned and leaded and the glass had that grey look that was found only in old houses. The paintwork needed decoration and some replacements might be needed for the frames and doors, but it had a timeless air of peace and beauty that made both Gordon and Maureen exclaim in surprise and pleasure.

'This one? Is it really for sale?' Maureen asked, sounding breathless. 'I've always wanted to live in a house like this – is it expensive?'

'No, because it needs a lot done inside, so it is going for a song,' Able told her with a smile. 'We'll do all that for you if you want it. Let's go in and look round, shall we? I've arranged to meet the agent – and here he comes now.'

A man in a brown suit carrying a briefcase hailed them, a smile of anticipation on his face.

* * *

Half an hour later, they emerged, having arranged to purchase the property. Maureen's face was glowing and Gordon looked quietly content.

'It's wonderful, Able,' Maureen told him as they went back to their cars. 'How can I thank you for giving us the offer of it? Will Tom mind that you've let us have it? He wanted to buy it himself.'

'Only to do up and sell on. Besides, Tom would love it that he found something you could be happy in, Maureen. You know he thinks the world of you, always has done since he was a kid.'

'Yes,' she agreed. 'You're right. I am sure he will be pleased...' She looked at Gordy, who was kicking a ball in the square with Jon. 'Did you like the cottage, Gordy?'

He glanced up at her. 'It's all right once it's decorated,' he said with a shrug and she laughed. 'I like the river and there's a football ground here where they play matches most weeks in the winter.'

'Kids,' she said and held out her hand to Gordon. 'I think it is just right for us, don't you?'

'It will be perfect once we get a new kitchen and bathroom – and replaster the whole house. The garden is huge, so we can build an office somewhere for Gordy,' Gordon said. He looked at Able gratefully. 'I don't think I'd have dared tackled it if it hadn't been for you – but I know your work and it is always sound. I have no worries about whether it will be done properly.'

'Tom's work, not mine,' Able said and laughed. 'I just do background stuff. Tom finds all the skilled men and his firm has a good reputation. I know he will come down and instruct the men we need and inspect it now and then to make sure it is right. I'll order the materials and keep a check on the money, just as I do in London. That's my side of it – and we make a good team. We've made a profit on every property we renovated thus far, but we'll be doing yours for the cost. Tom won't want to make a profit from you, Maureen.'

'You have to charge us something,' she said. 'I don't want you and Tom to lose by it but you can give us mates' rates.'

Able laughed. 'Yes, we'll do that, Maureen.'

'Have we seen everything we want then?' Peggy asked. 'Shall we head back home?'

'We can make enquiries about schools another day,' Able said, nodding his head as they all piled into his big, comfortable car, Jon squeezing into the front passenger seat next to Peggy. 'You all right, Jon?' He nodded and Peggy squeezed him to her shoulder. 'You enjoyed yourself by the river, would you like to live here with us?'

'Yes,' Jon said and laid his head against Peggy. 'Mum can come and stay sometimes, can't she?'

'Your mum's home is with us,' Able told him. 'She will go away for her work – when she needs to – but she will always have us to come back to.'

'That's good,' Jon said and accepted a wrapped toffee from Peggy.

'That is what I call a good day,' Peggy said with a sigh. 'At least we all know what we want to do – and we are lucky. We can buy the lease without waiting for the compensation, though Able thinks it will be quick once we agree it. The council want to get on with purchasing the properties so that they can start the demolition. I think Mulberry Lane is due to be one of the first from what Able has heard – isn't that so, love?'

'Yes, it is what I've heard. I was surprised, because I expected them to hang about procrastinating for a couple of years, but it seems the plans have been simmering for a long time but they kept it quiet until they were sure they had the funding.'

'If you'd known, you might never have bought the Pig & Whistle and done it up,' Maureen observed.

'I wouldn't have done so,' Able said. 'I wonder now if that was why the brewery were so obliging as to let us have it at a reasonable price.'

'You think they might have known of the clearance and didn't tell you?'

'It's possible,' he said. 'My lawyer says the council should have told me of their plans when I applied for planning – he thinks we have a good chance of getting every penny I spent and compensation for a thriving business.'

'I wonder how soon we'll get our letters,' Maureen said.

'I think they've already started to go out,' Able told her. 'Tom said one of his customers had had a letter telling him his house was due to be knocked down and offering him a new flat in compensation.'

'I didn't know they did that...'

'He doesn't own his home. The council is under an obligation to offer a home to those they make homeless – but I'm not sure how they intend to deal with the landlords of rundown properties. I imagine it will be the price of the land only. It has to be more if a house or shop is in good condition.' He glanced in the driving mirror. 'You haven't received anything yet, Gordon?'

'Not officially. My lawyer says he thinks I'll get full value on the shop, but perhaps not as much on Gran's house.'

Gordon spoke of the house they lived in, which had been left to Maureen by her grandmother. Although they had made repairs to keep it right over the years, it was an old house and they had not done any big renovations recently, as they had to the shop.

'It's as well we sold your old house years ago,' Maureen said. She opened a tin of biscuits and offered them round. The children took a couple each, but the adults refused, saying they'd had enough to eat with the picnic. 'Perhaps later—Yes, I think your old house wouldn't be worth much now, Gordon.'

'The money was better invested in the shops,' Gordon replied. 'I'm hoping for somewhere between twenty and thirty thousand for the lot, if I'm lucky.'

'Do you think as much as that?' Maureen asked him and he nodded. It was a small fortune, leaving them money to invest after they had bought their new home.

'Most of it is for the shops, perhaps only three for the house,' he replied. 'They are thriving businesses, Maureen. We need compensation as well as the price of the property.'

Maureen shook her head over it. 'The whole thing seems nonsense to me,' she said. 'How can the council afford to just knock down people's homes and their businesses like that? I should have thought they would have better things to spend their money on.'

'I suppose there is a case for it,' Gordon said thoughtfully. 'Too many slum houses makes for poor health amongst the children. Mildew on the walls, rats under the floorboards and cockroaches in the walls... they need better sanitation, a lot don't have a bathroom, just an outside toilet.'

'When you put it like that...' Maureen sighed. 'Why couldn't they have just knocked the worst down and left the rest in place?'

'That wouldn't occur to them,' Able replied with a laugh. 'They just go through an area and knock it all down and build fresh. I suppose when the grand plans are drawn up, they don't think about all the history and lives they will sweep away.'

'Well, it is just plain daft,' Maureen said. 'I wish they would consider folk more.'

'Ah, but it is *progress*,' Able murmured and they all laughed.

* * *

It was just two weeks after they returned from their successful visit to Cambridgeshire that Maureen's letter arrived. It was to inform her that someone from the council would call on the following Monday to assess her house for compensation under a compulsory purchase order.

'Just look at that!' she cried, showing it indignantly to Gordon. 'Out of the blue. We knew what was going on, but they might have sent warning letters out to give people a chance to make their arrangements.'

'Those living in rented houses have been getting letters offering them alternative accommodation for weeks,' Gordon replied. 'I suppose it has taken them longer to check on who owns what.'

Maureen nodded but she was fuming inside. She went round to Peggy's as soon as she could, clutching her letter.

Peggy took one look at her face and burst out laughing.

'I'm sorry, Maureen,' she gasped when she took breath. 'Your face – so indignant. I feel just the same. We had our letters this morning.' The laughter drained from her face suddenly. 'It makes it all so real, doesn't it? I know Able and I left once before, but I always knew Mulberry Lane was here and we could come home if we needed to...'

'I've accepted the move and I understand the need for modern houses.' Maureen sat down, her expression grumpy. 'It's just the officious way they write to you. No "by your leave or anything." They didn't even call a meeting to discuss how people felt...'

'Able says they did, sometime last year, but we were away – and I was in hospital. We knew nothing about it at the time. Tom went along, but he said there were only a handful of residents and he was the only one that asked any questions. He said it was all very vague and he thought it would all be forgotten. At the time, everyone had more important things to think about.'

Maureen sighed. 'I suppose we only have ourselves to blame. If we'd got together and created a fuss back then, perhaps they would have looked elsewhere.'

'Able did ask me if I wanted to oppose it when it was brought up again earlier this year. I think his lawyer wrote a letter pointing out that there were several successful businesses in the area and he was told they would be fully compensated. He thought it would be a matter of years, though, and it may still be by the time it all gets sorted.'

They sat looking at each other, lost in shared memories. 'Oh, damn them,' Maureen said and sniffed as the emotion caught up with her. 'It's just all the memories – the fun and laughter, all our friends...'

Peggy got up and fetched out a new bottle of sherry. She poured them both a large glass. 'I think we need a bit of something to cheer us up,' she said. 'I do know how you feel, Maureen. I was looking forward to the move and then I opened this and...' She sighed. 'It will be the end of an era. Old London is vanishing. What Hitler didn't destroy is gradually being replaced by all this modern stuff – high-rise flats and big shopping centres. We're being swept away by the tide...'

Maureen sipped her drink and then downed it. Peggy poured her another and did the same. 'Do you remember Alice that night... the way she showed her drawers to Hitler after that bomb went off and we were all fine?' Maureen asked. 'She was always so full of spunk and laughter.'

Peggy chuckled. 'As if it were yesterday. It is all crystal clear. I never did forget that – it was what happened after...'

They sat in silence for a moment, and then Peggy poured them another large sherry. 'I shouldn't,' Maureen objected. 'You know what I'm like and I've had two already.'

'Go on, I am,' Peggy said and took a mouthful. 'I don't think we've ever done this together, Maureen. We've always been busy, responsible women, looking after others. Let's sit here and drink and talk about ourselves.' She gave a little giggle, finished her glass, and poured another, lifting it in a salute. 'To old friends and good times—'

'And not so good,' Maureen murmured. 'Remember when poor Tom's brother went on that bombsite and got killed?'

'His father was in prison and his mother blamed him, even though he got hurt himself trying to get his brother away from the unexploded bomb.'

'She nagged him and he did all he could to help her,' Maureen said, shaking her head. 'He was always trying to earn money for her...'

'She was an old misery. Gave poor Tom and Jack a bad time – I liked Jack. Tom has always been a good lad.' Peggy lifted her glass. 'I'll drink to that.'

'So will I.' Maureen lifted her glass and drained it. Peggy topped them both up. 'Do you remember Violet.'

'You didn't like her. She only married your dad to get her hands on the money.'

'She didn't get it, though...' Maureen giggled and drank another glassful straight down. She held it out without thinking and Peggy filled it. 'Gran owned it all and I never knew... all the time I worked for dad for pennies and I never knew he didn't own the property...'

Maureen finished her drink and Peggy poured them both yet another.

'We did have some good times, didn't we, Peggy? Remember when that hairdresser first came here – Ellie her name was...' Maureen looked at her earnestly. 'Do you reckon the lads went for her husband after he murdered Mrs Tandy and attacked me?'

'He didn't do it... it was that hired assass... ssassin...' Peggy hiccupped. 'He only paid him... least that's what Mike said at the time... they bashed him up, you know?' She poured more sherry into both glasses and they both emptied them.

'No, no, it was Ellie's husband killed Mrs Tandy... you're thinkin' of somethin' else... the hired killer was meant to murder the one that raped poor Ellie...' Maureen protested and drank the last of her sherry.

Peggy poured another for them both.

'Was'h' it?' Peggy considered. 'Praps... Poor Mike... Here's to Mike,

God bless him... He was a good'un, too.' She looked at the sherry bottle, which was now empty. 'Thass funny... I'll get another one...' She got up and swayed across the kitchen to fetch another. After two unsuccessful attempts to open it, she went to the fridge and brought back half a bottle of white wine, pouring them both a glass and lifting hers in a toast once more. 'Remember when Rose nearly died over that bloke she fancied, getting her pregnant... and then he died and she married Tom.' She raised her glass again. 'Tom's a good'un... Drink to Tom, Maureen...'

Maureen stared at her glassily. 'I think...' she pronounced very seriously. 'I think you're drunk, Peggy...' And then she put her arms on the table and laid her head down and was gently snoring within seconds.

'No, thass you thass had too much,' Peggy said and smiled in satisfaction as she finished another glass of wine and then got up, staggered over to the settee and lay down, closing her eyes as she drifted into sleep.

* * *

'And that's how I found them,' Able said to Fay when she came round that evening. Jace had gone off on the first stage of his tour alone, after deciding it would be too much for her in her condition to be dragged all over the country. 'Your mum was sound asleep on the sofa and Maureen with her head on the table. They'd drunk a whole bottle of that strong sherry and nearly a full bottle of wine between them.'

Peggy said, 'We were talking about the past and old friends – we just got carried away.'

Fay looked at her mother's pale face and gave a short laugh. 'Mum! After all these years as a pub landlady, I thought you knew better than to get drunk.'

'There are times when it is necessary,' Peggy replied with dignity. 'Sherry is lethal stuff. I should have remembered. I normally only ever drink one in an evening. Wine is much less lethal.' She closed her eyes in pain. 'Remind me never to drink it again, Able. My head is drumming.'

'I had to take Maureen home in the car,' Able said, still amused.

'Gordon was making her black coffee when I left. He says in all the years he's known you, you've never got drunk together.'

'There's always a first time,' Peggy told him firmly. 'We needed cheering up after those letters came.'

'But, Mum,' Fay said, 'you're excited about getting that pub in Ely. You know you are.'

'Yes, I am.' Peggy smiled gratefully at Able as he handed her a cup of black coffee with two aspirins. 'Thank you.' She swallowed them and looked at her daughter and husband, both of whom seemed to be waiting for an explanation. 'Maureen was angry over it all – the way it was written so pompously got to her – and I was too when the letter came. It made it all so real...'

'If you're unsure, we can look for something here,' Able said. 'It's not too late to change your mind, Peggy.'

'No, I am looking forward to it,' she assured him. 'It will be an adventure. It is just that Maureen and I have so many memories here.' She smiled wryly. 'It seemed like a good idea...'

'After all the times you told me never to get drunk,' Fay pouted at her and then laughed. 'Oh, Mum, your face. Does your head ache dreadfully?'

'It's awful,' Peggy said and managed a strained smile. 'Good thing I'm not needed in the restaurant this evening.'

'I don't suppose you would have done it if you'd intended to work,' Able said. 'I think you both needed to get it out of your system and perhaps this will do the trick...'

'I shan't do it again,' Peggy replied fervently. 'The first thing you learn when you become a landlady is not to drink more than one glass in an evening. You would soon lose your profits if you drank them away.' She pressed a hand to the back of her head and moaned softly.

'Why don't you go up to bed?' Able asked her.

'I should ring Maureen, see if she is all right,' Peggy said. 'I ought not to have got her drunk.'

'Oh, I think it was six of one and half a dozen of the other,' he said with a little smile. 'Have an early night, love. Fay is going to stay for a few weeks longer now, so you'll have plenty of time to talk to her.'

The phone rang and Fay got up. 'That will be Jace checking on me,' she said. 'Go to bed, Mum. I'll see you in the morning.'

'I think I shall,' Peggy looked at Able apologetically. 'Sorry you had to find us like that – it must have shocked you.'

'I was worried for a moment, then I saw the bottles and the letter Maureen had dropped on the floor.' He looked at her seriously for a moment. 'You are sure you're all right with what we decided? It is easy to get carried away when you're having a nice day out.'

'Oh no, I am quite happy with things the way they are,' Peggy said. 'It was just... nostalgia, I suppose. And I wanted to cheer Maureen up. I should have stuck to wine. I'd forgotten how disastrous sherry can be if you drink more than a couple of glasses.'

'Never touch it,' Able said and helped her as she stood and half stumbled. 'Are you all right, hon?'

'Yes, fine,' Peggy said and smiled up at him. 'You've asked me if I am happy – what about you? Will it suit you to move there?'

'I'm happy anywhere you are,' he replied simply. 'You know that, hon.'

'Thank you. I am so lucky. Now I think I had best go to bed...'

27

'Mum got drunk? I don't believe you,' Freddie said when Fay told him on the phone later that evening. 'Are you kidding me?'

'No,' she said. 'Maureen was upset when she got her letter saying her gran's house was subject to a compulsory order and Mum thought it would be a good idea to have a few drinks to cheer her up – but they drank sherry and had a bit too much. Dad found them both fast asleep.'

'That's better than if they were both dancing naked in the street,' Freddie quipped.

Fay giggled. 'Dad said it was funny. Anyway, how are you?'

'Fine. Happy. I'm doing well in my tests and getting good grades for my written work as well as the physical – so it all looks good. I've applied for a teacher-trainee post at a school just a few miles from Cambridge and I've been accepted. That's what I was phoning about, to tell Mum and Dad. I start after the long summer holidays, but I'll still go into college two days a week for lectures and take my final exams next year. After that, I'll try for a job in the area.'

'That is all great,' Fay said, 'but I meant you, Freddie. Are you happy with Greta? Dad said the flat is tiny but in reasonable condition.'

'It's fine as it is for now. We're lucky to have it,' Freddie told her. 'Greta loves having her own home – and I love her, so we're good.'

'You really are?' Fay asked again. 'I felt for a while you were uneasy – but now it's OK?'

'Yes, there was some unpleasantness at college,' Freddie told her. 'It is over now and all settled.'

'Good. I might get up again soon. I'd like to spend some time with you before we go home.'

'Is America your home now?' Freddie asked and she was silent for a moment.

'Well, yes, I suppose it is, for a while anyway. Once we get back, I shan't want to go far, because of the baby,' she admitted. 'I know Jace promised we would come back here – but I enjoy the life out there, Freddie. I know that sounds selfish because I shan't see Mum and Dad much and they will miss out on a lot of my children's lives but—'

'It suits you and Jace, I suppose,' Freddie said. 'You mustn't feel bad about it. I shan't go far, for a few years anyway…'

'You wanted to travel!'

'Yes – but that was before—'

'Freddie! You shouldn't give up your dreams because Greta wants something different.'

'I gave up my football to take you skating,' Freddie reminded her sharply. 'I love Greta. She is loving her own home so much. We'll get married and I dare say we'll have a family…'

'You don't have to,' Fay objected and then, 'Oh, I know I am and it is quick, but it's what we wanted…' She laughed. 'I just wanted you to see what it is like in the big wide world, Freddie. We had a good life as kids – but there's so much more.'

'We shall travel, as and when we can,' Freddie replied. 'It will be a struggle for a while. I know all the things we talked about when we were kids – but I wouldn't change a thing.'

'I love you, twin,' Fay said. 'I'm being selfish. I hoped you'd come out to us later this year and spend a long holiday with us – I want to show you so much, Freddie.'

'You will one day,' he promised. 'Is Dad there – can I have a word with him, please?'

'I'll get him,' Fay said. 'I think he went down to the bar.'

* * *

'Freddie is pleased with his placement for his pupil-teaching year; he says it is juniors and just outside Cambridge. He can catch a bus or even cycle if the weather is decent,' Able said when Fay joined him in the kitchen for a cup of hot cocoa before going to their beds late that evening. 'I'm planning on giving him and Greta the money for a trip out to stay with you in the summer, but it is to be a surprise, so don't tell him, Fay.'

Her face lit up and she hugged him. 'That's wonderful, Dad, thank you. He was thinking he couldn't afford it now that they are saving to get married.'

'Well, I can and I shall,' Able told her. 'I've had the first offer on this place. It isn't bad, but my lawyer is trying for more. I'll have enough to help Freddie get started as well as everything we want to do.' He paused, looking at her thoughtfully. 'Your turn will come one day, Fay, but I know you and Jace have plenty of money – so I am going to give Maggie her share of the compensation, since she has worked so hard in that business, and I will let Freddie have as much as I can manage, but I don't want you to feel left out – you'll just have to wait for your share.'

'Oh, Dad, you don't know how glad I am that you are going to help Freddie. Besides, you've always given me everything I wanted,' Fay said and hugged him. 'I earn pocket money with my cooking and Jace gives me more than I can spend – I wanted to give Freddie some, but he refused it. He'll take it from you.'

'I hoped you wouldn't mind.' Able looked at her fondly.

'Darling Dad,' Fay laughed. 'How could I when you've spoiled me all my life? Please help Freddie. He gave up a lot to help me when we were young and I want him to have some fun.'

'Well, I'll start with the holiday for both of them – and, when they're ready, I'll help them buy their first house – but not a word of it to Freddie or Greta.'

'I'll keep your secret,' Fay said and popped a kiss on his cheek. 'Did anyone ever tell you you're the best dad ever?'

'Get on with you, miss,' Able said and grinned. 'Freddie is a good lad. He's worked hard at college and it hasn't been easy—' He broke off as he heard the doorbell ring. 'Who on earth is that at this hour?' He got up, telling her to stay put. 'I'll check and see.'

Fay nodded but went to the head of the stairs, listening as her father opened the door. She had wild ideas of rushing down to help him if whoever was there tried to force their way in, but then she heard her father's voice inviting someone in and they went through to the restaurant.

Fay hovered at the top of the stairs, straining her ears, but there were no untoward sounds. She drank her cocoa but lingered, unwilling to go to bed until her father returned.

He did so about twenty minutes later after seeing his late-night visitor out and locking the door. He looked at Fay, smiling as he saw her hovering.

'Miss Inquisitive...' he said and the tone of his voice told her that he was not displeased.

'Well, are you going to tell me?' she asked.

'I suppose – though I should tell your mum first...'

'What? Nothing wrong...?'

'It was about Freddie. He saved someone's life – one of the other students. That was the student's father. Mr Crawford is a busy man and he has been sitting in the House – parliament, that is – until now. He came to tell me how grateful he was and... he told me that there will be a big building contract coming up, as good as told me it could be mine if I put my estimate in...'

'Dad – that sounds a bit odd, doesn't it?' Fay said and Able nodded. 'Will you put an estimate in?'

'Tom may, I shan't,' Able replied. 'I was pleased to hear what Freddie had done, though. Mr Crawford said he had no influence with any school governors so could not help Freddie in that way but would be happy to give him a monetary reward.'

'What did you say?'

'I politely told him my son needed no reward for saving his son's life – that's when he told me about the contract. More or less said it was mine for the asking.'

'That isn't legal,' Fay said. 'It should be open to all-comers to tender.'

'And will be,' Able assured her. 'My name will not appear on the contract – we only need what is right and proper, no favours. I wouldn't want to live in any man's pocket and if I took something like that, I'd feel obliged...'

'Good for you,' Fay told him. 'You and Freddie are the same – as honest as the day is long.'

'Best way to be,' her father said. 'Now off to bed with you. I'm going to try not to wake your mum...'

* * *

Peggy was sound asleep when Able crept in beside her. He smiled, chuckling softly to himself as he remembered the scene where he'd discovered Peggy and Maureen sprawled out after drinking a bottle of sherry between them as well as a couple of glasses of wine. It was something Peggy never did, despite having been a pub landlady for years, and he knew she'd been feeling it when she went to bed early. She would be pleased when she heard what Freddie had done and he would tell her in the morning.

Peggy was just as delighted at the news as Able had been. They were both proud of Freddie and agreed that it was just what they would have expected him to do. Able didn't mention the offer of a large building contract because he knew she would fly off the handle at any hint of anything slightly bent. It happened in the world of business. Able was well aware that some big government building contracts went to those with friends in high places, but neither he nor Tom were interested in that kind of thing. They got all the work they needed without bribes or favours and would keep it that way.

Able had wondered whether Peggy was regretting her decision to move away from London, but she'd convinced him that her little drinking party with Maureen was just a spur-of-the-moment thing. For himself, he liked the idea of a slightly quieter life. They'd worked hard these past years and he thought the country pub would be less of a tie; they would no doubt build a good circle of customers and friends, but the pace of life was slower in the country and Able intended to find staff who could manage when they went on holiday.

It wasn't just Freddie who would be taking a nice long holiday in the sun that year. He'd already looked at some dates for a leisurely cruise that would get them out to America for the event of Fay's first child. Pip, Sheila and Sarah would be travelling there in September.

They had to sort out where Janet was going to live and what she would do after her stay at Pip's. Maggie would be fine. She and Greg had their own flat in London and a house in Cornwall. Maggie had talked vaguely of setting up a restaurant, but Able didn't think they had decided where it would be just yet. He felt sorry for Maggie, because her business had been doing really well and it seemed unfair that she should have to start all over again.

Able nodded to himself as he went downstairs. He would have a little chat to Maggie and see what she felt about things, tell her how much she would get when the sale of the Pig & Whistle was complete, and ask if there was any way he could help her.

* * *

'I've been talking it over with Greg,' Maggie told him when he asked her what she planned for the future. 'We think we will look for premises for a restaurant in the Padstow area. I think we'll keep it small and intimate at the start and see how it works out. Greg's home isn't far away and I shan't be working full-time as I do now.'

Able smiled and nodded. 'I can see you've thought about it, Maggie, but will that suit you? Obviously, you want to be with Greg more now that you're married, but you love your cooking.'

'Yes, I do,' Maggie agreed and smiled at him. 'Fay and I were chatting and I've decided to spend some of my time writing cookery books.'

'Cookery books?' Able looked at her in surprise. 'That's a new idea for you, isn't it?'

'Yes, it is,' Maggie agreed. 'I discovered such wonderful food when we went to Italy. Since I came home, I've been trying the recipes and inventing my own variations. They have been popular in the restaurant and, when he paid us a flying visit the other day, Jace was impressed; he suggested Fay and I should write cookery books together. He says he can find us a publisher in America – so that is what we are going to do.'

'Good for you,' Able said and smiled at her. 'You will have an exciting life, Maggie.'

'Yes, I think so. I still want to cook lovely food and to have my own restaurant, but I also want to travel the world with Greg. Wherever we go, I shall discover new ways with food and incorporate them into my menus – and the books if they work out.'

'And there was I worrying what you'd do when the Pig & Whistle is knocked down,' Able said. 'I can see I have no need to worry about you, Maggie love.'

'No – though I was very happy here,' she told him and gave him a little hug. 'It was so good of you and Granny Peggy to help me get started – but it was only ever going to be a starting point. I always had plans for the future and the restaurants are only a part of my life.'

Able nodded and smiled. 'That is as it should be, Maggie. I am glad that you have so much to look forward to.'

'Mum is looking happier too,' Maggie observed. 'She has had a talk to Tom and he has asked her to furnish the show house on that new estate you and he are building. She is very excited about it – and she has also found a lovely cottage near Pip's that she wants to renovate.'

'Ah, that's good news,' Able said. 'When did she tell you?'

'Just this morning,' Maggie said. 'She told me that Chris and his friends have their contract as a backing group for a long-playing record. So she will be going down to stay in late August and I suppose she will buy the cottage in the meantime…'

'Well, that sounds promising all round,' Able said and looked at Maggie thoughtfully. 'How good are you at keeping secrets?'

'Very good,' Maggie said her eyes sparkling. 'What are you up to, Grandad Able?'

Able looked over his shoulder. 'It's a little surprise for Peggy. Something I think she will enjoy and I shall need your help to set it up, Maggie.'

28

'So,' Martha Jones said, eyeing Greta with suspicion. 'You are the young woman who my nephew sent to take over my shop. I suppose you think it is yours now?'

Greta's heart sank as she looked at the elderly woman's face. She seemed so angry. Taking a deep breath, Greta answered carefully. 'No, Miss Jones. I know it is your shop. I am only here to help you – but I do like it very much.'

'I imagine you do – living in those rooms upstairs for free.' Martha Jones sniffed, her eyes moving round the shop as if preparing to find fault. 'You've moved things,' she accused.

'Yes, I put the full jars of boiled sweets on the top shelves and the ones we are using on the lower shelf so they are easier to get – and I put all the boxed chocolates on the other top shelf and the bars on the lower one, again, because we sell more bars of chocolate than we do of the boxes. I can just stand on these little steps of yours when someone asks for a nice box of chocolates.'

Martha sniffed again loudly but said nothing. 'I suppose the stock-room is almost empty?'

'Mr Jones asked me what we were running low of last week and the new stock arrived this morning. I have six big boxes to unpack in my lunch hour.'

'Have you indeed?' Martha's eyes seemed to snap with rebellion for a moment and then her body sagged a little, as if her energy had suddenly run low. 'Why don't you do them now and put the kettle on while you are there? I can manage here for a while.'

'Are you sure you feel up to it?' Greta asked and the fierce little eyes glared at her again. 'If you need me, just call my name—'

'Go along, girl, and stop fussing,' Martha said. 'I've got a chair and a tongue in my head. And I take milk and one sugar in my tea.'

Greta nodded and went off to start unpacking the boxes of sweet jars and boxed chocolates. She hoped they were busy in the shop the next few days because she really didn't want to be told she wasn't needed any more. She and Freddie had settled nicely in their little flat, but if Greta lost her job and had to start paying rent for her home, she wasn't sure they would be able to afford it for very long.

* * *

'So how did you get on working with Martha Jones then?' Freddie asked when he arrived that evening. He placed his heavy satchel, bulging with textbooks, on the desk and looked at her expectantly as she brought mugs of tea for them both. 'Was it awful?'

Greta looked at him for a moment and then laughed. 'No, it was fine. I thought when she first came in that it would be awful. I was sure she was going to sack me, but we were so busy all morning and she looked tired by the end of it. I asked her if I could do anything and she wanted to have a look up here. I came up in our lunch break and she was so pleased with what we'd done. I made some tea and we had some soup and a sandwich – and she told me she was glad Billy had saved her shop by asking me to work here.'

'Ah, that was nice,' Freddie said and smiled at her. 'I wondered if it would be all right. The first time I helped her out she was prickly, but then she warmed to me and we were fine together.'

'She admitted it was getting too much for her even before her "accident" – as she calls it.' Greta frowned. 'Some teenage lads came in after school and I saw the colour leave her face, but I don't take any nonsense from them. They made their choices, paid and left. I think Martha understands now that she needs some help if she wants to keep her shop.'

'And she likes you, so your job is secure for as long as you need it,' Freddie said and kissed her. 'I'm glad, Greta. If you'd had to find another job, you might not have liked it as much as you do this one.'

Greta nodded. 'Martha saw my typewriter and asked me what I use it for. She told me that she loves to read and would have liked to write but never had the courage to try.'

'I expect she would like your romance stories,' Freddie said. 'You must let her read some of them.'

'Yes – when I write another one, I will,' Greta said, looking thoughtful. 'I've been working on my book for a while now. I think I have nearly finished it...'

Freddie looked at her with interest. 'When do I get to read it?'

'Not yet,' Greta told him. 'I'm not sure it is any good...'

'If you don't let anyone read it, you'll never know.'

Greta laughed. 'I suppose you are right. I'm just so nervous in case you hate it – and you must tell me the truth, Freddie. Promise you will?'

'I'll always tell you the truth,' he said. 'What is it about?'

'It's a murder mystery set in and around the colleges,' she said and smiled nervously. 'I set it back in the thirties, just before the onset of war...'

'That sounds intriguing,' Freddie replied. 'When do you think it will be ready for me to read?'

'Well, I suppose you could now,' Greta said hesitantly. 'But you're busy revising for your exams...'

'I need a little time off now and then,' Freddie told her. 'I'd love to read your book, Greta. I really would.'

'You can look at it while I cook our meal,' she told him and fetched a pile of typed pages from the cupboard. 'I got us some lamb chops today and I've put a jacket potato each in the oven – oh, and some real fresh peas with mint sauce.'

'Sounds lovely,' Freddie said, looking at the title page. '*Murder Within Hallowed Halls*,' he murmured. 'I like the sound of that...' He lifted the first page and sat down at their little table, becoming quickly immersed in the story, to the sound of sizzling chops in the background and the delicious smell of mint.

* * *

'I love it, Greta,' Freddie said as he handed her the manuscript back with a cup of tea the next morning as she yawned and stretched, sitting up against the pillows. 'I sat up all night to finish it and I never guessed the ending, not for a second. I thought the porter or the Dean had done it – I never suspected the real culprit, not for one moment. It's very clever the way you made it all tie into the start of the war.'

'Really?' Greta's face lit as she sipped her tea. 'Did you truly like it, Freddie?'

'I didn't just like it,' he told her, sitting on the edge of the bed to drink his own tea from a mug. 'I loved it. I mean it, Greta. I think it is one of the best mysteries I've read for a long time. Gruesome in places, but thrilling and a satisfying end.' He smiled as he saw her look of relief. 'Now we have to find the right publisher for it.'

'Publisher?' Her voice was a frightened whisper. 'I'm afraid, Freddie. Supposing they say it is no good or—'

He leaned forward to kiss her on the mouth before she could go on.

'If one publisher doesn't like it, we'll try the next and the next,' he told her. 'It's good and I won't give up until someone takes it.'

'You do like it,' she breathed and then laughed. 'It was you that made me write it, Freddie. All your talk about the college and the dons and the students. I could never have done it without all the information you gave me.'

'If I helped with the background stuff, I'm glad,' Freddie told her. 'But your characters are what make the book shine for me. They are so believable and the Dean is funny, with his glasses on the end of his nose and his gown falling off his shoulders all the time.'

Greta giggled. 'I think he was based on your history tutor...'

Freddie nodded and arched his brows. 'I shall have to be careful what I say to you if you can draw people to life just like that.' He smiled. 'We must go to the library and look at the mystery books on the shelves – discover who publishes a lot of them and then we'll know who to send it to. We must send it by registered post, too, because we don't want to lose it.'

'I made two carbon copies,' Greta told him. 'One of them is a bit faint, but I can just about read it.'

'I suppose we could get a fast typist to copy it, if need be,' Freddie mused. 'But let's hope it won't get lost – after all your work.'

'Perhaps we could take it to the publisher ourselves – if they are based in London, it would be easy when we go in the summer holidays.'

'I think Dad is coming this way next weekend,' Freddie said, his frown clearing. 'It is something to do with the pub lease they are buying. If we have it all parcelled up ready, he will take it back with him and deliver it by hand.'

'Oh yes,' Greta said, smiling happily. 'If your dad took it himself, we would know it was safe.'

29

'Ah, there you are,' Peggy said when her husband entered their private kitchen where she was preparing a meal for Jon. 'I'd expected you back an hour ago.'

Able smiled and dropped a kiss on the top of her head. 'I had a commission from Freddie – well, it was for Greta, really. She has written a mystery novel and I dropped it off at William Collins, the publishers, on my way home from Cambridge. Freddie says it is brilliant – and he's read enough of them to know. He says it is somewhere between an Agatha Christie and John Le Carre.'

'I like Agatha Christie, never heard of the other one,' Peggy said, putting a plate of scrambled eggs in front of her grandson.

'I haven't read him,' Able admitted, 'but Freddie has. You know he always had a nose in a book when he wasn't playing football.'

'Oh, well, I hope it will get published,' Peggy replied. 'Why did they ask you to bring it with you?'

'Because it might have got lost in the post and she only has one good carbon copy. It would be such a lot of work to type it all up again for her.'

'Yes, I suppose it would,' Peggy agreed. 'I hardly ever read a book. I don't have time. I liked her short stories, though. I thought they should have sold better than they did.'

Able nodded. 'Apparently, Freddie gave her the idea to write the book. She wasn't getting much luck with selling the stories, and one of the magazines said she should try writing longer pieces so she decided to write a mystery about dark doings at the colleges.'

Peggy nodded. 'It sounds interesting. There's something you will want to see over there.' She nodded towards the dresser. 'It arrived by the second post today.'

'Is it the letter from the council?'

'I think it is from your solicitor, but probably telling you of the council's final offer.'

'Why didn't you open it?' Able asked her. 'It concerns you as much as me, hon.'

'I didn't want to. I preferred to wait until you came,' she said, smiling at him. 'Shall I make you some scrambled eggs or would you prefer a pork chop?'

'I'd like the same as Jon,' Able replied, ruffling the lad's head as he passed him to fetch the letter. He picked it up and opened it reading it in silence. 'Well, that's it then,' he said and looked at Peggy. 'We've got the full compensation for the building – and a satisfactory amount for the loss of business. That will be Maggie's, of course. It won't cover the cost of setting up her new restaurant, but it will give her a few thousand in the bank – and we'll have enough to do all we want, give Maggie and Freddie some money and still be in pocket.'

'That's wonderful, Able,' Peggy said and went to him to read what the letter had to say. 'Twenty-five thousand pounds... that is a lot of money, Able.'

'So it should be,' he said. 'In a few years, this place will probably be worth far more – or it would if they hadn't decided to knock it down.'

Peggy nodded, then, 'You mentioned Maggie and Freddie – what about Fay?'

'I've talked to her and she knows hers will come later,' Able said. 'Janet is all right at the moment, too – and Pip will be earning more than any of us once he moves to America. Excluding Jace he's the one who earns monopoly money...' He laughed. 'Well, that is certainly a relief. I knew we had a strong case, but my solicitor says it helped that we negotiated immediately instead of trying to fight it. The council want to get on and it will cost them far more if everyone contests it.'

Peggy looked at him, catching her breath. 'That's it then, isn't it? We are really moving, all of us?'

'Yes, we are,' Able said and put his arm about her waist, pulling her in as he looked down at her. 'I signed the lease of the Dog & Duck this weekend and we can take the pub over in one month. I've agreed with Tom about the work we need doing there and he'll give it priority as soon as it is ours.'

'Good.' Peggy smiled up at him, feeling a spurt of excitement. 'It will be an adventure, Able. The start of a new life. I am looking forward to it.'

'So am I.' Able bent his head and kissed her.

'Hi Mum – Able,' Janet said as she walked in. Jon looked up at her and she smiled. 'Hello, darling, how are you?' She deposited some parcels on the table.

'Oh, good, you're back,' Peggy said. 'How did you get on?'

Janet had been to a country house sale, where the contents were being auctioned. 'Really well,' she replied, looking pleased with herself. 'I got some gorgeous brocade curtains and some other bits and pieces – for the show house.'

'I'm glad you're back, Mum,' Jon said and made to get up, but she walked towards him.

'Eat your tea, Jon. That looks good.' She gave him a small parcel and bent to kiss his cheek. Jon opened it and looked delighted with the model kit inside, saying that his grandad would help him put it together. 'There is a good cowboy film on this week at the Gaumont, Jon. Would you like to go and see it on Saturday afternoon?'

'Yes, please, Mum,' Jon said and finished his scrambled egg on toast. 'Can I have a piece of cake now, Granny, please?'

'Of course you can, Jon,' Peggy said and smiled as she went to fetch it from the dresser. She opened the tin and took the large seed cake out, turning to Janet as she cut a generous slice. 'We've heard from the council and the compensation has been agreed...' She looked at Janet. 'Have you thought what you will do when we move out of here?'

'I'm going back to Pip's at the end of next week,' Janet told her. 'Chris is away with friends just now and Pip has finished working for his old firm. He and Sheila are taking some time off together – and he wants to know if you and Able will come down for a few days at the end of the school term.'

'That won't be long,' Peggy nodded. 'Yes, we had planned on visiting Pip before he leaves for America. It will be our last chance of seeing him for a while.'

'When Chris follows them to America – probably next Christmas, I might come down to you for a while,' Janet went on. 'I haven't decided where to settle yet, and I'll be staying in London some weekends with Lars, but I know I can come to you whenever I want.'

'Of course you can,' Peggy said, pleased to see Janet looking more relaxed at last. She seemed to have reached a place of peace for herself and that was a good thing. 'You must be hungry – unless you ate on the train?'

'Oh, I had a limp sandwich and a cup of tea, but I wouldn't mind some of what Jon just had, Mum.'

'Take your things to your room and I'll have it ready,' Peggy told her. She turned to look at Able as Janet went out, Jon following behind, busily munching his cake. 'I think I want to give a party at the pub, or perhaps we'll do it in style this time and have it in the restaurant. It will be a farewell to friends and customers—' She broke off as she saw Able's face. 'What have I said?'

Able sent her a rueful smile. 'It was supposed to be a surprise,' he said. 'I'd arranged it all with Maggie – and it will be in the restaurant. She is going to make a big splash for all your friends and regulars, Peggy. We thought you would enjoy that...'

'And so I shall,' Peggy said and laughed. 'I'm sorry I spoiled your surprise, Able. When is it to be?'

'This weekend,' he told her. 'Pip, Sheila and Sarah are coming, too – though Chris can't because he has some gigs or whatever he calls them. Freddie and Greta are coming up on Saturday evening and the party will be Sunday afternoon. Fay will be here and Jace is going to try to get here.'

'That is wonderful,' Peggy said and put her arms around him, embracing him. 'I am so lucky to have you, Able. I'd only just thought of it and you had already arranged it. Were you so sure it would all work out?'

'I was pretty sure – but after all, you love a party, so it wouldn't have been wasted. We don't need an excuse to celebrate; we have more than enough reason.'

'Thank you,' Peggy said and hugged him and then gave a little cry. 'I'd better watch that toast. I think it is burning...'

* * *

'Pip, it is lovely to see you – and you, Sheila my love, and Sarah. Oh, my, how you've grown. You're a young lady now, Sarah.'

'It is lovely to see you, Granny,' Sarah said and hugged her. 'And you, Grandad.' Sarah hugged Able, too. 'I want to stay with you for a few days if I can? Mum says it is all right if you agree. It isn't long until the end of term and I got good grades in my exams.'

'Of course you can stay – for as long as you like,' Peggy told her. 'You can come and stay when we move too.'

'I thought it would be a good chance for her to see a bit of London,' Sheila said when she and Peggy hugged. 'She's young and she assures me that this is all where it is going on now – whatever that means?' She laughed and Peggy nodded her understanding. Sarah had moved on to Fay and Jace, and was asking lots of questions about Hollywood; she was a young bright girl, full of life and curiosity about the world.

'Well, Mum, so it is finally goodbye to Mulberry Lane this time?' Pip said, giving her a kiss on the cheek.

'Yes. There will be no reunion this time,' Peggy said and laughed. She looked around her family. 'It doesn't matter – because this is what matters, the people you love. You are going to America, and Fay lives there now – but we shall visit and one day you may come back here to live. We shall never lose touch with one another because we are family.'

Pip put his arms about her and lifted her from the ground in a bear hug. 'You're my mum,' he told her. 'You'll always be my mum – and home will always be here, but I'm glad you're not unhappy about things.'

'Why should I be?' Peggy asked him. 'Life is an adventure and this is just the next little bit of it. I'm looking forward to my new pub. Maureen will be living close by and she will see more of Matty – and they are building an annexe so that Gordy can have his own plumbing business once he has completed his apprenticeship.'

'It will be fun if you make it so,' Pip agreed and turned to Able. 'I know you will look after her. If I didn't know she was happy with you I'd think twice about going, but I've always understood how much you loved her.'

'That's right,' Able replied, glancing at Peggy as she moved from one to another of her family, talking, laughing and embracing them all. 'As long as I am around, she will never be alone.'

Pip nodded and went off to talk to Maggie who had just entered with Greg. Janet and Jon joined them and Jon was picked up by his uncle and was soon laughing and chatting.

Peggy felt tears prick behind her eyes as she reached for Able's hand. 'I couldn't have asked for a nicer surprise,' she whispered.

'Just wait until tomorrow,' Able told her. 'I think there will be quite a few tears when your regulars say goodbye, hon. It is the end of an era – for them as well as us. Goodbye, Mulberry Lane... there is bound to be a lot of emotion...'

30

The restaurant was packed with family and friends that Sunday afternoon. Maggie and her staff had decorated it in shades of turquoise. There were garlands of flowers and posies on the tables, balloons and silver crackers, and packets of pale pink sugar almonds beside each plate. The food was a fantastic buffet of cold meats, prawns in coral sauce, tiny sausage rolls, cheese and pineapple on sticks, all kinds of salads, crusty bread rolls and little tarts with fillings of mushrooms, cheeses and salmon. A huge three-tier cake graced one side table, and the desserts Maggie brought out later were chocolatey and gooey, topped with whipped cream and flaked almonds, or luscious strawberries in a sweet custard dribbled with burnt sugar strands, and individual pavlovas topped with toffee sauce and thick cream.

Peggy gasped in wonder as she saw the tables just before her friends arrived. She looked at Able with misty eyes. 'I think this must be the most sumptuous party the Pig & Whistle has ever seen. We had some good ones in the past, but we could never have dreamed of food like this...'

'You had to battle through the hardships of the war,' Able said, smiling at her affectionately. 'You gave people the best food available, and you made it taste good even when times were hard. It is only right that you should have this opportunity to give the kind of party you love now that we're all leaving for good.'

Peggy nodded, her thoughts drifting to the past when it had been such a struggle to find enough decent food to keep her regulars happy – but she had and there had been a spirit of sharing and companionship. It would not be the same once it had all been swept away in the tide of progress. For a moment, she felt sad, but then she heard voices and turned to greet her guests with a smile. Today was a time to be happy, not sad.

'Oh, Peggy, isn't this wonderful?' Maureen cried and came bustling in to hug her and exclaim over the way the restaurant looked. 'It's like an underwater sea cavern. I've never seen anything like it.'

'Isn't it lovely?' Peggy agreed. 'Fay and Maggie put their heads together. I think Fay had seen something similar in Hollywood – but this is all their own effort. I love it...'

'Yes, so do I,' Maureen said and then handed her a large bunch of flowers. 'I wasn't sure what to bring – somehow a bottle of wine didn't seem appropriate.'

'We have plenty of that,' Peggy said and laughed as she saw the look in Maureen's eyes. 'It was the sherry. I'd forgotten how quickly it goes to the head, love.'

'I had an awful headache the next day,' Maureen said and smiled. 'It was naughty of you, Peggy, but it was fun just the same. I don't think I've ever done that before in my life.'

'Nor I,' Peggy agreed, 'but there is a first time for everything.'

Maureen smiled as Gordon came forward to greet Peggy with a kiss on the cheek. Gordy had gone off to talk to Freddie and there were some squeals coming from where the younger members of the family had gathered. She had a sudden thought, 'I haven't told you that Gordon got full compensation for the shop – and Ginger is going to work for Tom Barton.'

'Oh, that's wonderful,' Peggy exclaimed. 'We shall all be gone before they come to tear down our homes. I don't think I'd like to see the bulldozers move in.'

'I certainly wouldn't,' Maureen said, but she was smiling. 'It's going to be fun, Peggy. A new life and yet we'll still be together.'

Peggy nodded and hugged her.

Rose and Tom arrived next, together with their children. Rose had brought Peggy flowers too and she hugged and kissed her.

'I am going to miss you and Maureen,' she said. 'Tom says it is nice up there and I can take the kids and visit you when they are out of school – there is a hotel in the high street and some other places do accommodation.'

'We've got plenty of room at the Dog & Duck,' Peggy told her. 'You will stay with us if you come, Rose. We're close to the river and it's nice to walk there – and I think the youngsters can take a boat on the water in the summer.'

'All Jack wants is to play football,' Rose said. Her eldest son had gravitated to Freddie, who seemed to have most of the younger people grouped around him and was telling them something that kept them amused.

'I hope you will come and see us,' Peggy said. 'I think there is a football ground up in the Paradise area of Ely, so Jack could watch a game there if he comes in the autumn.'

'We'll let you get settled first,' Rose said. 'Did Tom tell you he's bought us a nice house out in the suburbs? We decided it would be as well to move out a bit and have something with a garden. I'm thinking of finding a part-time job now. The kids are all old enough to look after themselves if I'm not home – Tom isn't keen, but I thought I might ask Janet if I could help her dress the show house.'

'Go and talk to her,' Peggy suggested. 'I am sure she would be glad to have a partner in London. Once she gets her interior-design business up and running, she will be sure to need help in sourcing what she needs.'

Rose nodded and drifted off to speak to Janet as more people began to arrive.

Now it was the turn of all of Peggy's friends and neighbours to greet her; so many faces from the lanes, some of them quite elderly now. They came in, smiling and excited to have been asked to what they knew from experience would be a good do – but were gazing about in wonder. No one had expected anything quite like this…

'I wonder what Alice would have made of this?'

Peggy looked at the man who had spoken and laughed. '*A right bloody posh do,*' Peggy said with a fair imitation of her late friend's voice. 'She would have asked where the port was – loved her port and lemon, didn't she, Alf?'

'Ah, she did that,' Alf agreed with a grunt of approval. 'Them were the days, Peggy. We shan't know 'em again and that's a fact.'

'No perhaps not – but life is easier now, isn't it?'

'For some mebbe,' he conceded. 'I've been offered a flat in Basingstoke. Don't know as I shall take it. It will be like prison, stuck up there in the clouds, away from anyone…'

Peggy looked at him anxiously. 'What will you do then, Alf?'

'Mebbe I'll go and live with my grandson. He's got a little place down near Southampton. Runs a fish and chip shop and his wife is a hairdresser. They say I can live in their spare bedroom – or they will find me a nice bungalow with a garden. I'd like that; I could grow my own vegetables.'

'You liked your allotment,' Peggy agreed. 'You used to bring me vegetables during the war when they were short. Onions, too, and you could never get them in the shops. I made some lovely soups with your veg, Alf.'

'Fancy you remembering that…' He looked at her and grinned. 'You were always a right 'un, Peggy lass. Come 'ere and give us a kiss…' He put his arms around her and planted a smacker on her lips. 'If I'd been fifteen years younger, I'd 'ave cut Able out…' He gave a cackle of laughter and moved on to shake Able by the hand. 'You look after our Peggy. We shall miss her wherever we end up.'

Peggy was greeting the next of her guests, an elderly lady who had been one of Alice's friends. She seemed very emotional and was escorted by her granddaughter, Sally Ann, who told Peggy her grandmother was coming to live near her in her house in the suburbs.

'It was that or go in a residential home, and we didn't want that, did we, Granny?' Sally Ann looked at her fondly. 'Granny is getting rid of most of her stuff – and she wanted you to have this, Peggy.' She handed Peggy a parcel done up in brown paper and string.

Opening it, Peggy found a photograph taken after the Armistice. It was of the street party they'd held in Mulberry Lane and showed Peggy and all her friends and neighbours toasting the end of the war.

'Oh, Lily, that's lovely,' Peggy said and bent to kiss the papery white cheek, her own eyes brimming with tears. 'I shall treasure it, thank you.'

'I wanted you to have it,' Lily told her. 'You were the spirit of the lanes in those days, Peggy. Many a day I felt like giving in and then I'd see your smiling face, and you'd tell me to come over and have a cup of tea and a slice of your apple pie. It made me feel as if I wasn't alone after my Pete was killed and then the boys, I don't think I could have carried on. I had my Susie, but she was away doing her bit as a nurse – and now I have Sally Ann, so I'm luckier than many – but I doubt I'd have made it through without you, Peggy.'

'Oh, I'm sure you would,' Peggy told her. 'We are both lucky, Lily. I have my family and you have yours.'

'Aye, it's all that matters,' Lily agreed and walked a little unsteadily into the restaurant to the table she'd been allotted.

On and on they came, until every table was seated and the rooms were filled with people, all talking, laughing and remembering. Peggy's gaze travelled round the tables, her heart swelling with love for these people, her family and her friends. Shirley and Ray were there, though the twins had been left at home with the nurse. Maggie and Greg were smiling at each other, and Fay was looking happy with Jace by her side. Most of all, though, today was a day for Peggy's friends from the lanes.

When everyone was seated, Peggy stood. 'I want to make a toast,' she said. 'To friends and family, those who are no longer with us, and old times, the good times, the bad times, all the fun and laughter, and the tears.' She lifted her glass. 'To the folk of Mulberry Lane. Thank you for being my friends and I wish every one of you a happy life in the future.'

A little ripple of applause ran round the room, and then Alf stood up, holding his glass, which contained beer and not that fancy wine stuff. 'To our Peggy,' he said. 'There ain't one of us that hasn't had cause to thank her for something – so good luck to yer, gal. Yer a good 'un.' As he raised his glass, a roar of approval greeted his words and everyone drank to Peggy.

'We will miss you but we shall never forget you...' someone said and the words were repeated again and again, bringing tears to Peggy's eyes.

'I'll miss all of you, too,' she said and smiled. 'So if you need a chat any time, come and see me at the Dog & Duck.'

There was some laughter and Alf piped up, 'I might just do that.'

It was a fitting ending, Peggy thought. Something they would all add to their memories of the place that had been home to them all.

* * *

'Tired, hon?' Able asked later that evening. Everyone but family had left now. Jon was in bed, and the younger adults had all gone out as a group. Janet had gone off on her own, probably to meet Lars, and Pip and Sheila were helping Maggie and Fay to finish clearing up. Jace was with them. He had one more show to do and then he and Fay would be going home to America.

'Yes, a little,' Peggy agreed. 'I think it was the emotion, Able. So many memories... and some of them were upset when they left. Lily isn't well. She would never admit it, but Sally Ann told me she insisted she come to her because she doesn't think she would survive more than a few months in an old folks' home.' She sighed and looked sad.

'People get old, hon,' Able said. 'Lily had as good a life as most – though I know she lost a lot in the war.'

'She battled through,' Peggy told him. 'She and Alice were great friends – but you should have heard them swear at each other when they fell out, which they did at least once a week.' She laughed suddenly. 'It was so funny the way they'd stand in the street and go at it hammer and tongs – and then the next day they'd be in the pub drinking a port and lemon together as if nothing had happened.'

Able nodded. 'You loved them all,' he said. 'They knew that – and that is why they all love you and wanted to say goodbye properly. It was a good party, Peggy. Maggie and Fay did us proud.'

'I am so proud of them – of all my family,' Peggy said. 'They've all got on and they are all doing something they want to do, planning for the future and spreading their wings. Even Janet seems to be happy at last.'

'She is certainly content now,' Able agreed. 'I think she has come to terms with herself.'

'I believe she has forgiven herself at last,' Peggy said. 'She and Jon are getting on better now, too. Yes, I think she is mending inside. Maggie was very clever to give her that idea for her new business. Janet and Rose will make a good team, I think.'

'So now you can think about yourself,' Able told her. 'What are your plans, hon? We have three months or so to finish up here, though I think we can move sooner if you're ready. Maggie will continue the restaurant until she is ready to make her move. She says she will stay until September and then close down. She is going to Italy again in October with Greg and then they will go to his home in Cornwall, and I suppose that's when she'll look for a new restaurant.'

'We'll go down and stay with Pip when school breaks up,' Peggy said decisively. 'Jon can stay there with Janet then and we'll come back and pack up our things here. I think Tom will have completed the renovations to the pub that we asked for and then we can move to Ely...'

'No regrets?' Able asked and she shook her head.

'None at all,' Peggy said. 'It was good. I wouldn't change any of it – except for the bit when I didn't know whether or not you were alive – but other than that I am content. It was a full life, is still a full life, Able. Some of the past wasn't happy, but that's the way it goes, ups and downs. I was lucky. I found you.'

Able smiled and kissed her. 'We're both lucky,' he replied. 'I think we should be pleased with ourselves; the children have all done well in their own way and should have happy lives. As far as I am concerned, these next years are our golden times. We'll run a quiet pub, make new friends and take long holidays – and we shall always be together.'

'Yes, always,' she said, smiling up at him as he bent his head to kiss her.

'And now we turn the page and begin again...'

'That's right,' Peggy replied and smiled. 'It is a whole new story, another chapter of our lives...'

ACKNOWLEDGEMENTS

This is the last book of the *Mulberry Lane* series. When I began it was just an idea for a trilogy that I wasn't sure would be published. I would like to thank my editor, Caroline Ridding, for believing in me and the books and helping me to make them the success they have been. I would also like to thank my readers for believing in my family of friends at *Mulberry Lane* and my publishers for giving me the pleasure of seeing my books in print and continuing to publish all ten of them.

ABOUT THE AUTHOR

Rosie Clarke is a #1 bestselling saga writer whose most recent books include *The Mulberry Lane* series. She has written over 100 novels under different pseudonyms and is a RNA Award winner. She lives in Cambridgeshire.

Sign up to Rosie Clarke's mailing list for news, competitions and updates on future books.

Visit Rosie's website: https://www.rosieclarke.co.uk/

Follow Rosie on social media here:

facebook.com/Rosie-clarke-119457351778432

x.com/AnneHerries

bookbub.com/authors/rosie-clarke

ALSO BY ROSIE CLARKE

Welcome to Harpers Emporium Series

The Shop Girls of Harpers

Love and Marriage at Harpers

Rainy Days for the Harpers Girls

Harpers Heroes

Wartime Blues for the Harpers Girls

Victory Bells For The Harpers Girls

Changing Times at Harpers

The Mulberry Lane Series

A Reunion at Mulberry Lane

Stormy Days On Mulberry Lane

A New Dawn Over Mulberry Lane

Life and Love at Mulberry Lane

Last Orders at Mulberry Lane

Blackberry Farm Series

War Clouds Over Blackberry Farm

Heartache at Blackberry Farm

Love and Duty at Blackberry Farm

The Trenwith Collection Series

Sarah's Choice

Standalones

Nellie's Heartbreak

A Mother's Shame

A Sister's Destiny

Sixpence Stories

Introducing Sixpence Stories!

Discover page-turning historical novels from your favourite authors, meet new friends and be transported back in time.

Join our book club Facebook group

https://bit.ly/SixpenceGroup

Sign up to our newsletter

https://bit.ly/SixpenceNews

Boldwood

Boldwood Books is an award-winning fiction publishing company seeking out the best stories from around the world.

Find out more at www.boldwoodbooks.com

Join our reader community for brilliant books, competitions and offers!

Follow us
@BoldwoodBooks
@TheBoldBookClub

Sign up to our weekly deals newsletter

https://bit.ly/BoldwoodBNewsletter

Milton Keynes UK
Ingram Content Group UK Ltd.
UKHW041825240124
436610UK00002B/5

9 781785 131066